# THE ROMANEE
# VINTAGE

# THE ROMANÉE VINTAGE

Book 3 in the Inspector Truchaud Mysteries series

by

## R.M.Cartmel

All characters in this novel are fictitious and any resemblance to real persons, living or dead, is purely coincidental - apart, of course, from Mme Christine Tournier, who is incontrevertibly real.

THE ROMANEE VINTAGE © R.M. Cartmel
ISBN 978-1-9996652-0-0
eISBN 978-1-9996652-1-7

Published in 2017 by Crime Scene Books

Book design by Clockwork Graphic Design

Cover design George Foster Covers

Printed and bound in Great Britain by Marston Book Services Ltd, Oxfordshire

## Dedication

This is dedicated to Pierre Vincent, winemaker extraordinaire, from whom I learned so much, and from whom I lifted the line about winemaking not being a competitive sport,

and to

Sylvie Poillot and all at Domaine de la Vougeraie, for allowing me to spend the 2014 vintage with them, and for being responsible for that diamond among the nest of rubies, Le Clos Blanc de Vougeot, the author's favourite white Burgundy.

Paris

BURGUNDY

# La Bourgogne

- Auxerre
- Montbard
- Dijon
- Nuits-Saint-Georges
- Beaune
- Nevers
- Autun
- Meursault
- Chalon-sur-Saône
- la Saône

# The Côte de Nuits

Nuits-St-Georges

TREELINE

To Beaune
(Premeaux-Prissey, Aloxe-Corton)

Nuits Saint Georges

D974

Clos de Vougeot

Vosne-Romanée

Vosne

Échezeaux

Vougeot

Chambolle-Musigny

Morey-St-Denis

Gevrey-Chambertin

Fixin

Couchey

Marsannay la Côte

D974

To Chenôve

VINEYARDS

N

# Nuits-Saint-Georges

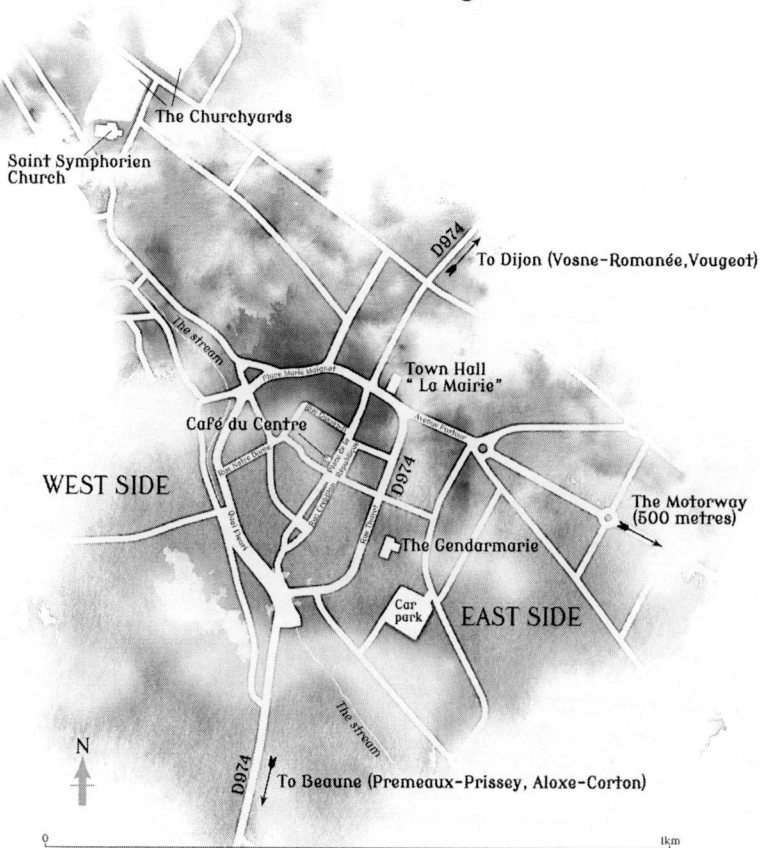

The Churchyards

Saint Symphorien Church

D974

To Dijon (Vosne-Romanée, Vougeot)

The stream

Place Marie Malefiat

Town Hall
" La Mairie"

Café du Centre

Rue Gosterit

Place Caston Ravel

Rue Thurot

D974

Avenue Pasteur

WEST SIDE

Quai Dumas

Rue Claudine Bauvain

The Motorway
(500 metres)

The Gendarmarie

Car park

EAST SIDE

The stream

N

D974

To Beaune (Premeaux-Prissey, Aloxe-Corton)

0                                                                          1km

# Contents

## Dramatis Personae

Commander Charlemagne Truchaud, *Our hero. A detective*

Other Paris-based police who crop up in the narrative

The Divisional Commander, *Truchaud's ageing boss. One day we must give him a name*

Natalie Dutoit, *A stunningly beautiful detective sergeant whom Truchaud secretly adores*

Commander Lucas, *An urbane Parisian whom Truchaud secretly loathes*

Nuits-Saint-Georges based gendarmes

Captain Duquesne, *The chief, who is also Truchaud's friend*

Sergeant Lenoir, *who might have a thing for Mac if he hadn't been promoted*

Constable 'Mac' Montbard, *A strawberry blonde gendarme who probably also resents Lenoir's promotion*

Constable Savioli, *A gendarme who drives the main desk at the gendarmerie*

Solange, *Another constable whose name only Mac can remember*

Municipal police aside from Truchaud, based at the town hall

Constable Fauquet, *who makes singularly bad coffee*

Truchaud's family and friends working at and around Domaine Truchaud

Michelle Truchaud, *His widowed sister-in-law*

Bruno Truchaud, *Her son, age twelve*

Dad [Philibert] Truchaud, *A faded force*

Members of the Laforge household

Simon Maréchale, *A master winemaker*

Dagmar Witter, *Old Mr Laforge's great-niece and Simon's new girlfriend, learning French rapidly*

Suzette Girand, *Simon's previous girlfriend, but still big enough to help at the vintage*

Hairy Eddie, *Suzette's flatmate at University who is also helping at the vintage*

Old Mr [Emile] Laforge, *who sits at the end of the table at dinner*

Marie-Claire Laforge, *His granddaughter*

Jacquot Laforge, *His great-grandson, growing up fast*

The Parmentier Dynasty in Chambolle-Musigny and Meursault

René Parmentier, *The elder brother who looks after the white vines in Meursault*

Jeanette Parmentier, *His wife and the mother of,*

Lucien Parmentier Jr, *10 years old and nobody knows if he has the 'Gift' yet*

Marine Parmentier, *8 years old, who has inherited a gift*

Pierre Parmentier, *The younger brother who looks after the red wines in Chambolle*

Yvonne Parmentier, *His wife, who definitely has the Gift*

Mehdi Akhbar, *Pierre's right-hand man from Algeria via Morocco and Corsica*

Walid Akhbar, *who appears each vintage to help his brother out*

Arifa Akhbar, *Their sister, who also arrives at the vintage to run the household*

Other characters around and about

Jean Parnault, *Truchaud's late elder brother's great pal. Suzette's uncle*

Dr Girand, *The village GP, and husband to,*

Genevieve Girand, *Truchaud's teenage sweetheart and mother to Suzette*

Madame Clermont, *A ferocious woman and the coroner's officer. Appears roaring at every murder scene*

Mr de Castaigne, *The investigating magistrate*

And a real person who crops up from time to time

Christine Tournier, *who really does own and run the Café du Centre in Nuits-Saint-Georges*

# CHAPTER 1

*Nuits-Saint-Georges, early September, Monday morning*

Truchaud was sitting motionless at his desk in the town hall, gazing without focusing past the phone on his desk. Was he hoping for it to ring? Perhaps, but only if the call was from his old office in Paris. The untouched and unloved cup of instant coffee on his desk was getting cool and Fauquet, having delivered his sympathies, was tactfully keeping out of his way.

The day before, Philibert Truchaud had joined his son Bertin in the family crypt in the Saint Symphorien Churchyard up the hill. The commander, Philibert's surviving son, had received commiserations from the great and the good of Nuits-Saint-Georges, and from one or two of the lowly and the bad as well. At his brother's funeral, six months before, he had been right in the middle of an investigation, and he had been feeling driven by what was going on around him. This time it had been his father, who had died predictably after a long illness — 'bravely borne' as it would say in the paper — and had done so right in the middle of absolutely nothing. The vintage was on the way, and the family *domaine* would soon become a hive of frenetic activity. Everywhere he could sense the tension in the air; it was not just his sister-in-law who was forever looking out of the window checking the clouds. As he walked round the streets of the little town of Nuits-Saint-Georges, everyone seemed to be looking upwards. What were they looking for? Rain, hail, anything to threaten the precious grapes that were so nearly ready for harvest, and would be the main source of a family's income for the years to come. That's what they were looking for. The grapes needed just a spot more sun to bring them to full ripeness. 'Ninety-six per cent,' the family's wine master, Simon Maréchale had told him at the funeral. 'It would be a good year if we harvested them now, in a week's time,' he added a silent Gallic shrug into the sentence, 'Pouf! A great one perhaps?' Right now the vintners and their crews were standing in their doorways, holding their collective breath and watching the skies suspiciously for every passing cloud in case it turned into the hailstorm that would turn those ninety-six per cent grapes into worthless mush. It was surely too late for one of those now, although some of the villages to the south of Beaune had already been singularly unlucky that year. Soon the winemakers would drop their flags and everyone would rush out to pick the grapes to make the wine that was the major industry of that small, picturesque part of France.

There had been no presence from Truchaud's office in Paris at the funeral. Even Natalie had been unable — or unwilling perhaps — to attend. His mind passed wistfully over the sergeant whose electrifying presence had suddenly and so unexpectedly captivated him last summer, and who had all too quickly disappeared back to Paris leaving him with more unanswered questions in his personal life than he had ever known in a criminal investigation.

There had been plenty of the local force present of course, both from his own Municipal Police force, who formed a sort of Guard of Honour, and the gendarmes who also turned up in uniform to pay their respects. There were a number of faces from the winemaking community who had taken time out from their preparations for the vintage to go to the little church to pay their respects to one of their own who, as one of them said in Truchaud's ear, had fallen before his time.

He still looked past the phone, still wondering what he would say if it did ring. Would he say that they would see him later that day, and he couldn't wait to get back into the squalor and bloodstains of the darker suburbs of Paris, or would he say that he couldn't leave here yet, as the vintage was about to start and his family and its business still needed his input. Anyway, nobody had found a replacement for the Municipal Chief of Police role he had been filling on a temporary basis for the past three months. He was unsure whether anyone had even been looking; he knew he hadn't.

He was therefore not even sure whether he wanted to pick up the receiver when the phone rang. He looked at the display on the handset, and realised it was a mobile phone that was calling his office direct.

'Hello?' he asked, 'Commander Truchaud, Municipal Police?'

'Good morning, Commander, I'm so sorry for your loss.'

'Thank you, what can I do for you?'

'Well if you were to get into your car and drive to the north for about five minutes, you would find yourself in the village of Vosne-Romanée. If you were to turn into the village itself and head up the hill apiece, you would find on your left the Grand Cru of La Romanée-Saint-Vivant. Once you have actually got there, if you look out of your window, you might see something that would interest you.'

'I'm sorry, who is this?'

'I wouldn't wait, it might not be there very long.'

'Who …?' but the phone disconnected. He did a last number redial on the phone, but it just rang and rang. The caller did not pick up. *How can you do that?* he asked himself crossly.

He called Fauquet on the intercom. 'Did anyone call the outer office a few minutes ago?' he asked.

'No *Chef*,' came the reply, 'why?'

'Well I've just received a very strange phone call on the office phone, and I've no idea how to take it.' He told his colleague about the call. 'Any ideas?'

'None at all sir, but if you want to potter over and have a look, I'll hold the fort here until you get back.'

Truchaud thought for a few moments and decided that a little distraction, even for a few minutes and for whatever futile reason, was probably what he needed right now. 'Thank you,' he said, 'I think I'll take you up on that offer.' He stood up and walked over to the hat stand by the door and grabbed his trench coat and felt in its pocket to see if his mobile phone was still there. It was. He threw the coat around his shoulders and left the offices and wandered down the stairs, heading for the car park. When he reached his old Citroën BX, he slipped the phone into his trouser pocket and tossed the coat onto the back seat. The car, as always, started immediately and he set off.

Heading north up the D 974 — or as he always knew it, the 'seventy-four', which dated back to his youth when the road still had Route Nationale status — he drove out of Nuits-Saint-Georges and through the vineyards. He drove through to the next village, just over the crest was Vosne-Romanée, a tiny village proudly hosting the vineyards where they grew the grapes from which they made the most exquisite and expensive red wine in the world. Truchaud's family owned *terroir* in the village, though sadly not among the most exquisite and ludicrously expensive group, merely in the really damn good group, nearer the seventy-four. He wondered whether he should be changing the possessive pronoun now from 'My family' to 'I'. He thought about that for a moment. *Ownership is one thing, but if I actually have to get down and do the viticulture myself is quite another thing altogether. Those grapes of mine deserve the attention of hands far more skilled than those of a jobbing policeman to realise their full potential.* That having been said, he had heard that the grapes from the greatest vineyards required the least attention to achieve perfection. That's a fundamental rule of *terroir*.

He had to stop very suddenly when he came face to backside with a tractor underneath it rounding a very tight right hand bend. He followed the tractor out of the village, noticing he had attracted the attention of the driver of the tractor, who had turned his plethoric face round a couple of times to look at the car that was following him. It wasn't the sort of car you would drive on a farm, so why was it following him now, hmm? The tractor turned sharp left up a track to follow the village round, and Truchaud drove slowly on along the track, watching the vines on his left, laden with fruit. Suddenly he saw it. There was a gap in the vines, which was about three car lengths long before the vines came together again to climb the hill. He stopped, and got out of the car and looked up the slope.

There was a sea of green all around him with the impression of deep purple in the mix as well from the grapes themselves. He felt a frisson of excitement, he was looking at potentially more money than any man could ever dream of earning in just one lifetime. The Romanée-Saint-Vivant vineyard was one of the larger Grands Crus in Vosne. The very fact that the patch of earth had been awarded that status meant that the potential of the vineyard was top notch. However, as with most of the many named vineyards of any size, the convoluted French inheritance laws had left the vineyard with many and varied owners. It was to Saint-Vivant's good fortune that most of those owners were class acts, or at least classy enough to allow the vineyard to achieve its full potential without unnecessary interference.

There were the vines all were stretching out in front of him. In the middle of one of the rows of vines, something caught his eye. It almost looked like a scarecrow; it was just that that wasn't the sort of thing that was put up randomly in between rows of vines.

He grabbed his coat from the back of the car and put it loosely round his shoulders, it was a very balmy early September day and didn't merit a coat. On the other hand, Truchaud felt that he, personally, did merit his coat. He walked up the hill between the rows of vines, occasionally casting an eye at individual vines as he passed. Under those deep green leaves, he saw the bunches of ripe, bulging, purple grapes with their powdery white bloom of natural yeast on their skins ready to turn those grapes into nectar, the drink of the Gods.

The scarecrow stood slightly taller than the vines on either side of it. It was almost like a man sitting on a chair between the vines, looking out over all he surveyed. You know something? As he got closer, that's exactly what it looked like, a man sitting on a chair in the middle of the vineyard, looking west up the slope to the woods beyond the vines. His mobile phone rang, and he pulled it out of his trouser pocket. It had a number withheld sign on the screen. That figured, but he was sure it would be about what he was looking at.

'Hello, Commander? Me again. What do you think?'

'Look who is this?'

'Far more important, who is that you're looking at and what are they doing there? I'll call you back when you've found out, but be careful.' The phone clicked off again.

A feeling of dread suddenly filled Truchaud, and he broke into a run as he climbed the slope up to what was certainly a wooden dining chair — not a very expensive or even a particularly new one, just a basic wooden dining chair — but the scarecrow, or whatever it was, was tied to it with thick rope. He edged round it, being very careful not to touch the vines behind him with his coat. He turned and faced the scarecrow.

It wasn't a scarecrow, it was a man, a very frightened looking man tied to a chair with his hands tied behind his back and lashed to the chair. Both ankles were separately tied to the chair legs in front of them with separate lengths of rope. Oh yes, one other thing: there were things that looked like votive candles strapped to his chest, and in front of them was a box with flashing lights on the front and wires coming out into the sticks. *Oh good God.* He realised the man was a bomb.

At that moment, a voice shouted up from by his car, 'Hey you up there! Who are you and what the hell do you think you're doing? If you're doing any damage to those vines, you'll be in really serious trouble.' The red-faced man from a few minutes ago was no longer atop his tractor, but he was a very big man, and he was coming this way. Truchaud did not take a great deal of notice; he was so appalled by what he was already looking at.

His phone rang again. 'Well done, Commander. Provided you can defuse that one without it going off, you might save a life today, but don't worry, we'll talk again soon,' and the phone disconnected.

He phoned Captain Duquesne of the gendarmerie, whose phone number was logged into the speed-dial of his phone. He explained breathlessly where he was and that he needed access to the local bomb-disposal experts.

'We don't have a bomb squad in Nuits-Saint-Georges, and that's for sure,' replied the gendarme genially, uncertain whether his leg was being pulled.

Truchaud assured him it was not. 'So, who would you phone if you needed to dispose of a bomb in Nuits-Saint-Georges?' he asked desperately.

'Haven't the faintest idea old boy, the question hasn't cropped up in my time here, but I'm sure I can find the answer in one of the files in my office. As soon as I can find who I'm supposed to be calling I'll get them out to your location immediately.'

He also contacted Fauquet in his own office and got a similar response. He supposed that if each of them contacted a different bomb squad then two bomb squads being competitive was far more useful than the number he had there at the moment.

He turned back to the man sitting on the chair in front of him and introduced himself. 'Who are you?' he asked.

Meanwhile the man from down the bottom of the hill was now running up the hill waving a knobbly stick, shouting. Truchaud could tell his face was getting redder by the moment, and he was panting. A unit that large was not designed to move uphill that fast.

The man on the chair still looked terrified but didn't say a word.

'What the hell are you doing up here in these vines?' roared the running man getting ever closer, 'I've a good mind to call the cops.'

Truchaud looked over the top of the terrified sitting man. 'I am the cops,' he said coldly. 'What do you want me to do?'

The one-man stampede slowed slightly for a moment. 'So what's going on here then?'

'Ssh!' said Truchaud, putting his finger to his lips as the man arrived.

'So what's he doing then?' the big man asked again, trying to slide between the man on the chair and the vines. There was a lot more of the red-faced man than there was of Truchaud in every direction, and as he tried to squeeze his bulk between the row of vines and the sitting man, there really could have been only one of two results. Either the grapes near to the man's posterior would have been knocked off their vines by the aforementioned posterior, or the other option, which actually did happen. The man's belly rubbed up against the sitting man's shoulder and the back of the chair, which started to topple away from him, and as the sitting man was tied to the chair, he was unable to prevent himself falling sideways into the vines.

The look of increasingly abject terror in the sitting man's eyes gave Truchaud just enough warning to dive face down to the ground before the explosion that followed. He stayed down under his trench coat until whatever it was that was raining on his coat actually stopped. He looked cautiously out, half expecting what had just happened to be a hoax. It wasn't. He surveyed the hole where the man had been sitting. In the row of vines on either side there was a penumbra of smouldering wood, stretching almost to where the soles of his feet ended up after his swallow dive. Of either man, there was no sign. Oh wait a minute, that was a hand over there, attached to a wrist with a watch on it, but the glass was broken. There wasn't much attached beyond the wrist. One other thing was that all the birds had stopped singing. Had they all been silenced by that awful noise?

He put his fingers in his ears and jiggled them about a bit. No, there was no noise there either. He looked at both fingers. Well, at least that was something: there was no blood on either of them. At least he hadn't burst his eardrums. He said something. Now that was most bizarre, he couldn't even hear his own voice when he spoke. It was going to stop his career in its tracks if he had suddenly gone deaf.

Truchaud's mobile phone was vibrating in his pocket. He pulled it out and its face had lit up. On the front it read 'Caller number withheld'. It was him again. He put it to his ear. He could hear nothing, no ringtone, nothing. He pressed the button to answer anyway and said, 'Your bomb has deafened me, you bastard! I can't hear a word you are saying.' He hoped he had said that loud enough for the man on the other end to hear. In fact, he hoped it was so loud it hurt. The light on the phone went off. A couple of moments later it signified that it had received a text. He pressed the display button. 'Oops!' it read, 'my bad. Forgot 2 tell U vibration sensor on device. triggered if he spoke.' It then went into normal speak, 'but clever old you found another way to set it off. Well done! Ta'ra, bye-ee!' He checked the sender, but once again it said, 'Caller number withheld'. Damn! He had already put the phone back in his pocket when he saw the blue flashing lights down the hill. And much to his relief, he faintly heard the two-tone siren of the arriving gendarmes at the bottom of the hill.

# CHAPTER 2

Sergeant Lenoir was very fast on his feet. The gendarmes that followed him were somewhat less agile as they were carrying material to block the scene off from inquisitive bystanders. The combination of a sharp salute to the commander and an elongated 'Shit!' as he looked at the devastation around him seemed a somewhat incongruous juxtaposition to a still rather stunned Truchaud.

'The captain is waiting for you at your office, sir, would you like me to take you there?' he asked.

That brought Truchaud back to the present. The thought of having nearly been blown to pieces and then subsequently to be hurtled about by this very amiable but utterly mad driver were enough to bring anyone back to their senses. 'No thanks, I've got my own car down there. What I need for you to do is secure the area, and don't let anyone, and I do mean anyone, apart from the coroner's team onto the site.'

'The coroner's team?' asked Lenoir, dismayed.

'Oh yes, in amongst that mess,' he said, waving a vague hand in the direction of the crater, 'there are the remains of two people, and if Mrs Clermont turns out to be the examiner in charge I imagine that she will be threatening considerable damage to the person in charge of the scene if she discovers clodhopping boot prints all over her crime scene.'

'Two people?' Lenoir's eyes widened even more. He focused on Truchaud again. 'That probably explains the state of your coat. Are you all right, sir?'

Truchaud pulled what was left of his trusty trench coat off his shoulders, and it came away in pieces from him. What was left of it was a mixture of reds, both the brick red of blood and the deep red of grape skins, but was also very severely shredded. Mixed in was clear but very sticky grape juice. 'I think I'd better leave this behind,' he said.

'I think you'd better stay with your car until you're cleared to leave the scene,' replied the gendarme gently. 'I'll let the captain know that you've been delayed.'

'Meanwhile, I'll contact the examining magistrate. I've got his number on speed dial, and he can contact Mrs Clermont.'

Truchaud had already worked with two of the local examining magistrates and had got on all right with the pair of them. He pulled his phone out from his pocket and dialled. 'De Castaigne here,' came the response from his phone. It was one of the magistrates he knew.

'Commander Truchaud here, Nuits-Saint-Georges.'

It had been some three months since the pair of them had even talked, and it took a moment for all Castaigne's cogs to slot into place. 'Oh Truchaud, of course, how are you? What can I do for you?'

'Are you busy?'

'Not especially,' he paused, and then continued, 'should I have admitted that? Why?'

'Well you are now, I've got a double homicide to report.'

'I have to ask this, not in any way doubting you, of course, but you are convinced in yourself that they're both dead?'

'Absolutely, they're both shredded. The only thing that vaguely puzzles me at the moment is why I am not a third fatality myself. It happened right in front of me.'

'Where exactly are you?'

Truchaud told him the whole story in gruesome detail and that Sergeant Lenoir from the gendarmerie was currently in charge of the scene.

'I'll get a coroner's team to you right away, and I'll see you in a few minutes myself.'

'I'll be sitting in my car at the bottom of the vineyard,' he replied.

Halfway down the hill he turned and looked back up. Lenoir's team was making a good job of fencing off the scene with barriers on tripod stands. He might not prevent any lollygaggers looking on from the outside, but there was no doubt where it was not permitted to go to avoid damaging the crime scene. Near the bottom of the hill, not far from where he was standing, he spotted the chunky form of Constable Montbard, who had been nicknamed 'Mac' because her red hair and freckles made her look like everybody's idea of what a Scot should look like. The fact that she spoke hardly a word of English and the only words of Gaelic she knew were *uisce beatha* and *sláinte* was irrelevant. Whether she pronounced the latter word right, she had no idea, but it was an appropriate way for someone of who looked like her to say 'cheers.'

'Constable?' he called.

'Oh Commander, sir,' she said turning on her heel. He beckoned to her and she trotted over.

'You see that tractor down there?' he said, pointing to the blue machine parked at the side of the road, just about blocking his Citroën in.

'Yes sir?'

'The man who was driving that machine five minutes ago was one of the two victims. He was a big man, red face, grey hair, angry looking; but that may just have been because in the moment that I saw him, he was pretty angry. What we need to do is find out who he was. With a bit of luck, it might lead us to finding out who the other victim was.'

'Two victims?' Her voice betrayed similar dismay as her recently promoted colleague for a moment. Then she snapped back into a professional mode. 'Right on it sir,' she said and trotted off down the hill between the vines until she reached Truchaud's car at the bottom. She then turned right and walked up to the tractor. She looked at the number plate at the back and then climbed into the car in which she and Lenoir had arrived. She tapped on her iPad and looked at it for a moment. She climbed back out again and walked out to Truchaud. 'Can you tell Sergeant Lenoir,' she said with extra emphasis on the 'Sergeant.' There had obviously been issues between them about his promotion. 'Can you tell Sergeant Lenoir that it was me who's taken the car. The tablet has given me an address to check.'

Truchaud meanwhile wandered slowly back down the hill, wondering where everyone was. Usually at the slightest hint of a disaster you couldn't breathe for bystanders of one persuasion or another. There were times when he wondered whether members of the press were magicked out of nowhere just to get under his feet. At this moment, there was nobody. He called Captain Duquesne. 'You may as well cancel the bomb squad,' he said. 'I seem to have sorted that out myself, though as no doubt Sergeant Lenoir will have already told you, there have been casualties.' Truchaud took a breath, and then continued, 'I'm still at the scene, and I'll be staying until I'm released by the examining magistrate. Once he's done so, I'll be with you.'

'Are you all right?'

'I'm fine, though I suspect that I've been very lucky, and I can't say the same for my coat. It appears that it took the brunt of what fate intended for me. Lenoir's hanging on to what's left of it up at the scene.' Truchaud explained that they were waiting for the forensics team to arrive with Mr de Castaigne.

*Where is everybody?* he wondered. He appreciated that he was very close to the explosion when it happened, but it was a fairly big bang. His ears were still ringing, and it had completely destroyed two people and created a fairly impressive crater in the vineyard. Yet, apart from the gendarmerie, still no one seemed to be taking any interest in what had just happened in the Saint-Vivant vineyard. It wasn't lunchtime. He wondered whether the complete population of the little village of Vosne-Romanée was in a committee meeting somewhere, discussing how the upcoming vintage was going to happen.

He had, a couple of days before, sat in on such a meeting at Laforges, chaired by Simon Maréchale around the dining table. Maréchale had sat in the chair at the head of the table normally reserved for old Mr Emile, the patriarch of the family. Around the table sat various family members of the Laforges and the Truchauds, their full-time employees, and a number of students and the like who had been taken on for the harvest. After a polite speech about the passing of Philibert Truchaud and everyone's indebtedness to his skills as a winemaker, he got on with the business at hand, making sure that everyone knew what their roles were supposed to be at any given time over the coming weeks, and that the sorting tables and the fermentation tanks were spotlessly clean in preparation to receive the magic juice in the next few days.

Lenoir stood exactly where he had been told to stand, and he was trying to work out what had happened. Truchaud was down by his car, leaning up against the front mudguard, and Mac and the Mégane had disappeared into the village. Savioli and the new girl were fencing the area off. Dammit, Lenoir had forgotten the girl's name; how come he had forgotten her name? He just gets promoted, and he then goes and forgets the name of one of his squad; this was not the behaviour that

26

was expected of a newly promoted NCO, he thought. He felt relieved that the vintners were obviously at lunch and oblivious to what was going on. He was relieved that he would get the area secured before any of them reappeared to make a nuisance of themselves.

He allowed himself to rotate on the spot, that way the dreaded Mrs Clermont would have minimal reason to bite his head off. To his left as he looked downhill was ground zero. That was where the detonation had actually taken place. There was a hole in the ground there and really nothing else. Everything else radiated from that point. Under his feet there was just earth, but on either side of his feet was a mixture of wood and other material. A few metres up the hill were the remains of Truchaud's coat. How had that happened? Truchaud had said that there were two men here, of whom there was little left to see, at least from where he stood, and yet Truchaud himself was unscathed. He spotted the hand under the vines on the left as he looked up the hill and shuddered. The arrival of the dark blue van up from the village was heralded by the flashing blue light on its roof. Lenoir was at least relieved by the fact that it wasn't playing 'blues and twos' music as well. It stopped next to Truchaud at the bottom of the hill.

*Well, that sorts that one out*, Truchaud thought, *If they can get that size of van between the tractor and the vines, then I should be able to squeeze my Citroën between that gap; that is, when I'm a little less dizzy.* A large, fierce-looking woman got out of the driver's side of the van, and at that point Truchaud wondered if the vines had leaned away from the van out of self-preservation. She had a quick word with Truchaud, who pointed up the hill at Lenoir, and she stomped up the hill towards him. From the bowels of the van three more people alighted. One of them, in a sharp suit that fitted slightly too loosely, as if the wearer had been on a recent crash diet and had not yet invested in a new wardrobe, stopped and talked to Truchaud; while the other two, dressed in overalls and hoods, looked like they were about to take on a swarm of bees that had lost its communal sense of humour. Both of them carried cases.

The woman was definitely Mrs Clermont. Lenoir could feel his anxiety level increasing as she stomped towards him. He mused on the Mrs title. It implied she was married, and that therefore hidden in the background there was a Mr Clermont. Was he still alive, or had she already crushed the life out of him? He was stunned at his own thought processes; here he was surrounded by gore, and he was conjuring up the image of a little man being suffocated by the harridan marching towards him.

'Name?' she shouted as soon as she was within earshot.

Lenoir waited until he was sure she would hear his reply and then announced that he was Sergeant Lenoir of the local gendarmerie.

'Yes, you fool, I know who you are, I wanted to know who the victim is.'

'I've no idea as yet,' he replied. 'Mac has gone off to find the owner of the tractor down there, Commander Truchaud says he'll be one of them.'

'One of them? You mean there's more than one?'

'Commander Truchaud said there were two, and as far as I can see, he was very lucky not to be the third.'

'Jesus Henry Christ!' she muttered under her breath, but was now close enough for Lenoir to hear what she had said. She looked at his feet and was pleased to note that he had been standing still in one place. She pointed at the shreds of Truchaud's coat at his feet. He reassured her that that was Truchaud's, which he had abandoned after the explosion. She called one of her 'beekeepers' and told them that the coat would need parcelling up separately, as it was a component of the survivor of the incident. Lenoir also pointed out the hand and wrist on his left.

'Heads?' she asked.

'I haven't seen one yet, but then, I haven't been tramping all over the scene,' he continued, 'I've been standing here protecting it until you and your team arrived.'

She looked drily at him. 'Okay young man, I think I approve of you. If you like, you can go down the hill and join Mr Truchaud, and I'll take over from here.'

'Handing over the scene to Madame Clermont,' he said, saluted, and slammed his heel into the ground beside his other boot. Both of them looked anxious for a moment, as there was the alarming crunch of hob nailed boot onto bone. Lenoir picked up his foot and looked at the ground beneath it. There was a shiny shard of bone in the print.

'I think you'd better leave the scene now,' she said coldly, 'and please don't salute again, heaven knows what evidence you might destroy next time.' She watched Lenoir move timidly off towards the vehicles at the bottom of the hill for a moment, and then her gaze went back to where he had been standing. Aside from the glint of bone in Lenoir's heel print, there was a small hole drilled in the earth at the edge of the crater, as if something had rotated there just before the explosion.

## CHAPTER 3

*Chambolle-Musigny and Nuits-Saint-Georges, almost immediately*

Truchaud watched the ferocious woman walk back up the hill away from him. He didn't really understand why she always made him feel so uncomfortable, but she did. All right, so he was already feeling uncomfortable; his shirt was sticking to his shoulders and back, and the glue was a blend of someone else's blood, his own sweat, and some very ripe grape juice. He took his phone out of his pocket and called Duquesne, explaining that he was just going to go home for a quick shower and a change of clothes, and he would be with him in twenty minutes, if that was okay. Needless to say, it was, and Captain Duquesne said he would help himself to a cup of coffee like he always did, despite his knowing the stuff at the town hall was of the synthetic variety. Truchaud decided not to waste any time; the thought of the captain's mood after a cup of the instant that Fauquet served up in the town hall did not bear thinking about. Captain Duquesne liked coffee. He liked coffee lots, but he invariably liked 'proper coffee' and his gendarmes knew this and had learned very quickly how to make proper coffee. Even the new girl, whose name Sergeant Lenoir couldn't remember, had learned how to make proper coffee to Captain Duquesne's taste before she had learned her way round Nuits-Saint-Georges. It was only a little town on the surface; it was underground where things got more complicated, and nobody had taken her down into a cellar yet.

Commander Truchaud walked through the door into his office just in time to catch the captain of gendarmes' grimace at the mug on his desk. 'Shall we wander down to the Café to replace that?' he asked. 'I'm sure Mrs Tournier could make an improvement on that stuff.'

Captain Duquesne did not need a second hint and was up in a flash. 'Thanks for the cuppa,' he said to Fauquet on his way out, 'didn't have time to finish it; Truchaud's got something he needs to show me.' Fauquet wasn't fooled for a moment, but smiled gently both to himself and at the backs of the senior policemen who were leaving. He would take the mug from the desk later when its contents had really gone cold. It was then that he would wash it up.

They walked out of the front door of the Town Hall and crossed the road before turning left. They crossed the junction into the Place de la République and headed for the Café du Centre.

The streets were busy still. The holidaymakers were now older than they had been a fortnight before, as throughout Europe the schools had reopened for business. The streets were nonetheless still full of people, it was simply that they were more mature and rather less noisy than they had been previously. They would probably consume less ice cream and rather more beer and wine while they were about it too. That would be when the bars and cafés were actually open for business. There was a little activity in the cafés of the Place de la République, but that was more in the way of getting ready to serve people than actually doing so. One of the girls outside the Café du Centre suggested vaguely that they might be ready in half an hour if they cared to sit down and wait, but the commander and the captain knew that they would find an acceptable cup of coffee within a five-minute walk from there in the gendarmerie, and so that's where they headed.

As the gendarmes themselves were all out and about, mostly in Vosne-Romanée, the captain unlocked the door and let them in. He also proved most adept in the use of the coffee machine too. 'Don't tell any of them I can do this,' he said, 'If they catch on I'll have to make my own coffee from here on in. So, if anyone asks, you made these.'

They were sitting in his office nursing their coffees when there was the sound of activity at the door. Duquesne got up and was about to walk through to the reception when the front door slammed shut and there was a tap on his door, and in walked Constable 'Mac' Montbard, her strawberry blonde locks somewhat awry.

'Well I think I've found out who one of the victims was,' she said, producing a photograph in a frame. She passed it to Truchaud. 'Was this your man on the tractor, sir?'

Truchaud looked at it for a moment trying to imagine the bucolic, smiling face in the picture in angry mode. Yes, that would fit. 'I think so, yes,' he replied. 'Who was he?'

'Well, the owner of the tractor was the man in the picture you're holding. His name was Pierre Parmentier...' she started.

'Parmentier,' he mused, 'I've heard of him. Don't remember ever meeting him though. Tell me more.'

'Well, I traced the tractor back to his address in Chambolle-Musigny by the registration number. His wife was at home, and I spent the last half hour with her. She's very upset, as you can imagine. I didn't give her any gory details about what happened, just that there had been an "accident" with the tractor.'

'Any kids?' asked Duquesne.

'No, they didn't have any, but he does have a mother who lives with his brother, René. I gather they all live in Meursault, to the south of Beaune. I gather he's also in the wine business.'

'As are they all,' remarked Duquesne drily. 'You know, I'm amazed you managed to escape to join the police at all. These families seem to be equipped with handcuffs to keep their children in the business.'

'I didn't escape,' replied Truchaud, 'there wasn't any room for me. I was the reserve on the bench who wasn't needed. If Bertin had decided to go off and write poetry or perhaps go into professional politics or something, then I would have been summoned in to the family firm, but as he showed no signs of musical talent or corruptibility, I was surplus to requirements. Anyway, Mac, you were telling us about Pierre Parmentier.'

'Late thirties, he was.' *Ten years younger than me then*, thought Truchaud, *I wouldn't have known him at school then*. He plugged back into what Mac was saying. 'He inherited his half of the family business when his father succumbed to lung cancer four years ago. I gather the ban on public smoking happened too late for the old man, being an inveterate forty-Gitanes-a-day man. She said Pierre was already the chief winemaker for the northern half of the estate, as he was better with the Pinot Noir grapes, and René got on better with the Chardonnays, so he ran the southern half of the estate. They were already the chief winemakers of their respective areas while their father was still alive. The old man just oversaw everything, including the running of the business. I gather the two families are on good terms. I spoke to René's wife on the phone and told her what happened, and she said she would come right over. She should be at the house by now.'

'Did she have any idea who the man with the bomb might be?' asked Truchaud.

'I didn't go into any details about what happened, so I didn't actually mention him. I think she'll still be hoping that you don't identify her husband and that someone stole his tractor and had their own fatal accident on it. What do you think we ought to do when she asks to see her husband?'

'We ought to discuss that with Madame Clermont, which of course she may be doing anyway.' He swallowed the remainder of his coffee. 'Can you run me back to the town hall to pick up my car?' he asked Mac.

'And meanwhile I'll contact young Lieutenant Saint-André in the Gevrey-Chambertin gendarmerie,' said Duquesne, 'just to let him know what's going on and that we've got it covered. When you get out to the village, can you send back one of the kids to man the front desk?'

'Will do, sir,' she replied, wondering whether he now considered her too old to be one of 'the kids' and smarted a little at that. And with that, she and Truchaud left the gendarmerie. She drove them over to the car park behind the town hall. As he got out, he put his head in through the passenger door again. 'Presumably you're going to return this car to Lenoir,' he said.

'I imagine he'd like that, yes, sir,' she replied.

'Well, if I follow you, once you've given the car back to Lenoir and told him to ship a constable back to the gendarmerie front desk, you and I can go and see Madame Parmentier. I think that would only be polite.'

'If that's okay with you, sir.'

'Lead on,' he said and climbed into his BX and followed her out back onto the seventy-four. The handover to Lenoir only took a couple of moments, and having got his hands back on what he considered to be his car, he wasn't going to risk losing it to anyone else. It was the young constable, Savioli, who drew the short straw to get driven by Lenoir back to the gendarmerie. The new girl — damn it what was her name? — was following Madame Clermont around rather too closely to be interrupted anyway. Meanwhile Truchaud was guided into the very narrow and twisting streets of Chambolle-Musigny. He was convinced that the road was less threatening once he had got through the gates into Domaine Parmentier. There were another couple of tractors parked in the courtyard and a fairly large Peugeot up by the steps up to the front door of the house. The car wore one or two scars on its paintwork that suggested that it was perhaps too large a car for that village.

Truchaud was unable to decide which Mrs Parmentier was the recently bereft one, as they were both full of tears. Mac introduced the woman she had met before and said, 'And you must be René's wife?'

'I am, now please tell me exactly what happened.' Both women focussed on the gendarme in uniform rather than the somewhat older man in civilian clothes she had brought with her. Truchaud thought he really must get into the habit of putting on his Municipal Police uniform once in a while. He introduced himself, and the presence of a senior police officer did not seem to make the two women any happier.

'My husband was murdered?' asked Pierre Parmentier's widow.

'Not exactly,' replied Truchaud. 'I think the technical phrase is "unlawfully killed". The whole picture is somewhat more complicated than how my colleague originally painted it. There were two casualties in the incident, and your husband got involved unfortunately because he was trying to find out what was going on in his vineyard. He does have a parcel in the Romanée-Saint-Vivant vineyard, doesn't he?'

His widow nodded. 'And if he hadn't?' she asked.

'I would like to think, being the good man that he was, he would still have got involved,' said Truchaud gently. 'There was an incident going on right in the middle of the vineyard, and he walked over to investigate.'

'What sort of incident?'

'I was just about to interview a man with a bomb strapped to his chest who was, himself, strapped to a chair in the middle of a vineyard. Everybody's vines are just about ready to pick at the moment, and everybody is looking out for everybody else. If you see something unexpected going on in the middle of a vineyard, you go and investigate. That's what I was doing too.'

'You're a winemaker too, Commander?' she asked.

'In a manner of speaking. My family is, in Nuits-Saint-Georges. On another occasion it might be you and your vineyard that someone is doing something strange in.'

'So, my husband was killed and you survived. May I ask why it happened that way round?'

Truchaud looked at her sadly. 'Pure damned luck,' he replied. He told her what had happened at the vineyard, only leaving out the strange conversation he had had on the telephone.

'So, who was the man on the chair?' she asked.

'At this moment, we've no idea. I don't think your husband recognised him either, as far as I could tell, although it all happened too quickly to ask him.'

'Am I going to be able to see my husband?' she asked.

'I will ask the coroner whether that will be possible, but I might suggest anyway that perhaps you would be better off remembering him how he was,' he said, waving a hand at the framed photo Mac had returned to the mantelpiece, 'rather than how he is now.'

Perhaps it wasn't the most tactful thing to have said, but sooner or later she would realise exactly the extent of what had happened. Both women wailed and clung on to each other for a moment.

'Would you like me to make a cup of tea or find a bottle of cognac or something?' Mac asked the air.

'I've got a bottle of Marc here,' sobbed Mrs Pierre and walked over to a rather ornate cabinet and took out a very dusty half-empty bottle with a sticky label on the front with Marc 1976 handwritten on it. 'I don't drink myself, apart from tasting the odd drop that I put in the cooking, but you're welcome to one if you want.'

Mac backtracked hurriedly, 'No, no, no,' she said, 'I wasn't suggesting that I or the commander would like a drink, I was wondering whether you or your sister-in-law might like one.'

'Oh,' she thought for a minute, 'Jeannette? Would you like a shot of Marc?'

'Only if you're going to have one,' Mrs René replied, 'otherwise no thank you.' The widowed Mrs. Parmentier put the bottle back in the cupboard. 'That bottle was distilled by my father-in-law back in 1976,' she said. 'He never bothered to make a lot of Marc, but he hung on to that batch. He said it was the first batch he ever made and put it into a little barrel down in the cellar and apparently forgot all about it. Pierre found it down there about twenty-five years later and wondering what it was, drew off that bottle. It was an interesting night, the night they found that. I had two very drunk Parmentier men on my hands to put to bed. Mami was having nothing to do with either of them.' She was brightening up slightly as she remembered this little episode in her husband's life.

Truchaud thought for a moment that this might be a good moment to take their leave. At this point he doubted that they would have anything instructive to tell him, and at the same time he didn't have anything more to tell them. That would all happen in the fullness of time, and he would no doubt meet up with the surviving Parmentiers over the next few days. He stood up just as Mac was thinking about sitting down again. 'May I offer my condolences to you both Mesdames and ask your permission to visit you again shortly. Constable Montbard here will be contactable at the gendarmerie should you need or want anything.'

Mac was fishing in the pocket of her uniform as he spoke. She pulled out a slightly tatty visiting card that had obviously been rumpled when she had stood up and sat down. 'My contact number's on that. It will get through to me directly, it's a mobile phone, and I carry it on me even when I'm not on duty.'

'You're on duty even when you're not on duty?' asked the less bereft of the two women, cocking an eye at her.

'In a manner of speaking, yes, I will always answer my phone. If I'm somewhere off patch and you're in need of a gendarme instantly, I'll take a message and get someone on duty round to you as quickly as possible.'

'Thank you, we'll try not to bother you unnecessarily.'

With that and polite farewells, the police left the house. Walking to the car, Truchaud remarked drily, 'Well, that's the uncomfortable bit over with for the time being. Now we have to get down to finding out who the human bomb was and why someone would want to kill him. I think we need to be talking to the forensics team and see if they can identify him. I think we need to talk to Mrs Clermont sooner or later to see if she's found anything identifiable, don't you? Though probably I think we need to give her at least a chance to get away from the crime scene and back in her office. Any ideas in the meantime?'

## CHAPTER 4

*Nuits-Saint-Georges, later that day*

Truchaud drove them back to the town centre. He parked out front in the empty parking slot labelled 'Free for People Visiting the Gendarmerie,' thinking that people would believe that the gendarmes would bother to report a car parked in that spot belonging to someone not visiting the gendarmerie to the municipal police. To park in all the other slots, you had to stick a Euro and some change into a small box, and it would give you a ticket, which you would stick in your windscreen. Truchaud knew all about that, as it was his municipal police department based in the town hall that was responsible for all the parking issues in Nuits-Saint-Georges. He knew very well that none of his coppers would know anything whatsoever about who might or might not have any business in the gendarmerie. Joe Average was probably blissfully unaware how rarely the different branches of law enforcement ever spoke to each other. Unless, of course, your names were Truchaud or Duquesne.

Savioli sat in reception, hoping for someone to come in or to call him on the phone or even to commit a robbery, anything to take his mind off the tedium and the oppressive heat. There was no breeze in reception like there was outside. He was in shirtsleeves, and he gave Truchaud a hangdog look when he walked in, rather like a puppy hoping he would be taken out for a walk in the fresh air. Unfortunately, Truchaud's only solution to reduce his suffering was to ask him if he had seen Constable Montbard recently. Crestfallen, Savioli told him she was out back, 'where it's cooler.'

Truth be told, it wasn't a lot cooler, but the humidity was reduced, as the window was open and a little air circulation was possible. Mac was writing a report on the laptop. She looked up at him as he walked in. 'Just thinking sir,' she said. 'The victim — you know, Pierre Parmentier — didn't have any kids. No, I know it isn't any of my business, but why not?'

'Why isn't it your business, Constable?' replied Truchaud, 'The man's just been illegally killed on your patch, I would have thought that anything to do with him was your business until we prove it isn't. You are his family liaison officer, so to speak.'

Her eyes opened a bit wider. 'Am I?' she asked. 'I've got an official job on a case?'

'Don't you usually have official jobs on cases round here?' He had worked on and off with this squad for six months, and he had never really thought about how the little gendarmerie actually organised itself.

'Well, no not really. A case crops up and the captain just takes it on, and we all pile in together so to speak. I expect it's considerably different in Paris than it is in Nuits-Saint-Georges. We wouldn't have even one detective here if you didn't happen to be around.'

Truchaud thought about that for a moment. The difference in scale was indeed vast. 'Going back to the point you brought up,' he said, 'kids. Why did you ask?'

'Well, I was thinking, just for the moment, just assuming that Parmentier's killing wasn't just a piece of collateral damage, so to speak, who would have a motive for killing him. The first question that then cropped up, "Who gains?" And from that I then thought, well who inherits the vineyard? He hasn't got any descendants.'

'And you immediately asked yourself, why not?'

'Well, think about it for a moment, sir, you own Domaine Truchaud outright after yesterday, and you haven't got kids.' It hadn't even crossed his mind for an instant that since yesterday's funeral he was now the legal owner of his family's wine business. 'Now suppose the bomb yesterday had taken you with it as well, what would have happened there?'

'Well Bruno, I suppose …' replied the detective uncertainly.

'But you've only had a day or so to think about that, and there is a very good reason why you've not got an obvious heir.'

'Oh?' he asked, rather uncertain where she was going with this.

'You're not married,' she replied.

'Quite,' he said, still uncertain where the constable's train of thought was headed and becoming increasingly uncomfortable about it.

'But he was. And we met his wife this afternoon.'

'We did,' Truchaud agreed. 'And…?'

'Well, she didn't appear to be a recent addition to his family. She appeared to have been married to him for a while, so why no children? That's what I was puzzling over. Now, there are various reasons why people who have been married for a while don't have children. Firstly, it could simply be because they don't want kids. Maybe they simply don't like kids, or perhaps they have other things to do with their time at the moment, and therefore kids will come along later. It could be that they can't have kids for one reason or another, or it could be that they did have kids, but something happened to them.'

'We definitely do know there are no children, don't we?' Truchaud asked thoughtfully.

'I did ask that, it was one of the first things I did ask. I wanted to be sure there wasn't some nice fluffy kid at school that day who was just about to walk in all bouncy from lessons and find to her horror that Dad had just been blown to bits. Definitely no kids, sir.'

'You've been thinking about this, haven't you Constable?'

'Oh, yes sir, and I couldn't find any scores that needed settling either. Nor could I find any evidence of Captain Jealousy raising his ugly head.'

'You mean you asked the new widow if she knew who might have it in for her husband or who might be homicidally jealous of him?'

'Not in quite so many words, sir, and I hope she didn't realise I was fishing at all, but I did have my notebook out and explained that I was on duty, and that I had to take notes to keep the captain and our new sergeant happy.'

'Oh yes, I remember having had a new sergeant myself back in the day. Is Sergeant Lenoir hard work?'

She grinned at him, the freckles over the bridge of her nose puckering up, 'Not really, he's still a bit of an old sweetie underneath it all, but please don't tell him I said that. He wants people to think he's a real hard man.'

'You can count on my discretion, Constable. Now, where do we go from here? I think you're right. I think we do need to investigate Pierre Parmentier's life as if he were the main target. Certainly, his vines were in the killer's sights at the very least.'

'Hang on sir, do we actually know that?'

'Well, he has got vines in the Romanée-Saint-Vivant vineyard, hasn't he?'

'But was the human bomb placed in his patch or in somebody else's, and was he just being supportive of a friend and colleague when he tried to find out what was going on? I understand that as far as Vosne-Romanée Crus goes, it was one of the larger ones.'

'I think you'd better get your notebook out, Constable. You're asking a lot of questions that are going to need answering, and we don't want to forget to answer them because they weren't written down.'

'Yes sir.' She smiled again, feeling very pleased with herself that she had got the commander from Paris's full attention. She had worked as part of the team over the past six months alongside Truchaud, but this was really the first time that they had been working this closely together, just the two of them. 'Just exactly which patch of the Saint-Vivant does Parmentier own, and therefore was he being protective of his own or a neighbour's patch, and if so who is that neighbour? And why haven't the Parmentier's got any kids? Anything else?' she asked while rapidly scribbling in her notebook.

'I think that will be enough to be going on with,' said Truchaud, 'and other questions may well crop up as a result. Shall we go?' he asked.

'What, right now?'

'No time like the present, Constable, if for no other reason than we need to get the Parmentiers used to seeing our faces until there is a solution to hand.'

'But isn't that harassment, sir?'

'Only if someone has actually started using the word. So, let's go now, you can do your bit for bureaucracy later when I'm otherwise engaged.' He put his nose round Captain Duquesne's office door. The captain was looking at the screen on his desk while absent-mindedly slurping on a cup of coffee. *That's interesting*, Truchaud thought, *I wonder who made him that? Poor old Savioli, not having much fun is he today?* 'I'm taking Mac out with me, we've got some questions to ask.'

Duquesne looked up, 'Still within our jurisdiction, I assume?' he asked.

'Yes. It's all this case, and they are her questions after all.'

'You'll be telling me next that you think she'd make a good detective one day,' Duquesne smiled over the top of his cup.

'I've always thought that,' said Truchaud with a smile. 'Anyway, we've got to go if you don't mind my taking her with me.'

'Be my guest, and Constable Montbard,' he tossed past the detective's shoulder, 'make the gendarmerie proud.'

'Yes sir,' she said, and Duquesne could almost have sworn that she skipped as she followed Truchaud out past the sweltering and despondent Savioli.

They stayed on the seventy-four till Vougeot, and when he reached the roundabout on the edge of the village itself, he turned left into what constituted a built-up area round there. He did a sharp right and then left dink, and set off up the hill past the top-ranked vineyards of Musigny and, closer to the road, Les Amoureuses. The naming of Les Amoureuses had always amused Truchaud when he was a child. A vineyard called 'The Lovers' was always romantic, but one that specified that the lovers in question were both of the female persuasion always made small boys giggle. More recently, he had wondered why the bureaucrats concerned had not awarded it Grand Cru status when the badges were handed out. He had always been seriously impressed on the rare occasions the stuff had passed his lips. Still, the fact that the vineyard only held a Premier Village Cru status didn't seem to affect the price very much. The stuff was still very expensive.

He wiggled the car though the narrow and twisty village streets of Chambolle, all of which had been constructed long before the invention of the motorcar, and it showed. They pulled into the wide courtyard that a sign on the wall outside said belonged to one 'Domaine P. Parmentier Père et Fils'. Ironic, thought Truchaud, there isn't a 'Son' at all. Still, it gives us an opening to discuss.

'Oh, that,' said Mrs. Pierre Parmentier, 'The "Fils" in the title was in fact Pierre and René's father. It may even have been his grandfather for all I know. Certainly, their Grandfather was Paul Parmentier, and he died not long after the Second World War. His son Lucien, who was Pierre and René's father, wouldn't have dreamed of changing the name of the firm during his lifetime. He was intensely loyal to his father's memory, and indeed equally proud of what the family achieved. Lucien was generally held to be a great winemaker, and he swore that everything he knew he had learned from his father, Paul. I don't offhand remember what Paul's father was called.' She looked across to her sister-in-law, who shrugged. She didn't appear to know either.

'It's not important,' said Truchaud, 'I was interested, that's all. Bearing in mind that you and Pierre never had a son.' He was feeling awkward, however circuitous the route he was taking to get to the question he wanted to ask. However, the Parmentier ladies didn't appear to notice.

When he finally got to the question that was puzzling him, the answer came through easily and painlessly enough, though the reason for the problem very obviously wasn't. 'Well, we had been trying for a while without success, and then I did fall preganant, and that was all very exciting for about a week, and then I started getting pain, and I was afraid I was miscarrying. And then I ended up being rushed into the Bocage Hospital in Dijon when the pain started getting worse. It turned out that my pregnancy was in the tube and the whole thing was about to burst.'

She took a breath for a moment, and her sister-in-law took over. 'It was awful for all of us,' she said. 'It was an emergency operation and they had to take the left tube out, and it didn't stop there did it love?'

'Go on, you tell them,' said the woman, who was becoming tearful again.

*Mrs René; I really must find out their own names, I can't go on thinking of them as appendages of their husbands*, Truchaud thought, though, for the time being, the woman he knew as Mrs René carried on with the narrative. 'Well, while the surgeons were in there they had a look around and discovered she had lumps in her womb; what were they called, dear?'

'Fibroids,' replied the other woman with a choke in her voice.

'Anyway, they told her that without further surgery, the only pregnancy she would ever have would be in the other tube, and that would be another disaster.'

'So, we thought about it,' Mrs Pierre joined in, 'and we decided to go for the surgery and have the fibroids taken out.'

'I never did fully understand, why didn't they do that while they were in the first time?' asked Mrs René.

'I wasn't very well, if you remember, so they didn't want to do anything more dramatic at that moment. They wanted to wait until I was very fit and healthy before they did anything else. Just as well they did, considering what happened.'

'Oh?' said Truchaud with a question mark in his voice.

'Well, yes, they did say that there was a slight risk that if after shelling out the fibroids they might not be able to stop the bleeding, and if that happened, then they might have to take the whole womb out to save my life. And that was exactly what happened. Anyway, no womb means there is no oven in which to cook a baby, so to speak. We were talking only last week about adoption…' And that was as far as she got before the tears got the better of her again. After a while she calmed down and said, 'At least René and Jeanette have children, so the future of the family *domaine* is intact.'

*Ah!* thought Truchaud, so Mrs René here is called Jeannette. That's another question answered.

'Oh yes?' chipped in Montbard, looking directly at Jeannette to try to take some of the pressure off the widow Parmentier, 'And what are they called?'

'They're Lucien, after his grandfather, and Marine after my mother.'

'How old are they?'

'Lucien's ten and Marine's eight.'

'Still very young then?'

'Not too young to be mobile hurricanes, very active the pair of them; still, one wouldn't have it any other way. It's a parent's nightmare, having dull children, don't you think.'

'I've never really thought about it like that,' said Montbard, 'I'm not married myself, so I don't have kids.'

'Yes, dear, but you're still very young.' Truchaud noticed that Jeannette called everybody 'dear', at least everybody apart from himself, and he hoped she wasn't going to start.

'We're hoping that at least one of Jeannette's kids shows a talent, or at least an interest in fine wine. We call it the "Gift". At least this "Gift" is not gender-specific. There are women with great reputations here in Chambolle.'

'Not just in Chambolle, dear, but up and down the Côte there are women who make fine wine and put their names on the bottles, so if Marine is a girl with the Gift, it's not going to be a problem. After all, dear, you've got it too.'

45

*Now that was an interesting comment*, thought Truchaud. Mrs Pierre is a skilled winemaker too. He wondered whether she was in fact the person responsible for the wine he had heard such positive things about since the case had started; no, that wasn't quite true. He had heard of Domaine J. Parmentier when he was still at school. When the usual pre-vintage buzz was up and running, and he could swear he could remember susurrations like 'I wonder how Parmentier's are going to do this year' out there on the wind.

'Yes, but I'm not related by blood to Marine, I'm just her aunt.'

'Maybe the Gift is as common as having blue eyes. It's just that we wouldn't know if someone had got the Gift if they lived, say, in Le Mans.'

Montbard giggled. 'Unless their Gift was being able to drive very fast round corners,' she said. Truchaud wondered whether she was thinking about her newly ordained Sergeant Lenoir when she said that.

'Quite,' said Jeannette slightly stonily, obviously not completely appreciating the feisty young gendarme chipping in.

The conversation was disturbed by the sound of a key turning in the lock of the front door. All four of them looked up. A tall, bullish, rather severe looking man appeared at the living room door. Truchaud looked at the two women to assess their response. Jeannette leapt up. 'René!' she said, 'Thank you for coming, I didn't know whether you would be able to get away.'

It was after he had greeted his sister-in-law that he appeared to realise there was a gendarme and somebody else in the room. 'Can I help you?' he asked, with an edge in his voice.

'We're the police,' said Truchaud, 'I'm from the municipal and Constable Montbard's from the gendarmerie.'

'You thought someone of my brother-in-law's standing only deserved a constable?' René replied drily.

'I am the municipal chief, so Constable Montbard is accompanying me. Is that a problem?' Truchaud became equally terse. He felt that Mrs Pierre deserved better than a testosterone test in her front room.

Apparently after a moment, so did René. 'I'm sorry,' he said, 'it's all been a shock. Please excuse me everybody.' He introduced himself, 'I'm René Parmentier,' and after a moment he added, 'Pierre's brother.'

The police then introduced themselves again, and the atmosphere calmed down somewhat. 'We're here just trying to piece together exactly what happened,' Truchaud told him.

'I don't get it, why would anybody want to kill my brother? I thought everybody liked him.'

'That's just it, sir. We don't know that anybody wanted that. It is possible that this was all a terrible accident,' were Montbard's first words to René.

'But I heard that someone just blew up part of the vineyard. Doesn't sound like much of an accident to me.'

'But the target might not have been your brother, he just happened to get in the way.'

'But why would he want to do a thing like that?' René asked.

'He might have been trying to save my life,' replied Truchaud softly.

'Without trying to sound harsh, I ask again, why would he want to do a thing like that?'

'Because I was there, and he probably didn't know what I was guarding was a bomb.'

'Didn't he ask?'

'No.'

'Didn't you tell him anyway?'

'We didn't have time. He arrived and bang; it was literally that fast.'

Everyone looked at each other wondering what to say next, and not having the faintest idea.

It was René who broke the silence, and ignoring the police presence, he said, 'Are you still able to carry on with the vintage?' he asked his sister-in-law. 'Do you know if you need people to help?'

'As far as I know, Pierre had it all set up. Most of the students are lined up, and we've got one or two foreign students already on site. I think we'll be all right.'

'And you think you can face it yourself?'

'I have absolutely no idea, but the only thing I can do is try. Can I call you if I run into trouble?'

'At absolutely any time at all. After all, when Pierre and I were children our father ran both *domaines* himself, and he made some pretty amazing wine in both areas. I suppose it was really only one *domaine*, but it had as many vines and grapes as the pair of them do now.'

'But he was your father, and they say he could turn a pig's ear into a silk purse at any time.'

Truchaud watched the two Parmentiers support each other's grief by talking viticulture and the upcoming vintage. They were going through the same major upheaval as had his own family's Domaine Truchaud earlier in the year: the loss of its prime winemaker. Truchaud's father had been lost to the Domaine much earlier than he had been lost to the world, of course. He had been probably out of it for last year's vintage, if the truth be told, but Bertin, Truchaud's brother, covered for him and his illness. It was only when Bertin died that his father's illness had become apparent. It would be interesting to see how each Domaine coped with the vintage that was about to begin. He would also be very interested to compare the relative quality of each wine that they made against other families that had not suffered such a major loss during the past year. In a point of fact Truchaud's loss had been greater, as it had lost both its winemakers in the past year; at least Parmentier's still had René aboard. He wondered whether René had the 'Gift'. He promised himself to try to find a bottle René's Beaune just to see what it was like. Sounds like fish was on order soon, after all, René was supposed to be the white wine expert in the family. A bottle or two of his Meursault and some trout for the barbecue and all of his extending family would be content for this evening. He started making a mental shopping list. The flat where his father had lived until he went into the nursing home six weeks ago had been fully cleared and cleaned and now had a couple of students resident in preparation for the next few weeks' frenetic activity. They were currently cleaning and sterilising the fermentation tanks in preparation to receive the products of nature's bounty. They may only have three wines of their own to work on, but Truchaud was justifiably proud of their Grant Cru and their two rather good village Crus, which would all be kept scrupulously apart from each other during the harvest, all the way down to different labels on bottles when they finally saw the market place in the best part of two years' time.

Perhaps it was the time to quietly leave the scene. They had no more questions to ask at the moment, and he didn't know what Mac was feeling, but right now he felt his presence was an unnecessary embarrassment. He knew that he would need to reappear at a probably inopportune moment during the vintage, so he felt that he might as well bid his farewell now.

He fished in his wallet for a few visiting cards, and handed them out. 'I will no doubt need to be seeing you again soon anyway, but if you feel you need to talk to any of us at any time, please get in touch. My mobile phone number is also on that card as well as my office number.' Mac Montbard was also handing out gendarmerie cards, explaining that the Nuits-Saint-Georges gendarmerie was handling this case, although neither of the houses were in its jurisdiction. Presumably René's house was in the Beaune sector, he wasn't exactly sure where it was that they lived, he knew it was south of the Beaune built up area. Mac Montbard jotted his address and telephone number down in her notebook, and they bade the Parmentiers a temporary farewell.

'Well, sir, what did you make of all that?' Montbard asked Truchaud once he had negotiated the gate without hitting either of the gateposts or scraping the exhaust pipe on the bump on the way out.

'I thought they were putting a very brave face on it all,' he replied and then added after a moment, 'probably for our benefit.'

# CHAPTER 5

*Nuits-Saint-Georges, lunchtime*

Truchaud picked one of the fish off the barbecue and turned it. He was finding it deeply soothing to be concentrating on something as precise and important as preparing a meal after the bewildering chaos of earlier events.

The fish smelled good, especially with the tarragon-scented smoke behind it. The wine, a Meursault from four years ago, he had put in the fridge, just to bring it back down to 'cellar temperature'. It wouldn't stay in there very long. He was beginning to realise he was becoming quite a 'winey', picking the food to suit the wine rather than the wine to fit the meal. Still, as this was police work, seeing what René Parmentier's wine was really like, he owed it a chance to show itself off at its best.

He had already made the salad dressing, being a blend of walnut oil, mustard, honey, crushed garlic and wine vinegar; he had mixed them together and stirred and finally put the mixture in a bottle and shaken it like a cocktail waiter. He had picked up the lettuce from the shop next to the fishmonger, and also some rather dark tomatoes, which looked delicious. He looked around and saw no one watching, and so he popped a slice of tomato into his mouth. It was everything a tomato should be.

There was bread and some fresh butter on the slab in the kitchen, and soon he would take the wine out of the fridge and pull the cork. All under control, he thought, and he just hoped that Fauquet wouldn't call him with an emergency that he had to drop everything and run. Hang on a minute, he and Fauquet were part of the municipal police. If there was anything that was that urgent it wouldn't be a municipal police problem, it would be one for the gendarmerie in Nuits-Saint-Georges, or even the civilian police in Dijon. He thought about that for a moment. How could he be happy about a situation where a case crossing his desk that was important enough to disturb his lunch was too important for someone like him to deal with? He thought about having an apéro just to calm himself down, he looked up at that bottle of Suze on the shelf above him that probably hadn't been disturbed for years. After a moment's thought, that's where he left it.

He walked back into the house and got out a pile of plates and took them out to the table in the yard, and went back and put a number of everyday wineglasses, tumblers, and cutlery on a tray, and took that out to the table as well. He got out a litre decanter from the cupboard in preparation for filling it with water and put it on the slab. He took the bottle of Meursault out of the fridge and put that on the slab too and then returned to the barbecue to turn the fish again.

The arrival of the family and the students at the gate showed Michelle's exquisite sense of timing. She marched them through the gate just as Truchaud was beginning to worry about overcooking the fish. Michelle, his sister-in-law, had taken over the fiscal side of the family business since the deaths of his father and brother; well maybe that's not fair, he had a sneaking suspicion that she had been running the business for some considerable time before that. Simon Maréchale, head winemaker of Domaine Laforge was now their head winemaker too, and Michelle and Marie-Claire Laforge, being the women behind the firms, were becoming close chums. Simon wasn't part of the lunch party, as no doubt he was busy at Laforge's, certainly the larger Domaine of the two. But another reason why he wasn't there might well have been the identity of one of the students who was.

He smiled at Suzette Girand, who hoped to be going off somewhere intellectually stimulating very soon, depending on the final conclusions of the examiners at Dijon University on her dissertation. She was the local doctor's daughter, but as far as Truchaud was concerned her far more important parent was her mother, who was someone who, in his youth, had been the girl of his dreams. She was also the sister of Jean Parnault, now the top man of the more prestigious families in the Côte de Nuits who had been a very close school friend of his brother's back in the day. As Jean and Bertin had been inseparable as kids, he had teamed up with the sister. Her daughter sitting in front of him, Suzette, had been, for a while anyway, romantically linked with Simon Maréchale, but that had gone the way of many things during the summer just past. It surprised Truchaud pleasantly that she had nevertheless chosen to come and work at his little Domaine that year, rather than at her prestigious family's larger operation. Especially as things could potentially get awkward with Simon and his new girlfriend, who had arrived out of the blue in the heat of the summer and blown his socks off. He was teaching the new girl, being a German, how to speak French, among a lot of other things, on a tit for tat basis so to speak.

Suzette, although born and brought up among the vines and barrels of a Nuits-Saint-Georges wine family with viticulture running in her veins, said she was more interested in the humanities than wine. However, she was an extremely useful person to have around. As an aside, she had brought her roommate from Dijon University whose real name was Edouard, but Truchaud knew him as Hairy Eddie. He too had finished his course at Dijon University and was thinking, in typical slow and steady Hairy Eddie fashion, about what he was going to do next. Suzette recruited him to come and work at Truchaud's for the vintage, and had reassured all concerned that he would be good and reliable, and would never be stoned in the vineyard. Eddie, from his side of the fence, was well aware that Truchaud's would be teeming with police a lot of the time and therefore maintained an appropriate discretion as to his non-viticultural activities. There were two other students, one who had just signed on at the viticultural University in Beaune, and another who was based somewhere else altogether and would have to disappear by the first of October come what may, as that was when his serious studies restarted. All of them looked at Suzette as their sort of foreman, as she knew all about this wine stuff, and at the same time she was one of their generation. And as for Bruno, Truchaud's twelve-year-old nephew who was still at school, turning up in the late afternoon, well, he was the real expert on the vines belonging to Domaine Truchaud.

Eddie came out with the decanter full of very cold plain tap water, Domaine Municipale, and parked it on the table. Suzette carried out the salad and one of the other two carried out the bread. Truchaud had himself pulled the cork from the wine already and parked that on the table before he served everyone with a fish each.

Michelle looked at the label on the wine bottle. 'Interesting choice,' she said, 'Any particular reason?' And Truchaud told his family enough about his day so far that he could ethically get away with.

'Oh, Uncle Charlie,' said Suzette, looking earnestly at Truchaud's rather battered appearance. 'You really do attract trouble, don't you?' Apart from her mother, she was the only person who called him Charlie, and he was very touched that she called him Uncle Charlie. Somehow, he knew that the girl totally understood what could have happened twenty years before, but somehow never did.

He poured the wine into his glass and gave it a sniff. 'May I?' asked Suzette from across the table. He poured a splash into her glass too. She too took a sniff, and Eddie had a chuckle. Pretentious or what!

'What do you think?' he asked.

She took a mouthful and ran it round her tongue. She looked at the others around the table, and as this was the only wine they were going to be asked to taste at that moment, she didn't look for a spittoon but just swallowed. She looked thoughtfully at Truchaud. 'Do you want me to be honest?' she asked.

'Always,' he replied, 'especially on matters of wine.'

She shrugged. 'I've tasted better,' was her considered opinion.

Truchaud took a mouthful and did the tasting manoeuvre too, pulling the same faces like Suzette, and, like Suzette, he swallowed the mouthful at the end of the facial gymnastics. 'I see what you mean,' he replied. 'If it was a branded "vin Ordinaire" called "Bacchus's Dream" it would be an excellent deal, but knowing it's boasting to be a "premier cru Meursault" then that little bottle is at a distinct disadvantage, it has something to live up to. Its report card would read "It could do better".'

'Have you tasted anybody else's wine from that vineyard?' Suzette asked.

'To be honest, I really don't remember. I don't drink Meursault often enough to know the fine-tuning of what individual wines taste like. Why do you ask?'

'Well, you have to remember that the rankings were handed out eighty odd years ago to that patch of ground.' She turned to Eddie and the other students. 'That's how the ranking system works. A piece of ground is awarded Grand Cru status for its potential ability to make great wine. It is up to the winemaker to make the *terroir's* dreams come true. Now those vineyards have probably changed hands several times since the thirties. The patch of ground may be in a very different condition than it was when it was originally ranked.

It would be interesting to see what other winemakers have made out of that vineyard.'

'Are you one of those who would tear up the current ranking system and start again?' Truchaud asked the green-eyed girl with a grin.

'I wouldn't dare, my uncle would be furious, and I suspect you and the Laforges would be too.'

'I would have thought your uncle's Chambertin would stand even the closest individual re-evaluation. I tasted some with him the other day.'

'Yes, I heard about that. I gather you and he did a swapsie tasting, him with his Chambertin and you with your Clos de Vougeot. I gather he was equally impressed. What I would like to know is why I wasn't invited.' She glared at him through her fringe and ended up looking fetching, rather than fierce. Maybe that was her intention.

'Ah, well, that was a session with a dealer from Paris, and Jean invited Michelle and me over and suggested we brought a couple of bottles with us. I think he is still trying to buy the *domaine* off us.'

'Is that on the table?' she asked somewhat surprised. Truchaud was aware that Michelle was listening to this conversation with considerable interest.

'Not in the immediate future,' he replied. 'I suppose that if Bruno and Michelle ever were to decide that they really don't want to do this any longer, then it's nice to know there is someone friendly out there who might be interested in taking it off our hands.'

'I'm sure the bargaining chip would be your Clos de Vougeot. Even if they broke that vineyard down into small individual parcels the size of La Grande Rue,' she continued, naming one of the smallest Grand Cru Vineyards in Vosne-Romanée, 'I have a feeling that yours would still hang on to its Grand Cru status.'

'Well, thank you Suzette,' said Michelle from the other side of the table, 'It's nice to know we are appreciated.'

'Anyway, shall I pour?' asked Truchaud brandishing the bottle of Meursault. He poured enough wine into everybody's glass, translating his and Suzette's opinions into everyday speak. 'An alright little wine, just not up to its boast on the label.' He tucked into a mouthful of grilled fish.

Michelle's thought of the wine was that it was more like a Chablis than a Côte de Beaune. It was far less mouth-filling than a Beaune and was a lot less buttery, but it did have a steely minerality about it that washed down grilled fish with a great deal of aplomb. It certainly wasn't unpleasant, it just didn't feel as warm and as full-bodied as it should be.

'Tell you what,' said Michelle, 'I'll pull out a bottle of what I think a premier cru white should taste like. If we're going to do wine tasting for the students here, then we should be showing them what they should be aiming at, and not the defaults.' She got up and walked down the steps into the outdoor entrance to the family cellar. She came back after five minutes with a dusty bottle whose label announced it to be a Le Clos Blanc de Vougeot Premier Cru. 'They grow this in a little walled vineyard on the other side of the little road where we make our red Clos de Vougeot. It's one of my favourites.' She pulled the cork and then went into the house and came back with another handful of glasses. 'Now I know that we haven't let it breathe very long, but I personally feel that white Burgundy should be tasted at cellar temperature.' She poured the wine into the new glasses. 'Now' she said, 'What do you think about that?'

'Oh,' said Suzette, 'That is something else altogether.' Again, she turned to her fellow students, 'You see what we mean by a fat mouth feel and a buttery taste? There is also a lot more going on in the nose too. This is altogether something very different, it has a swagger about it saying, "Hey guys, look at me".'

'Quite,' replied Michelle.

'Ahem,' said Eddie, after a moment. 'This is very nice and all, but am I missing something here? I thought we just made red wine at Domaine Truchaud.'

# CHAPTER 6

*Nuits-Saint-Georges, after lunch*

'Oh, it's good to see you're back,' said Fauquet's cheery voice as Truchaud walked through the office door. 'There's been a call from a divisional commander in Paris who said to call him as soon as you got in.'

*Oh good*, Truchaud thought as he sat down at his desk, *the Old Boy's decided he can't cope without me any longer, and he wants me to go back to Paris*. Despite the current excitement, Truchaud knew that was what he really wanted. He picked up the phone handset and dialled the number he knew by heart.

'Chief,' he said, almost jauntily, 'It's Truchaud, you asked me to call you when I got back.'

'Hmm,' came back down the line, 'It's alright for some, dossing out there in the countryside and taking time off for a leisurely lunch.'

'Oh, the process did involve work too,' he replied defensively.

'No doubt drinking some interesting wine to go with it, I know, I know.'

'Well, as a matter of fact, yes, how did you guess? Has Fauquet been letting the cat out of the bag?'

'Not at all, dear boy, you can rest assured he's been the model of discretion. I just know you, that's all.'

'Anyway sir, what can I do for you? When do you want me back?'

'Is that what you think this is about, me summoning you back to Paris? Couldn't be farther from the truth, old boy. You're exactly where we want you. Seems you're sitting at the epicentre of whatever's going on in the world at the moment.'

'What do you mean?'

'This attack on French vineyards.'

'You mean the news has got back to Paris already? I'm stunned they even know about it in head office in Dijon yet.'

'Don't look down on your country colleagues, you'd be amazed how much they understand, whatever strange vocabulary it is that they're using. Anyway, we've had Rheims on the phone to us yesterday; I gather they've had a similar incident. There was a bomb placed in a cellar in Épernay, which I understand would have caused a bit of a mess if it had actually gone off.'

'It didn't go off?'

'No, fortunately, it didn't, but you see, you were the one policeman present at these incidents. And I was delighted to hear that you had lived to tell the tale. So, dear boy, what was the tale you lived to tell?'

Truchaud stuck to dry understatement. 'As this stage of the investigation, I really have no idea sir,' he replied, 'We appear to have identified one of the victims, a local winemaker called Pierre Parmentier. The crime scene boys are examining the scene for any remnant of the bomber such that he can be identified, but they certainly haven't come back to me yet if they have.'

'So, what else have you been doing? Apart from having lunch that is?'

'I have had a shower to get bits of vineyard out of my hair, and then I went with a gendarme to interview the family of the victim we have identified. Then, as you correctly surmised, sir, I had lunch with my family over a bottle of wine from the victim's brother's estate, just to see whether there might be any clues there.'

'And were there?'

'At this stage, sir, I have no idea.' He paused for a moment and then continued, 'May I take you back to something you said earlier?'

'Go on.'

'You said that someone had left a bomb in a cellar in Épernay.'

'I did.'

'That was a totally different sort of thing than happened here. Here there was an attempt to blow up a vineyard and kill a man in the process. It also killed another man and nearly made a mess of a third. However, a bomb in a cellar, now an explosion in a confined space like that would shatter any number of bottles, especially when you consider those bottles contained champagne. I wonder how many more bottles the flying fragments would shatter too. That was a definite attack on the wine, the one here was an attack.' He paused. 'Well, I'm not sure what this was an attack on, to be honest, it almost felt personal,' he said and told the divisional commander about the peculiar telephone calls he had received during the episode.

'Oh.' The divisional commander also went silent for a moment. 'Yes that did feel like it was an attack on you. Were they your family's vines?'

'No, not at all, we're still trying to find out exactly whose vines they were that got blown up. We know that Parmentier had a patch in that vineyard, but whether it was actually his plot that was involved I'm afraid I don't know yet.'

'Was it a prestigious vineyard?'

'It was a Grand Cru, but not one the man in the street has necessarily heard of …'

'Not one of your ludicrously expensive and "there goes my complete pension on one bottle" ones?'

'Oh yes, certainly one of those.'

'How far away might those have been?'

'Couple of hundred yards maximum, certainly the right village, but even the village wines in Vosne are something quite out of the ordinary in the right hands.' Truchaud smiled to himself, giving his family's own patch of Village Vosne a plug. Of course, the old man missed it completely.

Truchaud could hear a sharp intake of breath between the old man's teeth. 'So, we've had a couple of very near misses then?'

'Was anyone blown up in Épernay?' Truchaud asked.

'No, fortunately, the bomb squad got to it before it went off, and they got it out and defused it. It wasn't attached to anyone though. I gather, though, that they're very tense up there because they have no idea whether that was the only bomb or whether others are lying around in the "hundreds of kilometres of cellars" that Épernay boasts of in the local tourist spiel. One other thing, right at this moment in time, you're the only person who appears to have actually spoken to the bomber. What can you tell me about him, or is it her?'

'Him, boss. It certainly sounded like a man's voice. They were two very short conversations. He was certainly aware that we would be able to put a trace on him if he kept talking long enough, and he didn't fall into that trap.'

'So, what could you tell me about him.'

'You know something, I thought he sounded creepy, and I was fairly sure he was disguising his voice, you know, putting that voice on. It wasn't a synthesized voice changer or anything. It was more like a comedy voice he had learned to produce. I'm not sure I would recognise him if I heard him speak normally. However, the other side of that is that he had obviously practised it, and if he practised it that well, it was obviously a voice he was used to using, so he might just use it again out of habit. The only problem is that I would have to be in earshot to hear him.'

'That's why we want you to stay there. From what you tell me about the conversation, he's a local at your end.'

Truchaud thought for a moment. 'Boss, when did you hear about all this?' he asked.

'The Épernay story crossed my desk yesterday afternoon about three o'clock, and I heard from Dijon just before I was about to go off to lunch just now. So, unlike you, I didn't get any. Lunch that is.'

'Anything from Bordeaux?' Truchaud enquired.

'Nothing so far, but why do you ask? Surely you don't want someone to go around blowing up other areas of France?'

'Well, Bordeaux is the biggest of the prestige areas in France.' He paused. 'Hang on, just making sure nobody's listening to me coming up with what is tantamount to heresy round here.' He paused as if he was looking under his desk for little people hiding under it and then continued. 'And if one was going to start a campaign against the French wine industry, then disrupting Bordeaux would surely be the place to start. Up until you called it had felt a very local and personal attack on a particular small vineyard in a small area. Your telephone call has turned all that over. Where do we go from here? Do you need me back there?'

'No,' said the old man, 'I think we really need you down there on the spot. But I do think we need you to be contactable to go anywhere and see anyone at a moment's notice. I'll keep a helicopter on standby, just in case we need to ship you across to Bordeaux or somewhere. There is an airport of some persuasion to the south of Dijon, isn't there?'

'Yes, at Longvic, just between Marsannay and the motorway. I'm not sure how active it currently is; it doesn't seem to have any scheduled passenger flights anywhere. I can be there in about fifteen minutes from here, obeying speed limits, provided the traffic behaves. It might take a little less time on the motorway itself, but it's really too short a distance to make much difference.'

'And your old car doesn't go fast enough to break speed limits, I know.' The old man chuckled down the phone.

'May I discuss all this with Captain Duquesne?'

'The gendarme chap, yes, of course, and probably you will need to contact the other gendarmerie down there too. Have you got his phone number?'

Truchaud carried that number in his head and he trotted it out slowly so that the divisional commander could get it down.

He repeated it back to Truchaud, confirming he had got it right and then continued, 'Trouble with the village gendarmeries is that they're all so small and independent of each other. I'll let you know when I've spoken to their national headquarters. Can you and your captain talk to their regional barracks in Beaune? They should be more clued up than the one at the prefecture in Dijon about wine and stuff. Presumably their Paris command will be aware of all this.' The old man hummed a little as if he had had a further thought. 'Call you back later.' The phone clicked off.

Truchaud tapped the cradle to clear the line and redialled. 'Gendarmerie?' he heard down the phone.

'Is that you, Savioli?' he asked. 'Truchaud here, is the captain there?'

'Putting you through.' There was a click and a moment's silence.

'Truchaud, old man,' came Duquesne's bluff tones. 'It seems that it has all suddenly become part of a bigger issue,' he said.

'Are you free?' Truchaud asked.

'Always for you *mon ami*, especially as everywhere you go, the excitement seems to follow.'

'I'll be with you in five minutes, get the coffee on.'

Truchaud explained to Fauquet that he was going down to the gendarmerie, and that he could be reached there or on his mobile, and left. Rather less than five minutes later he was pressing on the *sonette* outside the door of the gendarmerie and Savioli was letting him in. A hot, steaming cup of coffee was already waiting for him on Captain Duquesne's desk.

'Well!' said Duquesne, greeting him and waving a hand at the coffee.

Truchaud sat down. 'You heard,' he said. 'My divisional commander said we ought to be getting in touch with the other gendarmeries locally so that they're all on the look-out.'

'Way ahead of you, Lieutenant Saint-André's already on his way over from Gevrey-Chambertin, and the major's sending someone over from the garrison in Beaune. He seems relatively okay about the local event being under our control at the moment, but if it all kicks off, well.'

'At the moment in time my lot are keeping the Épernay issue and this one separate too, but I don't think the old man is convinced one way or the other.'

'So, is your old man sending your wholesome sidekick down from Paris to hold your hand again?' Duquesne grinned.

'Who, Natalie you mean? D'you know something? I don't think she crossed either of our minds during the whole conversation.'

'Commander Truchaud, I do believe you're slipping or getting old or something.'

'Probably the latter,' he replied. Maybe it was just that nearly getting blown to pieces concentrates the mind a little. 'Tell you what, if we find we really need someone with her particular skills, I'll ask him to send her down to us.'

'As soon as I think you need someone to make you smile, I'll remind you of that. Anyway, any news from the lab?'

## CHAPTER 7

*Nuits-Saint-Georges, Friday lunchtime and Saturday morning*

Simon Maréchale looked at all the expectant faces around him. 'I have been round the vineyards this morning. Are you all ready? We start at the crack of dawn tomorrow.'

His announcement sounded as if it merited a triumphant cheer, and it duly received that from around the table in front of him. Then Alain, Truchaud's new student from the University of Viticulture in Beaune, waved his arm and introduced himself again. 'Not that I am questioning your decision, but one day I hope to be wearing your shoes somewhere, and these are things I need to know. How do you know that tomorrow will be the perfect time to start?'

Simon grinned, 'Well,' he said, 'I tasted them today, you see, and they weren't quite in perfect balance, but tomorrow they will be after just a drop more sun.'

'What does "in perfect balance" mean?'

'The tannins in the skin and the acidity are perfectly balanced. The sugar's been ready for a little while.'

'Why not start this afternoon?'

'Do you want to make wine that's nearly perfect when with just a drop more patience it could have been completely perfect?'

'And if we start on Sunday?' the boy continued.

'It will overbalance slightly, and you will be forever saying to yourself, "If only we had picked it sooner, like this chap did".' Simon mimed tasting a glass to the amusement of the others round the table.

'Tomorrow morning, we pick the two Grands Crus. Suzette, will you take charge of the Clos de Vougeot? And Armand, the Echézeaux?' The Echézeaux was the flagship vineyard of Domaine Laforge. It lay just a little bit further uphill from the southern half of the Clos de Vougeot, and was, needless to say, on the other side of the wall that surrounded and defined the Clos. Domaine Truchaud's Clos de Vougeot patch was up near the wall on the north side of the vineyard just down from the drive into the Château itself.

'I will drive both teams out to their separate vineyards and will leave you with your twenty-five kilo baskets. I'll then tour around picking up those you've already filled and deliver them back to their respective *domaines* where the sorting teams will be waiting for them. Don't worry if I get around to you before you've finished picking the vineyards, it will get the sorters busy that much sooner. In the afternoon, we pick the Truchaud Vosne and the Laforge Chambolle-Musigny. So, sorters, you will need to realise that the grapes will need to be kept apart. I'll tell the sorters when I start delivering the Vosne and the Chambolle.'

'And we do hope that you won't make a mistake delivering the wrong grapes to the wrong vineyard,' came the cheeky riposte in a crackling voice from the only person who would have got away with that sort of comment. Dammit, thought Maréchale, why isn't Jacquot in school?

'Commander Truchaud, I hope you won't mind being allocated to the sorting tables?' Simon said directly to the detective. 'Somehow, I can't help feeling that if you were suddenly called out to do police stuff, it would be easier if you were to be called away from the sorting tables rather than from the picking, we could just slow the table speed slightly.' He also thought, but didn't say, that if the detective suffered from any delayed reaction from the incident the previous day, then an ambulance could be called the whole thing being in the public *domaine*. 'Any questions?'

Truchaud was pleased that there didn't appear to be any bitterness between Suzette and Simon. They were just quietly getting on with the job. He hadn't noticed Suzette and Dagmar actually looking at each other though. He wondered if Dagmar knew anything at all about Suzette's place in her winemaker's scheme of things.

The following morning was still cool and crisp, but it wouldn't be that way for long. Suzette and Eddie, still a little sleepy at that time in the morning, were dragged out of the *domaine* by Maréchale and pushed into the big white double-cabbed van. In the back Suzette saw, piled to the roof, large flat plastic baskets. She was already looking forward over Armand's shoulder when Simon pulled out into the seventy-four. It appeared that every white van in Eastern France had suddenly been commandeered by the winemakers of the Côtes de Nuits and were buzzing around everywhere, from little Peugeot Bippers to big double axle Renault Trafics like the one in which they were seated. Suzette was saddened not to see any of those old corrugated iron sided Deux Chevaux vans that had still been very much part of the scene in her childhood when she was still goofy and skinny, which, come to think of it was not all that long ago. She still remembered seeing one or two 2CV's as recently as last year, but by then she would already be describing herself as serene and slender.

'Did you tell everybody we were starting today, Simon?' Suzette asked the driver from over his shoulder. 'It seems that everybody's got the same idea that today is the day to start.'

'We don't keep secrets between ourselves,' he replied, 'Winemaking isn't a competitive sport, you know. Anyway, there are a lot of five star winemakers round here, and if you're one of those, then you will instinctively know the right time to start picking.'

The 25-kilo baskets were unloaded and parked at the track at the bottom of the vineyard. Each picker was also equipped with a hand basket to fill from the vines, and once full, to take down to the big 'twenty fives'. The sun had just risen and Simon said the magic words 'Let the vintage commence'. He grinned across at Pierre Vincent from the Domaine de la Vougeraie, who was unloading his Clos de Vougeot team at exactly the same time as Simon. Simon felt totally vindicated now about his choice of picking time; if Pierre thought that now was right, then it was right. Maybe one day he would win a 'Winemaker of the Year' award too.

All the students set off up the hill to the base of the vineyard. Basket in the left hand and secateurs in the dominant hand, the students started work. The hand basket went down at their feet and they crouched at the vine. Each one took a bunch gently in their left hands and snipped the stalk at the top with the secateurs in their right. The bunch was then gently laid in the basket, and the next bunch got their full attention. Suzette looked at the next bunch and thought that there was a nice bit of millerandage in that one. The grapes were a variety of sizes within the bunch, and that was a good thing. It meant that the wine that was made from those grapes would show an increased complexity, with some of the grapes containing lots of juice, being the big ones, and the little ones with lots of pigments and tannins. Big was a matter of proportion, of course, even the largest of these was smaller than a queen olive, and the little ones were not much larger than a garden pea.

Suzette had chosen to remain with Laforges for this vintage although she was sure that her uncle would have given her a job at his vineyard. Simon had fairly obviously taken up with the German girl, but once Suzette found herself back at her own family's Domaine Parnault then that would be where she was stuck, and she was far from sure that she wanted to spend the rest of her life pleasuring grapes and vines. She was still waiting for the results of her dissertation, and a really good result from that would give her every opportunity she could imagine. Besides, she quite liked the Laforge Truchaud axis. Commander Truchaud and her mum had so obviously had a thing back in the day even though they really weren't letting on, and they were really rather sweet about it all. It was so funny watching old people discovering emotions they weren't really sure they had recognised before. Oldies, you've just got to love them, haven't you?

She clipped at another bunch, and it felt furry, so she looked at it carefully. There were a number of healthy grapes at the tip of the bunch, so she snipped them into the basket; the next chunk was hairy and didn't look at all well, so she snipped that off and left it in the field, and the bottom of the bunch, which had a fine healthy looking bloom on it, went into the basket.

'Er, Suze,' said a voice behind her, 'What was that all about?' Eddie had been watching over her shoulder, her selective cutting of that bunch.

'Well, the middle bit had got a touch of mildew, so I cut it out.'

'Simon didn't say anything about doing that,' said Eddie, alarmed, 'Are we supposed to do that too?'

'No,' said Suzette, 'They'll do all that on the sorting tables when the grapes get into the *domaine*.'

'So why did you do it then?' he asked.

Suzette gave him a brilliant smile, 'Because I can.'

'Aha,' said Eddie grinning back knowingly, ''Cos you grew up in this area, you know all sorts of tasteful facts about mildew and stuff.'

'Lots about mildew,' she said, 'yeah. I'm really into that. Come on, let's do this thing. Remember, we've got another plot to pick after we've finished this one.' They steadily climbed the slight westward slope towards the wall that bordered the drive to the Château, picking the grapes in bunches as they went. It was not hard physical work, as such, but because they were bent over, even young backs like theirs ached after a while, and they found they needed to stand up and stretch. 'This is the most painful work you will ever get working the vines,' she told young Alain. 'That is, unless you do something silly like falling off a tractor or stick a fork through your boot.'

'I imagine that would smart,' the viticultural student replied, 'that or getting blown up.' What had happened the day before was definitely not a secret. 'Not that your eyes would be watering very long if that happened.'

Surprisingly, the first full hand basket was Alain's, and he offered to take Suzette's down to the 25-kilo baskets at the bottom of the vineyard. 'It will balance me,' he explained at this unexpected demonstration of gentlemanly behaviour. Suzette watched him as he walked down, and her explanation of her watching him so closely, should anyone have commented, would of course have been to make sure he was suitably gentle with the precious grapes, worth probably nearly their weight in gold if unblemished, as he tipped them into the bigger baskets. Eddie followed him down, although his hand basket wasn't quite full, and they exchanged a few words and a chuckle while Suzette stretched again. Within moments they were bent over again with their secateurs poised at the vine.

# CHAPTER 8

*Nuits-Saint-Georges, later that morning*

Following his breakfast, Truchaud found himself back in his office in the town hall. Fauquet and a couple of the other municipal police were in there, as was Jean Parnault, looking slightly embarrassed.

'Hello Jean,' he said, 'what's all this about?'

'I think I'm supposed to report myself to you,' his brother's friend replied.

Truchaud looked down his nose at Jean pretending to look like a somewhat peeved schoolmaster. 'Oh?' he asked.

'There was a wild boar who obviously realised we were about to start harvesting the grapes today, so he thought he had better get on with his spot of harvesting first. Well, I was on wild boar duty last night, and I'm afraid I didn't miss.'

'You shot him.' Truchaud said that as a statement rather than a question.

'I'm afraid so. And I understand that if one shoots a wild boar, we have to come to the municipal police headquarters and give oneself up to the powers that be. And you, my old friend, are the powers that be, are, whatever,' he added, getting in an enormous mess with his grammar and pronouns in the confusion.

'And where did this "porkicide" take place?' Truchaud said, still trying, for the most part successfully, to sound piqued. 'You do have a permit to brandish firearms?'

'Up in the Grands Echézeaux,' he replied, producing the required permit from his pocket.

'A porker with some taste; do let me know how he tasted.' said Truchaud grinning, well aware that only a few yards downhill from where the boar breathed his last was the top end of the Clos de Vougeot. Okay, so there was a wall between them, but there were gaps in the wall, and it wasn't far from his own prize holding, and the actions of a ravenous wild boar could have done severe damage to a *domaine's* annual productivity, hence the rota of armed guards in the pre-vintage weeks. Even Old Mr Laforge had, until fairly recently, taken part in this guard, as indeed had many of the other few surviving members of the Maquis. It was a matter of pride among the old warriors that they could all shoot an apple off the top off a child's head. Truchaud was relieved that he had never had to prove that to the local Burgundians. The accuracy of his own shooting was more of the 'by luck than by judgement' class.

He understood that Fauquet had always volunteered to be part of the guard, and that it had been a matter of considerable pride to the police municipale when he had successfully potted one in Vosne-Romanée sneaking up on the prestigious Romanée-Conti vineyard down though the Beaux Monts a couple of years ago. 'The porker wasn't interested in that Premier Cru stuff, he knew exactly what he was going for: the Romanée-Conti, of course,' was how he generally described the incident, also proving to anyone who was listening that despite his outsider status, he had learned all about what Nuits-Saint-Georges and its surrounding area was all about. That, of course, had been before Truchaud's time, but it was still talked about both within and without the town hall. Legend has it that Aubert de Villaine gave him a bottle of the wine as a thank-you for his marksmanship. The bottle is still hiding discretely in his cellar waiting for a day of great celebration.

Truchaud was rummaging through the incoming mail on his desk looking for something that wasn't advertising spam when Fauquet appeared, having seen Parnault off the premises. 'The lab in Dijon was after you,' he said, 'I said you'd call them back when you'd finished with the current business.'

'When was that?' Truchaud asked.

'Oh, a couple of hours ago.'

'But I wasn't here a couple of hours ago.'

'No sir, but Mrs Clermont doesn't know that does she?' they exchanged grins, and then Truchaud picked up the handset and dialled the number on the bit of paper Fauquet had just given him.

'Ah, hello Mrs Clermont,' he said, 'Truchaud here, what can I do for you?'

'It's alright for some,' she said drily, 'satisfactory breakfast?'

Truchaud drew a breath and followed Fauquet's story, 'It's harvest time down here at the moment,' he said, 'and we do get invaded by wild boar. Every wild boar that goes on to the great barbecue in the sky has to go through the municipal police in transit, and you won't believe the paperwork that involves. All the farmers are itching to get back to their vineyards. Most of them started picking their best today.'

There was a grunt down the phone, as if she didn't believe any of it, but she carried on. 'Definitely got one character here,' she said, 'not yet convinced about the second one, but even the one I am sure about is going to need a closed casket funeral. I think you are a very lucky boy, Commander.'

'I don't understand, it wasn't that big a bang. You mean one of them just vaporised?'

'So it appears. I've drawn in a few more students to work on individual fragments. If we find two right radii, for example, then we'll know one belongs to one person and one the other, but we haven't found a single intact radius so far.'

'You know, Mrs Clermont, there are times when I don't envy you your job.'

She grunted, 'It'll be your job to discuss all this with the relatives, and to be honest, that is what I see as the harder of the two jobs. Mind you, it does help to be anosmic where I'm sitting.'

'Anosmic?'

'I have no sense of smell.'

'That must be terrible,' said Truchaud, thinking about all the dinner and wine experiences he had enjoyed over the years, which he would have never had without a sense of smell.

'It does mean that I don't go around wasting my income on fancy bottles of wine. I can, however, tell when someone's put a glass of vinegar in front of me, I've still got the basic taste senses, so don't think you can have a joke at my expense.'

'Perish the thought,' replied the detective, wondering who on earth would dare give Mrs Clermont a glass of vinegar. She was acid enough as it was. He changed the subject. 'So where do we go from here?' he asked.

'Well we carry on separating the tissue. How have you done?'

'Well, we're convinced now that the winemaker was Jean Parmentier, but as yet we have no idea who the other guy was.'

'Can you describe the mysterious other one again; you actually saw him?'

'The most memorable thing about him was the expression of abject terror on his face. His eyes were just too big for the rest of him.'

'Ethnicity, skin colour?'

'Caucasian, tanned. I suppose he could have been an Arab, but he was fully westernised in his dress.'

'Age?'

'From his hair colour — dark, no grey —and his lack of lines, mid-thirties I would think.'

'See, we're getting somewhere, and the fact that you've described the victim as "he" throughout, then we've excluded a further forty-eight per cent of the human race. Clothes?'

'Dark blue work shirt, darker than his jeans?'

'Shoes?'

Truchaud thought for a moment, trying to picture the man's feet. 'No, I'm afraid I don't remember them,' he said.

'Never mind,' she said, 'I've a lot more idea what I'm supposed to be looking for now. Talk to you again soon.' Click.

That conversation made Truchaud even more thoughtful. What was she telling him, that she couldn't find any remains of the human bomb? It sounded as if the bomb and Parmentier on top had protected him from the blast so completely that the epicentre of the blast, being the man himself, had been completely destroyed. But bones don't completely vaporise. It doesn't work like that, does it?

Fauquet put his nose round the door. 'Coffee?' he asked, and Truchaud noted that he was already holding a steaming mug in the hand on his side of the door.

'Perfect,' he said, and then the rest of Fauquet appeared, armed with a mug in either hand, and as he sipped at the mug Truchaud had seen first, he was obviously intent on staying. The other mug got planted on the desk by Truchaud's hand.

'Something you want to talk about?' Truchaud asked.

'Well, yes *Chef*. I don't think I've ever known a vintage that started as dramatically as this one.'

Truchaud was filled with a number of questions in response to that statement. He chose, 'How many have you actually seen since you've been here?'

'This is my sixth,' he said, 'up close and personal. The boar thing, well we see that most years, and usually more than one, so expect another before the week is out. But the bomb; well, if I were to say I had never expected to see that in my lifetime, it would suggest that I had thought of it but never expected to see it, if you know what I mean.'

'If it makes you any more comfortable, as far as I know it has never happened once in the history of viticulture.' He smiled gently. 'The Benedictines never even tried to blow up the Cistercians, and that's even though they never spoke to each other.'

'I didn't think the Cistercians spoke to anybody; weren't they a silent order?'

'You know, that may have been true. I'm pretty damn sure someone spoke to Napoleon when he arrived though. We owe the continued existence of the Clos de Vougeot to some sort of conversation when the little Corsican Colonel's squadron of men showed up here.'

'Colonel?'

'At that time in the early seventeen-nineties, he was a colonel in the revolutionary army, nothing more. But he was a colonel with very good taste in wine, and it was his intention that the vineyards should not be destroyed by the revolutionary caucus, even though the clergy and the aristocracy were to be dispossessed. From what I understand from the local history, the monks who were also skilled winemakers, and there were a fair few of them, were reinvented as owner-peasants before anybody else arrived from Paris. I'm sure he managed to procure himself a few barrels of his favourite wine.'

'I thought his favourite wine was Le Chambertin,' said Fauquet.

'I think it was, that and the Clos de la Perrière in Fixin. All Benedictine territory from the monastery in Bèze. Quite a distance for those monks to come, all the way from Bèze to here, it must be thirty or forty miles north, that monastery.'

'Well, Cîteaux is a similar distance to the east for the Cistercians to come.'

'Yes, but at least the Cistercians had the beginnings of the Château to sleep in. As far as we know, all the Benedictines had to rest their heads in was a little Cabotte. It was a sort of little stone shed where they kept their farming implements.'

'I'm sure the villagers of Gevrey would have put them up. It would have been a good ticket to heaven, looking out for a holy man, and it's not as if the Benedictine monks were a silent order. Nor were they particularly severe. They might well have been entertaining company for a rustic villager and his family and hopefully wouldn't have threatened the wives and daughters of the house.'

Truchaud grinned at the constable, 'You know, you have quite rascally thoughts on occasions,' he said. 'Do you think that our lady folk are more at risk today?'

'Absolutely sure of it. That's why the municipal police is here. We may not arrest many people, but we are the crime prevention unit. I like to think that our lads and lasses just wandering about in the streets keeps the real wrong'uns from misbehaving.'

'In which case, you lot buggered up big time yesterday,' was Truchaud's dry reply to that one.

'That's what I was worrying about a bit boss,' the constable replied, 'Are you blaming any of us for the bombing? Are you thinking that we should have in some way predicted it was going to happen and thus prevented it?'

Truchaud looked at him, surprised. 'Is that what's worrying you? Don't worry about that, what we will be doing is making absolutely sure that we catch the lunatic who did this, and make damn sure he doesn't get any opportunity to do it again.'

'Thank you, *Chef*, that does make me and the rest of us feel a lot more comfortable.'

'The rest of you? You mean you've all been worrying about this?'

'Well yes, me and the lads, we were all talking about it last night and none of them had any idea how you might be thinking. There was some anxiety that you might think that we were all a bunch of failures.'

Truchaud smiled at the constable gently. 'You tell the rest of the squad that I won't ever consider them a bunch of failures, even if we don't catch the lunatic who did this. The responsibility for that failure, I will put down fair and square at the door of the civilian police in Dijon, and the gendarmerie. You all can count on it.'

'Thank you, *Chef*.'

## CHAPTER 9

*Nuits-Saint-Georges, Saturday before lunch*

Captain Duquesne was sipping thoughtfully at a mug of coffee — what else? —when Truchaud walked through his door. 'Any news?' they asked each other, almost simultaneously. They then looked at each other and shrugged.

Truchaud thought about making himself a cup of coffee and then thought better of it; he really didn't have the time. 'I'm really only here to borrow a gendarme,' he said. 'I think I need to have an official word with our friend, the doctor. And I think that to prove to him that I'm not there as a relative or, God forbid, a patient, I probably ought to have someone in uniform with me. What, with seeing my father through his last few weeks and what have you, we've been seeing rather a lot of each other recently.'

'Quite,' said Duquesne, 'Mac's out the back if you want to take her with you.'

'She'll do fine, she even knows about the case, so I won't need to brief her in advance. Good choice.'

Truchaud walked though into the back office where Mac Montbard was busy typing up a report and nodded at her. 'Are you free to accompany me to the doctor's?' he asked.

'Do you really need a chaperone?' she asked with a grin.

'Now there's an unnecessary thought,' he replied, and then explained that he wanted to ask a few questions about Parmentier's health in case that gave them any leads on the case. He continued that he was still sure that poor Mr Parmentier was collateral damage, so to speak, but he would feel fairly foolish if he missed the obvious because he didn't bother to look.

Montbard saved whatever it was she was doing on the laptop and stood up. 'Now?' she asked.

'That's what I had in mind, yes,' he replied, 'shall we go?' And they left.

Five minutes later, they walked up to the surgery door. It was still open, so they walked in. The receptionist looked up and told them that surgery was finished for the morning even if they had booked an appointment. She was running her eye up and down the list in front of her, trying to work out who had missed their appointments and who, therefore, one of the two in front of her was. Certainly there wasn't a young gendarme on her list, and she couldn't immediately identify the middle-aged man standing beside her either. 'Sorry,' she said, 'and you are?'

Montbard told her that they hadn't got an appointment, but nevertheless they would like to see the doctor, and was he in? The receptionist looked horrified at them despite the fact that the woman who had made that outrageous statement was in uniform and probably armed. As if anyone could look at a doctor, let alone formally see one, without first making an appointment. Now that wasn't going to happen, was it?

Truchaud was aware that the tension was mounting between the two women, and he was relieved when Dr Girand appeared from his consulting room door, apparently on the way out, and was even more relieved when the doctor recognised him. 'Commander Truchaud!' said the doctor, not needing to be introduced. 'What brings you here at lunchtime?' Truchaud wondered whether the question was loaded with irony. Certainly, the receptionist's glare at Montbard seemed to imply she thought it was.

'Lunch,' he replied airily. 'We were wondering whether you had any plans for lunch, because if you hadn't I was going to stand you some.'

'The doctor does not take lunch with his patients,' said the receptionist pointedly, with an expression on her face like a bulldog who'd swallowed a wasp.

'No, no,' said the doctor, 'these two aren't patients, they're police.'

'I haven't done anything,' replied the receptionist dismayed.

'Nor have I, as far as I know; shall we find out exactly what it is they do want?'

'Well,' replied Truchaud, 'aside from offering to stand you lunch — which offer still stands incidentally — I was also hoping to talk to you about Pierre Parmentier, whom I imagine you know.'

'Chambolle-Musigny?' asked the doctor, mentally locating the patient in question.

'That's the one,' the detective replied.

'You know I can't talk about patients, don't you?' snapped the receptionist, 'We're restricted by confidentiality. You wouldn't like us talking about all your workings to all and sundry, now would you?'

'You know we're investigating his murder, don't you?' Truchaud replied in exactly the same tone.

The receptionist gasped; this was obviously the first she had heard of the man's demise. *Well, that was something anyway* thought Truchaud. The grapevine was obviously busy with something else that day. The doctor said, 'Well, perhaps we ought to get the business over before I think about lunch, don't you? Won't you both come through to my room?' He turned on his heel and walked back into his consulting room, and Montbard and Truchaud followed him through.

Dr Girand sat down behind his desk again, and the police sat down on the chairs in front of the desk. The doctor took out his wallet and produced a card that looked like a credit card. He stuck it in to a card reader attached to the computer terminal on the desk and typed something on his keyboard. The screen lit up and he typed some more, then waited a moment, and then said, 'Here he is, Pierre Parmentier, now what was it you needed to know?'

Truchaud hadn't really thought about any specific questions yet. The doctor had been considerably quicker off the mark than he had expected. 'Well,' he said, 'I suppose the obvious question is that you wouldn't know of anyone who might have wanted to kill him, do you?'

The doctor looked at the screen for a moment and said, 'No, there isn't anything up here about blood feuds or anything. From what I heard, he was caught in the crossfire in a manner of speaking.' So the doctor had his ear to the ground even if his receptionist hadn't. What else would there have been for him to talk about with his family over breakfast anyway? His daughter, Suzette, was picking the Truchaud Clos de Vougeot grapes while they were talking. 'Do you know who the other person was who died at the scene?' the doctor continued.

Truchaud shook his head slowly, 'Not at the moment,' he replied, 'Have you any ideas? Is there anyone you're missing?'

The doctor grinned at him. 'If I knew where all my patients are all the time, it would be a very bizarre world indeed. Nobody else has come in to the surgery today expressing grief or loss of anyone close to them, not who I didn't expect, if you see what I mean. I'm surprised not to have seen more of you all after your father's death, for example. How are Michelle and Bruno doing, by the way?' Truchaud realised what he meant. Truchaud's father had died very recently and they had just had his funeral. It had been a totally expected death and, in many ways, a relief to them all when it had happened. The last days leading up to it hadn't been easy on any of them.

'No unexpected deaths in the last twenty-four hours then?' said Truchaud.

'Not as far as I know,' assented the doctor, 'and I would like to think I would.'

'Hmm,' said Truchaud, 'So, what can you tell me about Mr Parmentier then?'

'To be honest, not a lot,' the doctor replied. 'Had all his childhood vaccinations and all the childhood illnesses all, fortunately for him, during his childhood.'

'What exactly do you mean by that?' Truchaud asked.

'Well, if you get German measles when you're pregnant it can seriously damage any baby you're carrying.'

'Yes, but he was a boy, so it's not very likely he'd get pregnant,' said Montbard drily, and the two men looked round at her, surprised, as if they had both forgotten she was there.

'Yes,' agreed the doctor, 'but it's very infectious, and often you've passed it on before you've really got any symptoms to speak of. There are times when I recommended to mums that they have a German measles party, or maybe a mumps or chicken pox parties, to spread them around the kids before they're old enough to come to any harm. Chicken pox is quite unpleasant to catch in adulthood.'

'And mumps can sterilise you if you're an adult too,' said Montbard, realising that she needed to keep herself in the conversation to keep reminding the men that she was there.

'And he had all those diseases in childhood?' Truchaud added, wondering what on earth the things he caught in childhood had any relevance to his getting blown up in his mid-thirties.

'All of them,' replied Doctor Girand. 'I hardly ever saw him after that apart from his TB test and vaccination and the occasional insurance medical. He was always very fit, even if he tended to be a little overweight. He tended to indulge himself a little in the good things in life.'

'Quite,' said Truchaud knowing exactly what the doctor was talking about, thanking his lucky stars that he had his own finely tuned senses of smell and taste. 'So he was basically very fit and hearty and the only reason that he didn't have kids was the problem that his wife talked about?'

'Oh, she told you about that, did she?' He didn't bother to wait for the detective to answer and continued. 'As far as I know, that was the case. Why are you asking all this? Do you think that this was actually an assassination attempt on Parmentier and that he wasn't just an unfortunate casualty?'

'We have to look at all eventualities,' replied the detective obliquely.

'Well, Commander, if you feel you need to see me again professionally, you know how to find me. Socially, may I thank you for giving my daughter a job over this vintage; I know she's been really looking forward to it. She was very excited this morning. Do you know that today is the first time she's picking a real Grand Cru! Her mother's excited too. We'll have to buy a few bottles off you.'

'I'll hold you to that,' grinned the detective, 'meanwhile, I think Constable Montbard and I have other things we need to do.' He stood up and shook the doctor gently by the hand and led the gendarme out of the consulting room.

As they walked back to the car, Montbard looked at him. 'That was an interesting observation you made back there,' she said.

'How do you mean?'

'Well, there were various possible targets that the bomber had in his sights. The John Doe who actually had the bomb strapped to him, Pierre Parmentier, his vineyard, and you were all legitimate targets. We don't know the identity of the man who had the bomb strapped to himself, but we do know the identity of the other three. It's the difference between Cluedo and real life.'

'How do you mean?'

'Well, Cluedo gives you the choice of Professor Plum in the billiard room with the lead piping, but you don't need to have any motive to solve any particular game. Here we've got Mr Parmentier in the vineyard with the bomb, but we're nowhere near solving the puzzle.'

'Especially as it might just as easily have been the detective instead of Mr Parmentier,' replied Truchaud with a shudder. 'What we need to think about is to see what the gain is with each one's destruction. Who gains if I were to be killed, for example?'

The gendarme paused for a moment, trying to stifle the grin that wrinkled the freckles over the bridge of her nose. Truchaud raised one interrogative eyebrow, and she replied, 'My immediate answer to that, for which I apologise unreservedly, is Bruno, your nephew.'

'That is actually the sort of thinking we're going to have to do. He may not be a serious suspect, but I suppose he needs to be on a list.'

Montbard looked aghast at Truchaud, 'But sir,' she protested. 'He's your nephew and he's only twelve.'

'As I said, he's not a serious suspect, but if we eliminated every twelve-year-old from a list of suspects only because they are twelve, then a fair number of homicidal twelve-year-olds would be free to kill again.'

'Are there that many?' she asked surprised.

'Probably not round here,' he assented, 'but there are some very strange kids with some very strange behaviour traits in the *banlieus* of Paris. I would not assume their innocence simply on the grounds of age.'

'But he's your nephew, he's Bruno.'

'I would certainly assume his innocence on the grounds of his being Bruno, yes, and who knows, that might be my mistake.' Truchaud looked at the gendarme quizzically for a moment, and then smiled gently. 'Sorry Mac, that was uncalled for, I was teasing.'

'You know sir, I think that's the first time you have called me by my nickname.'

'Yes, I never really understood what that was all about.'

She grinned for a moment and then answered, 'With my red hair, they all think I look like a Scot, so they call me Mac. Funny really, as I only speak about five words of English.'

'I'm not sure that the Scots would admit to speaking English unless you really pushed them. My father had an interesting business link with a Scottish family.'

'Oh yes?'

'Yes, when his barrels had finally worn out and really weren't really imparting any oak into the wine, he sent them up to a little distillery in the Highlands, and the distiller would use them to mature his whisky in for at least twelve years. Dad had the odd bottle of it lying around. It had a strange slightly pink hue to it, and a slight aroma of pinot noir.'

'I'd like to try that one day,' she said thoughtfully.

'I'll see if I can rustle out a bottle some time and we'll have a snifter, but only when you're off duty, that stuff is strong.'

'Yes sir!'

## CHAPTER 10

*Nuits-Saint-Georges, after lunch*

Truchaud walked through the door of the family winery. He was delighted to have the chance to spend the day thinking about something other than bombs and bits of bodies. The sorting table was laid out and the crew were milling around awaiting the imminent delivery of grapes from the vineyards. The soft susurration of conversation belied the excitement that their part in the vintage was shortly about to start again. He milled about slightly apart from the others, perhaps a little concerned that he couldn't actually remember how he had got there. It couldn't have been more than ten minutes since he had left the surgery, but during that time he had parted company with Mac Montbard, presumably at the gendarmerie, and he had either walked, or perhaps had driven home. He looked out of the double doors, well, there was his car in the yard, but that didn't actually tell him very much. Either it had been there all the time or he had driven it here just now. While he was looking at his car, a white Renault Trafic van drove through the gates and blocked his eye line by reversing up to the loading dock. A young man, presumably one of the students but not wearing anything from the waist up, appeared out of nowhere and threw open the doors of the van, and then nimbly leaped up onto the loading dock and called out numbers loudly. Presumably they were metres, as when he shouted, 'Stop!' the van did so. He then climbed into the back of the van and unloaded large twenty-five kilogram plastic baskets onto the dock with the minimum of effort, but with just a gleam of sweat.

Truchaud felt a tug at the back of his shirt, and he nearly swatted it, but as he turned to see what it was that was hanging off his shirt, he was relieved that he hadn't; it was Bruno, wearing a very earnest expression on his face.

'Uncle, follow me. Now, you stand here.' The commanding tones of his nephew did not brook argument. The boy led him to the end of a conveyor belt near where the half-naked student — rippling for the entertainment of those who were entertained by such things, probably just himself — was emptying one of the white baskets of grapes onto the first bit of the conveyor belt which was shaking the bunches down in preparation for the second part of the grapes' adventure on the conveyor belt. By then, the bunches were just one layer thick, so that when the humans in the room took over they could all could be surveyed. There were a half dozen other people at the sorting table, including Michelle, Bruno's mother, who had not commented on Bruno's suspiciously early return from school that day. Mrs Albrand from next door, who was known to appear when the family Truchaud's need was great, and had obviously decided that it was needing time for the Truchaud family that day, so she was piling in too.

'I think the only people in Nuits-Saint-Georges who aren't working in the vintage are the gendarmes,' Mrs Albrand told him. 'See, we've got one of the municipal police here ourselves. So, if you want to park anywhere in Nuits-Saint-Georges today, you'll probably get away with it.'

Truchaud grinned at her as he turned to talk to Bruno; as Simon didn't appear to be about, Bruno was the dominant Truchaud winemaker on the premises, even though he was only turning thirteen. The commander did not feel in any way competitive with his nephew in this. This would be Bruno's life, the boy had already made that clear. 'So what do you want me to do, boss?' he asked his nephew.

'As the grapes pass in front of your nose, take those secateurs and cut off as much wood as you can,' the boy replied. 'Also, can you look out for grapes that have gone bad or aren't in any way ripe.'

'How can I tell those?' the policeman asked.

'Well, the bad ones are all wrinkled and furry and the unripe ones are not dark purple.'

'How do I know it's not the famous noble rot?'

'Uncle, we're not in Alsace growing Riesling or Gewurztraminer grapes. Pinot Noir grapes don't rot nobly.' Bruno's voice had a little tiredness in it.

'What if I miss one?' Truchaud wasn't going to let him get away with it.

'Then Mum or I who are further up the table from you will

hopefully catch it before it goes in the hopper.' Beyond the conveyor belt, the bunches dropped onto a rather more rapidly climbing stepped conveyor which separated the bunches individually and fed them into the destemmer, which separated the individual grapes from the stems. The grapes fell through the floor of the destemmer into a hopper, and the stems, leaves and anything else that the device didn't think was a grape was spat out the back, where it was collected in another 25-kilogram basket.

'And what do I do with the ones I have picked up?'

'Drop them in the basket at your feet. They'll go to the distillers. They may even make some marc with it. If that marc is really lucky they'll send it over to the Gaugry people in Brochon to roll your favourite Époisses cheese in.

'And the baskets that Jean-Paul there is emptying onto the conveyor belt comes from?' Truchaud asked his nephew.

'All of this is the Vosne,' he said. 'All of these grapes will go into that tank over there,' he said pointing to the tank that was not wearing a lid. 'Tomorrow we do the Nuits-Saint-Georges.'

'What about the Clos de Vougeot?'

'We did our most valuable wine first,' said Bruno. 'We did that this morning.' He pointed to a tank, which appeared to be wearing a muslin bonnet to the left of the tank that they were going to tip the grapes into. 'While you were out doing policeman stuff.'

'I may yet have to rush off now and do policeman stuff,' the commander said, tapping his pocket where the phone lay.

'But is this the first time you have worked in the vintage, Uncle Shammang?' Bruno asked him, absent-mindedly separating some grapes that looked distinctly hairy, from some healthy-looking ones with bloom on them. The hairy grapes Bruno dropped in the basket at his feet.

'It's the first time since I was a youngster,' he acknowledged, thinking that it must have been a quarter of a century ago. He picked up a bunch of grapes and cut the end of the stem off. There was one pale green grape among the small dark berries, and Bruno nodded at him, so the green grape went into the box at his feet. 'If you look at all those grapes in that bunch, they're all different sizes. That's millerandage, and that is a good sign.'

Truchaud looked at the bunch. Yes, he could see the variety of sizes among them, but every single grape was far smaller than a table grape that you got at a fruit shop, even the biggest of them.

'Try one,' said Bruno.

'What?'

'See what you think of the taste.'

Truchaud picked one off a bunch of grapes he had just passed as fit, and had let travel on down the conveyor. He popped it into his mouth. The skin was quite tough as he bit into it. The juice was sticky and sweet, but there was a sharp tang to it as well. The pips in the middle of the mouthful tasted nutty.

Bruno, having clipped the end off another bunch and checked it carefully, turned to his uncle and said, 'Well, what do you think?'

'Doesn't taste anything like wine,' he said after a moment. 'Doesn't even have that cherry-ish pinot noir taste that is the reason we all like this stuff so much in the first place.'

'That will all come in during the fermentation process. The juices will pull the colour and the alkaloids out of the skins during the first fermentation that turns the sugar into alcohol. Sometime in the new year the malolactic fermentation, which turns the malic into lactic acid, will change the taste too. The timing of that was up to Dad or Granddad last year. I suppose Simon will make those decisions this year.'

'He would be a fool if he doesn't include you and Michelle in the decision-making process too,' said his Uncle.

Bruno looked at his uncle and smiled. He was aware he had been paid a compliment. This boy already knew a lot about making wine.

The destemmer made a bleeping noise, and Michelle pressed all the buttons on the various bits of machinery, and everything stopped. Two of the lads pushed the hopper out from under the destemmer; Truchaud could see the hopper was full to the brim with grapes. The lads pushed the hopper on its little casters towards the fermentation tank, which wasn't wearing a muslin hat. Standing beside that tank was a device that looked like a forklift truck. They slid the hopper onto the forks and then pushed a button, which settled the hopper comfortably onto the forks. 'May I watch this?' Truchaud asked.

'Of course,' said the boy, who was wheeling an empty hopper

into place beneath the destemmer so that the sorting process could start anew. One of the men had a pad in his hand, connected by a cable to the forklift. He pressed one of the buttons on the pad, and the forklift lifted the full hopper up alongside the tank. Up went the hopper until it reached what appeared to be a very precarious altitude. Truchaud wasn't sure that he wanted to be standing underneath, but the operator looked as if he felt safe enough. He wasn't even wearing a hard hat. Maybe that was just bravado. He had already stopped the climb by releasing the pressure on button. The two men looked up at the hopper and nodded to each other in agreement, and then the hatless man with the pad pressed what was presumably a different button and the hopper began to tip to its left. Out of the hopper and into the tank fell the grapes, with the prongs of the forklift staying firmly in the holes at the bottom of the hopper. When they were both happy that the hopper was empty, the process was reversed, and the empty hopper was brought back to the ground level again, where one of the men wheeled it back to wait in line until the second hopper was filled.

Truchaud looked into the second hopper and was amazed to see it was already a third full. As soon as Bruno had pushed the hopper into place, his mother had switched on the sorting tables and the process had restarted all over again. Meanwhile, another truck had arrived with another dozen baskets on the back which were being unloaded by the driver and the shirtless student onto the loading dock.

'We've got four students working out in the vineyard itself, and I am sure Simon is travelling from vineyard to vineyard making sure it all goes to plan,' said Bruno. 'They're picking Laforge's Echézeaux today, so I guess most of his attention will be on that, but Jacquot and his mother will be involved as well.' He continued without appearing to take a breath, 'Are you coming to Laforge's for supper tonight? They're planning to feed both teams, and I gather Dagmar is going to make a German pea and ham stew like they serve to all their people in Germany when they do their vintage. She calls it her Winemaker's Pot.'

'I didn't know they made wine in her part of Germany.'

Bruno grinned. 'Oh but they do, fairly near Chemnitz along the rivers Saale and Unstrutt, so she told me. She claims it's the northernmost vineyard in the world. You see, she's awfully proud of her German roots, and that they also make wine in Germany. I don't think she knows that much about France that doesn't involve wine, or perhaps cheese, so she is trying to show all and sundry that she has wine in her veins too. We'll see how good she is at cooking for forty people, won't we? I hope it works out for her, I do like Dagmar you know, uncle.'

'I think we all do,' replied Truchaud thoughtfully, trying to remember exactly what the girl looked like. 'I think we all do.'

# CHAPTER 11

*Nuits-Saint-Georges, Saturday evening*

Truchaud looked at the round bowl in front of him. Without dipping his spoon in, he could see the pieces of bacon bobbing about in the green soup as well as the unmistakeable peas. The most obvious thing on display was the long Bockwurst sausage suspended across the bowl like a jungle bridge. A slightly surreal image arose in the back of his mind of his trying to walk across the sausage and falling into the soup

'The traditional Winzertopf should be eaten with the wine that is being made in that place,' said Dagmar from one end of the table. 'I asked Uncle Émile about this and he said he would approve of making this a German evening, and therefore we are drinking German wine tonight.' She giggled and then added, 'at least until it all runs out.' She smiled at the old man sitting at the other end who sent back a smile of his own in return. 'The wine you are drinking was given to me by one of my brother's friends in Boppard. He said that Horst really liked this stuff, and could I give him these bottles when I next saw him.' She stopped for a moment, and Truchaud wondered if she was going to break down. She took a breath, cleared her throat, and then started again. 'But I never saw him again, so I thought this would be a good time to drink them, as a gift to the new family he found for both of us. To Horst.' She raised the glass to the light in the middle of the room and then sniffed the glass, just like Simon would have shown her. She then continued, 'This wine is nothing like what we have been making today, but I hope you like it, it's a gift from little Germany to father France.' She picked up the glass and toasted the present company. Everybody watched at her carefully. Truchaud was becoming ever more impressed with the girl's mastery of French. Three months ago, she hadn't spoken a word, now she was standing at the end of the table making a speech in the language, and her accent behind it did not make it any more difficult to understand.

Finally, Simon couldn't wait any longer. 'How is it?' he asked.

She smiled at him. 'You know, it really isn't bad at all,' she replied. And the rest of them took their cue and tasted the wine.

Suzette asked her, 'What grape is this made from? It's a deep red wine with a lot of mouth feel and a lot of body, but it doesn't taste anything like the wine we make round here.'

Dagmar picked up the bottle in front of her. It was a bottle with shoulders like it came from Bordeaux, except that it had been closed with a screw cap. She looked carefully at the label. 'It says here, Bopparder Hamm Michael Schneider Cabernet Dorsa.' She looked at Simon. 'Is Dorsa a type of grape?' she asked.

'Cabernet Dorsa is,' he replied, 'though I don't think I've ever tasted it before, most interesting. Michael Schneider must be the name of the man who made it.' He looked up at the paterfamilias seated at the end of the table, and dumped the responsibility for approval onto him. 'What do you think?' he asked.

Old Mr Laforge was also giving it the professional once over. Before he said anything he also tasted the thick green soup in front of him. 'Tell you something, the wine and the dish go extremely well together. You do realise, my dear, that you're going to have to get some more of this wine for our cellars. It will be an interesting little conundrum that we will keep as a house secret to confuse the visiting tax inspectors.'

Truchaud grinned across the table at Simon. The old man was obviously quite taken with Dagmar. For a Burgundian winemaker to have complimented a German wine whose grape had been created in a laboratory to mimic the Bordeaux style was a rare compliment indeed. But he was right, this was a nice mouthful, and it went very well with the bacon and spice flavours of the Winzertopf, and indeed, now he had broken the Frankfurter Bridge across his bowl it also added to the taste of the smoked pork sausage very well.

The ceremony, such as it was, now being over, the two families and their friends and acquaintances all tucked into the supper. Truchaud was impressed that the two girls, Suzette and Dagmar, did not appear in any way tense in each other's company despite the fact that they had, at least some time during the previous summer, been competing for Simon's affections, and that Dagmar had won. He wondered about Suzette's feelings now. Maybe she had found someone else, though if she had, he knew nothing about it. Perhaps she was taking a break from affairs of the heart. He knew all about taking emotional breaks — his had lasted the best part of a quarter of a century — and, truth be told, he would much rather that Colonel Heart-Strings had not paid him an unwelcome visit last summer. He took a warm, friendly sample of pea and ham soup and tried to work out how a German supper at the Laforge's house had brought Natalie back to the front of his mind. Maybe it hadn't, the Parisian detective was never very far from his thoughts anyway, and somehow, he was relieved that he had not got a photograph of her anywhere. The memory would in time fade, well, until he got back to Paris anyway.

'You're not saying very much, Uncle,' said Bruno from across the table.

The detective looked up. 'Sorry, just mulling over the case,' he said. 'Not getting very far actually, but one always hopes that the idea that cracks a case wide open will come to you during moments of quiet contemplation.'

The boy grinned at him and nudged Jacquot Laforge sitting next to him and said, as far as Truchaud could interpret the burst of teenaged-boy-speak, 'See, I told you he was thinking about work!' The detective was relieved that nobody yet had perfected the skill of reading thoughts, at least without recourse to the assistance of torture, and with that rather tasteful thought, he put another spoonful of Winzertopf into his mouth.

It was at that moment that there was a crash of falling plates from the kitchen. Truchaud looked across the table for an explanation. Bruno was mouthing at him but he heard nothing. 'Don't pull faces at me Bruno, tell me,' he said, and realised he couldn't hear what he was saying either. Everybody was looking at him. Had he shouted at Bruno just now? He tapped the bowl in front of him with his spoon. No, he didn't hear that clink either. What was this all about?

Was there an eclipse of the sun on the way? That was the first he had heard of it. If not, why was it all getting darker? *Bruno, you're going out of focus, will you get control of yourself and stop doing that.* Had he just said that? He closed his eyes and then opened them — nothing at all — so he closed them again.

He opened them again. Ah, that was better, a bit of faint light again. Hang on, that hurts. His right shoulder was really very sore when he moved it, and now someone was flashing a light in his eyes. Oh, that was very bright, not clear, just bright. That was strange, he felt he was in a completely different position. His feet were at the same level as his head, and he didn't feel like he was sitting at a table. 'Commander Truchaud, can you hear me?' That was strange, it sounded like Dr Girand's voice in the distance, but that couldn't be right, he wasn't even there at the staff dinner. Was he hallucinating? That might be it. Had Dagmar put something, shall we say, interesting in the soup? No, that couldn't be it, everybody else seems okay. The face behind the light was coming into focus now — it was Dr Girand, how had he got there? 'Where did you come from?' he asked, and then the question as to where he was, bearing in mind he was no longer sitting at the dining table but lying on some sort of couch. 'Where am I?' he asked, 'What happened?' He was suddenly aware he was firing off questions very rapidly.

'You're still in the Laforge household,' said Dr Girand, 'lying down. Can you tell me what happened?'

'How did you get here?' Truchaud replied.

'You fainted, so I called my Dad,' replied Suzette's familiar voice from somewhere nearby.

'I what?' Truchaud replied. 'I have never fainted in my life. What actually is going on?' He was beginning to sound quite starchy, at least that's how it sounded from the inside.

'You fainted,' said Michelle's voice from somewhere nearby too. 'And fell off the chair. Dagmar put you in the recovery position and I did a test on your blood sugar, quite normal incidentally, and Suzette called her Dad.'

He felt that Dr Girand was probably the person in the room who was in command of the situation and looked at the face in front of him. 'What?' he asked, slightly more softly.

'I don't know yet,' replied the doctor, who turned to the rest of the room and asked, 'Anybody else got something to add?'

Truchaud had become aware that there was someone sobbing in the background. 'Oh, Mr Truchaud, Mr Truchaud, I'm so sorry, I didn't mean to ...'

'What?' he asked again, beginning to feel quite foolish about his repetitive 'whats', so he added, 'is she apologising for?'

'Don't know,' replied the doctor. 'What are you apologising for?' he asked the sobbing voice, 'What did you do?'

'I dropped the plates,' said the voice in the background. Who was that? Truchaud wondered. It wasn't a voice he recognised. 'I stood on something and I slipped and the plates went everywhere, I'm so sorry.'

'It's all right, Mélodie, it's not your fault, they're only plates,' came Marie-Claire Laforge's voice from somewhere else again. Ah, Mélodie, he remembered now, she was the girl who works in the Laforge shop. Presumably she was on their sorting table that week, and had been at the table for supper too. Everyone was there that day. So, she had been carrying plates or dishes or something and had dropped them. He was beginning to remember what had been going on. There was that crash before everything went silent and dark a moment or so ago. A moment or so ago … he thought. It had to have been longer than that. How long would it have taken Dr Girand to get there from wherever he had been before Suzette had called him? 'How long was I, um, out?' he asked.

'You were unconscious for about fifteen minutes,' said his sister-in-law from behind the doctor's head, and then he could see her looking over his shoulder. She was now clearly audible, as well as in focus.

Truchaud's inner voice screamed, 'Wha-a-t!' but as far as he could tell, he made not a sound. Once he had his emotions back under control, he asked, 'What exactly happened, Doctor?'

'That I don't know,' was the reply. 'You lost consciousness, and then some time later you regained consciousness. How do you feel now?' he asked while pumping up a blood pressure cuff on his left arm.

'As far as I can tell, fine,' replied the detective, 'How's my blood pressure?'

'That looks fine too,' said the doctor. 'Do you want to try sitting up?'

Truchaud sat up. The doctor took his blood pressure again while asking, 'How does that feel?'

'No problems my end,' said Truchaud.

'Mine neither,' said the doctor. 'Do you want to try standing? There's loads of people here to catch you if you feel dizzy.'

"Let's go for it,' said Truchaud and stood up, well aware that the doctor was pumping up the blood pressure cuff again as he did so.

'How does that feel?' came the question from the other end of the cuff.

'Fine,' said the commander.

'Blood pressure's fine too. So, what do we do from here? We could admit you overnight for observation to see what happens.'

Truchaud interrupted before the doctor got any further, 'Must we? This has never happened before, and I feel just fine now. It was probably just a faint.'

'Have you ever fainted before?'

'No, but there's always a first time for everything.'

'Well, I can't force you to go in.'

'Charlemagne, don't be so silly and do what the doctor is telling you.' That was his sister-in-law putting in her threepence worth.

'No,' he replied, 'I think I'll just go home and go to bed.'

'Well, that is fair enough,' replied the doctor, 'especially as there are other people with you in the house. There is one thing I must insist on: until we see exactly what happens, you don't drive a car. You lost consciousness unexpectedly, and we would all hate for it to happen again while you were driving, and you were to end up with one of our fellow citizens painted all over your bonnet.'

'Is that really necessary?' Truchaud asked.

'I'm afraid I must insist. I'm not saying you shouldn't work or anything, you just need someone like that gendarme you visited me with today to drive you. That won't be a problem, will it?'

'I suppose not,' replied Truchaud with a bit of a pout.

'That's settled then.'

It was only a few minutes walk from the Laforge household to the Truchaud *domaine*, and once he was in his room he sat down on the bed for a few moments. He then picked up the headphones and put them on, turning on his stereo. He pressed 'play'. The rapid fade in of 'Touch of Grey' greeted his ears. One day he would settle down and work out what the song was all about. It would have been helpful if they had printed the lyrics on the sleeve, but the Grateful Dead never did. He could have plodded through them, translating them into French as he went. That would at least have given him something to do.

# CHAPTER 12

*Nuits-Saint-Georges, Saturday night*

Truchaud opened one eye and then shut it again. He thought about what he had briefly seen and then opened both eyes this time. He was definitely in his room. His feet felt odd, so he cast his eyes down at them. Ah well, that explained something: his left foot still had a shoe and sock on it. The toes of his right foot waggled back at him without being covered by anything. He lay back and drew a bead on his little stereo using his strangely disparate feet as a sight. The device was still plugged in and switched on, as the front panel was lit, but there was no sound was coming from it and he could see that the disc inside was not whirling.

He was still wearing last night's shirt and trousers, but he could see he had thrown his jacket in the direction of the armchair, but that it had missed and was now spread-eagled on the carpet as if it had been shot. He thought about what the evidence told him so far. He had come into his room and put a record on. He had thrown his jacket at the chair and started to get undressed, starting with his right shoe and sock as he always did. At that point, he had apparently gone to sleep. The question he had to ask himself was: had he simply nodded off or had he had another attack of sudden unconsciousness? He doubted whether he would ever know the answer to that, and was not entirely unhappy not to know either. That was one advantage of not sharing one's sleeping area with anyone else, you don't get any ready replies to uncomfortable questions.

He knew that there was one other piece of evidence that might help his detective work should he actually want to know: what was the music he had put on last night before suddenly going to sleep? He took the CD out of the player and looked at it. It was a Grateful Dead Dick's Picks concert. Would he have gone to sleep with that on? Well, there were certainly times when he had felt he had gone into a trance-like state when listening to one of their longer extended jams, and he had let the music flow over and through his crevices. For example, a half hour workout to 'Eyes of the World' was one of those numbers, which could take him 'into his space.' So, from being in his deep personal space, it could be just one stop from actually going to sleep. But then again, it was just as easy to say that he had become unconscious. No, the identity of the record didn't prove anything.

Next piece of evidence to check, had he wet himself? He was very relieved to find the answer to that one was 'no'. In fact, that was why he had woken up; he needed a pee. He took his left shoe and sock off and thought about it for a moment, and then got into his pyjamas, just in case he met anyone. Michelle and Bruno would be around the house somewhere, and he wasn't sure that he wanted to be found still half wearing what he had worn last night for Dagmar's *Deutscher Abend*. He then looked at the clock on his bedside table, and it said 2.40, so if he ran into any of them he would be surprised, provided he was quiet.

That little excursion took place without incident, and he crept back into his room and then folded everything up and turned off the stereo. Then he climbed back into bed, even though he felt seriously wide-awake. What else was there to do in the middle of the night, on his own with a house full of sleeping people?

He went through the case so far in his head. What did he actually know? Pierre Parmentier had been killed. The winemaker could have been the target, but that appeared far from likely, bearing in mind that when the incident happened he had arrived on his tractor out of nowhere; so it was certainly arguable that the unfortunate man could be described, using the unpleasant phrase so beloved of military leaders when far from the front line and when being interviewed on television, as 'collateral damage'. It was Truchaud himself who was invited to the scene by the man on the phone, who was presumably the killer. *Now who would benefit by killing me?* he asked himself. The old adages — one thinks of include revenge, silence, lust and money. *Well, who would gain financially by killing me*, he mused, *apart from Bruno and Michelle? Who wants to silence me right now? What do I know right now that someone would rather I kept to myself? Well, that could be anything. I know all sorts of stuff from the wrong side of the law; that's my job after all. Now, if revenge is the motive, there are twenty-five plus years' worth of the work I've done that could have produced a candidate there. But if that's where they came from, why now? And as for lust, why me? I've never been that lucky. So basically, what is it that I know the significance of which I am totally unaware?* He chewed over the language of that last sentence, wondering how he could work in a subjunctive in there for the benefit of a press briefing.

He lay back on the bed and closed his eyes for a moment. When he opened them again, the room was light. He looked at the clock on his bedside table, and it said 8.30. What was that all about? He had slept for another six hours without realising he had felt drowsy.

'Uncle Shammang,' came a voice he recognised so well through the door, 'are you coming down for breakfast?'

'Be down in ten,' he replied, realising that he had just committed himself to surfacing forthwith. Well, that wasn't such a bad thing, he thought, and stretched.

He wasn't sure it was exactly ten minutes later that he joined his family and the students who were sleeping in his father's old flat. Breakfast was usually a fairly silent affair that involved the munching of croissants and the swallowing of caffeine-rich coffee. Today, it felt it was doomed to be less silent than usual. 'Feeling better?' his sister-in-law asked across the table.

'I'll let you know after I've finished the second cup,' giving back his regular first-thing-in-the-morning response. He wasn't aware that he was particularly grumpy first thing in the morning, although Bruno regularly assured him he was. That morning, he felt he had every right to be a little out of sorts.

'You're not still suffering from yesterday, are you?' Michelle continued.

'Um, no' he replied, not really listening, but concentrating on the buttery richness of the croissant in his hand.

'I was just wondering whether you had had a hypo or something. I've had one or two of those things in my time.' Ah yes, thought Truchaud, the Insulin dependent diabetic. 'And I had one when they changed the insulin I was using to human insulin. However, the vial they gave me was all soluble and there wasn't a slow release component in it, and I didn't notice. Did you know that the human insulin doesn't give me the warning that the old beef and pork insulins used to give me when I was going into a hypo?'

'Uh-uh,' he said trying to listen and failing completely.

'I was wondering whether you were having a hypo and I should give Doctor Girand the sugar I always carry in my bag to rub on your gums.'

'What?' Truchaud looked quizzically at his sister-in-law, thinking that it was far too early in the morning for this sort of conversation, and certainly he was in need of another cup of coffee to make any sense of what she was talking about.

Two cups of coffee later, he was awake and, as far as he could tell, alert. That was when Suzette's caramel bob and Hippy Eddie's unkempt mane appeared round the door. It may have been shorter, but it was certainly no tidier first thing in the morning. 'Simon's out here with the truck,' said Suzette cheerily. 'He's taking us to the Nuits-Saint-Georges vineyards with the baskets, and he's then taking the Laforge crew on somewhere else. He did say where but I didn't catch it.'

'And I couldn't even pronounce it if I tried,' added Eddie, who was probably still as sleepy as Truchaud had been an hour ago, complete with hooded eyes.

'Do you think Simon would drop me off at the gendarmerie?' Truchaud asked the youngsters.

'You could always ask, but I don't see why not. Provided you don't mind sitting on a basket in the back.' Suzette grinned at him for a moment.

Truchaud harrumphed for a moment but did follow them out. Needless to say, it was Truchaud who got the seat up in the front and the students who sat on the floor of the van with the plastic crates. Suzette realised that that was one advantage of being a part owner of a vineyard. The seating plan of the van all reorganised itself immediately after Truchaud got out, though who it was who actually got to ride shotgun after he got out he didn't notice, as he didn't look round until after the van had pulled off again and disappeared round the side of the building.

He pushed the bell to announce his arrival and walked into the front office. Savioli looked up from his usual place behind the front desk. 'Morning Commander,' he said, 'I'll let the boss know you're here.' He walked through the connecting door, and tossed over his shoulder, 'Coffee?'

'Why not?' replied Truchaud, despite his recent huge caffeine fix. He knew he needed to stay awake and had no idea how easily he might suddenly fall asleep again. He followed Savioli through and found himself face to face with Captain Duquesne. Savioli trotted off to busy himself with the coffee machine.

'I heard about your problem last night,' said Duquesne, 'How are you feeling today?'

'As far as I know, fine,' replied Truchaud. 'How did you get to know so quickly?'

Duquesne repeated his favourite joke about grapevines being exceptionally fine in Nuits-Saint-Georges and added 'I suspect everyone will know about it by now.'

Truchaud thought about groaning and tactfully decided against it. 'So, what we want to do is to use that to our advantage. Assuming that our killer is a local, then he will no doubt think that I'm incapacitated now. How do we do that, I wonder?'

'If you are publicly seen being driven and not driving, that'll be a start.'

'I've been told not to drive by Dr Girand anyway,' replied Truchaud.

'I know,' replied the captain. They looked at each other silently for a moment and Savioli chose that moment to come in with the coffee. Truchaud wondered whether he had been tactfully waiting outside, waiting for a pause in the conversation.

'So, what's new?' asked Truchaud, 'Have they got any closer with identifying the other victim?'

'No,' replied the captain grimly, 'So far they haven't found any of his tissue at all.'

'What? How is that possible?'

'Well, so far they've only been identifying the larger body parts, and they all belonged to Parmentier. They haven't found anything that belonged to the other victim. Incidentally, the plant biologists have only identified one vine, does that make any sense to you?'

'Well that I probably can explain,' replied Truchaud. 'When vines get planted, they are pretty much all clones of an original plant. The original winemaker decided on which clone to plant and then did so. It makes the taste of the wine more consistent too. The interesting thing is that there was only one clone. Every plant is made up of two distinct parts: the rootstock, which will have come from a species originally from the United States, and the half above the ground, which in our case is a French vine. Pretty much every vine in France is a hand-grafted French vine onto American-sourced roots. That is because American roots are far more resistant to the Phylloxera mite, which are still in the soil munching on anything organic that takes their fancy.'

'Every vine? Throughout France, you say?' Duquesne's eyebrows went up in amazement. 'That must be millions and millions of vines.'

'And the rest,' replied the detective drily. 'I believe there is an island in the middle of the Gironde to which the mites haven't managed to get to yet, and they still have ungrafted French vines, but I don't think anyone is particularly thrilled with the wine they produce. They may be original plants, but the *terroir* isn't up to much.

'Why don't you winemakers import American vines complete and then plant those?'

'The plants from which the American rootstocks come don't make any decent wine either, so every vine in America is a combination of an American Rootstock and a European-type plant, even the traditional American vines like Zinfandel. But anyway, why should we want to make American wine over here? Burgundy must be made from French Pinot Noir and Chardonnay grapes. A little of our white wine is made from Aligoté grapes, and I am pretty sure that the Americans don't have any of those anyway. Next time I meet an American, I'll ask him.'

'Is that something you are likely to do?'

'Once we have stopped work on the new wine and moved on to the bottling and then marketing of last year's wine, you'd be amazed who'll come out of the woodwork. There will be all sorts of strange people appearing on our doorstep to taste our wine to see what we've been getting up to.'

'I never realised what a complex society you lived in,' replied the gendarme.

Truchaud grinned and stirred his coffee. He took a mouthful and was internally grateful that Duquesne was so picky about the taste of his drinks. That was a very good cup of coffee. Truchaud thought he would have to keep an eye on what wine he liked. He couldn't possibly be able to afford to become such a connoisseur of wine on a policeman's salary, certainly not red wine from the village of Vosne-Romanée anyway.

'Going back to the victims,' he continued, 'No sign of any parts of the other victim at all?' He mused for a moment and then thought out loud, 'The bomb was strapped to him, and if Parmentier fell onto the first victim's back, then the first victim would have taken the full force of the blast before it started ripping Parmentier apart. I have to say I must have been extremely lucky.'

'I think that is a fair comment.'

'May I make a suggestion, Captain?'

'Go ahead.'

'Will you ask the lab to concentrate on the smaller and less obvious parts to see if they can identify anything from the second victim? I have this feeling that until we can identify who he was, we may well not get any further with solving this crime.'

'I can certainly ask them, though you know as well as I do that the labs are very much a rule unto themselves.'

'You have the charm, my friend, persuade them that it is something they might actually want to do. Meanwhile,' he added, and swallowed the rest of his coffee, 'I think I have to go out and talk to Mrs. Parmentier again. Is Mac free to do a spot of driving?'

'I'll call her.'

# CHAPTER 13

*Chambolle-Musigny, Sunday morning*

'Where to, chief?' asked the woman sitting on his left. Truchaud looked at her for a moment. The light dusting of freckles over the bridge of her nose made her face look gently pretty that morning. She wasn't stunningly beautiful, not like that Natalie woman about whom Truchaud thought about far too much, especially at times when he should have been thinking about something else altogether. Moreover, despite her gently pretty face, Mac was stockily built. If she had played rugby, Truchaud thought, she would have been a lock forward, though he doubted she carried more than an ounce of spare flesh. She was potentially a very powerful young woman, and Truchaud was perfectly happy about that, as long as she remained on his side. Natalie, the radiant Natalie, the sharp-witted Natalie of his dreams was as graceful and as slender as a doe in a wild pasture somewhere. That wasn't to say that Constable Mac of the Nuits-Saint-Georges gendarmerie wasn't as bright as her short reddish hair, but she wasn't as brilliant as Detective Sergeant Natalie of the Paris National Police topped with her glorious golden mane, but then who was? Truchaud wondered how she would become the chief of police she was destined to be without that face getting in her way. Mac could go unnoticed if she wanted to, although dressed as she was in the uniform of the gendarmerie it wouldn't be that easy. Natalie couldn't go unnoticed no matter how she dressed. When she stood up, or even just arrived, people of both genders just watched and wondered who she was. Natalie, gorgeous Natalie, however she was dressed did not immediately conjure up the idea of 'that's a policeman'. She was quite happy to be a distraction while her colleagues did whatever they were planning to do. So why, Truchaud asked himself, did this beautiful colleague, whom he had known for at least a couple of years without so much as an emotional blip, suddenly have this dramatic effect on him? He was a little old to have developed a teenaged crush. Dammit, the last time he had developed a teenaged crush, he was in fact a teenager, and it was vaguely appropriate then. And once he had developed those feelings about the Sergeant, where had she gone? Back to Paris of course, leaving him in Nuits-Saint-Georges without a second thought. Well, no, that wasn't fair, there was no evidence whatsoever whether she had actually thought about him or not. He hadn't actually asked her or anything, he just assumed that she had been a carefree goddess when she was on her way back to the city further north.

'Domaine Parmentier, Vosne-Romanée,' Truchaud replied to the gendarme at the wheel. 'I have one or two more questions I want to put to the unfortunate man's widow.'

'Right you are, *Chef*,' she replied, much in the same way Natalie had said it. Had Mac spent so much time with Natalie when the Sergeant was down in Nuits-Saint-Georges? He couldn't remember any time that they had spent together, but then there presumably were times when Natalie was not basking in the gaze of her enraptured superior. It was just that he couldn't remember them.

Still thinking about the girl with whom a relationship was singularly inappropriate for a senior police officer, Truchaud looked out of the window of his car at the vineyards around him. There were people everywhere and white vans parked on tracks, which you couldn't see unless you were perfectly in line with them. As they drove into the tiny village of Vosne and he looked between the small gaps between the houses, he could see vineyards as far as the eye could see. Further up the hill, he glimpsed in passing the stone cross at the bottom end of the vineyard that was deemed the nonpareil in exclusivity by everyone who claimed to be in the know. He had never tasted the famous Romanée-Conti himself, but should the opportunity present itself, he doubted that it would be one he would reject, even if he were on duty at the time.

They pulled into the yard, and Montbard got the car as close as she could to the front door, avoiding a rather tatty minibus that was parked up to one side. Truchaud got out and tapped on the door, and a face appeared around the side of it. The face appeared to be labouring under the delusion that there was a chain holding the door ajar. There was no such chain, and moreover, it wasn't a face that Truchaud recognised. It certainly didn't look like a Parmentier face, but then he had only seen Mr Parmentier once, and rather dramatic things were going on at the time, and he was far from sure that he remembered everything exactly as it was anyway. The face belonged to a woman in her early middle age, younger than Truchaud but somewhat older than Mac, or Natalie, for that matter. She had long black hair tied behind her head in a bunch. She wasn't smiling, but then, she wasn't scowling either. It was a non-committal expression. The eyes were dull, and she was wearing a long, shapeless one-piece dress that was probably quite comfortable if it was really warm.

'Yes?' she asked in a distinct accent, was it Algerian perhaps? Ah, that explained it, yes, she would pass for Algerian.

'Is Mrs Parmentier in?' he asked.

'Not at the moment,' the woman replied, 'Who shall I tell her called?' She began to look alarmed as Mac, in full uniform of course, got out of the driver's side of the car. 'You're police?'

'Commander Truchaud of the municipal police, yes,' he replied, waving his identity card at her. 'This is Constable Montbard of the gendarmerie.'

'Oh dear,' said the Algerian woman, not really giving the card more than the most cursory glance, but appeared far more impressed by Mac's uniform. 'Do you want to come in?'

'That would be good,' Truchaud said noncommittally, wondering what would be the point if Mrs Parmentier really wasn't there.

They were shown into the same living room where they had all met before. 'I shall get some tea,' said the woman, and walked out.

Mac looked at the commander and raised one eyebrow. 'Did you say, "yes" to her offer of tea?' she asked. 'I must be going deaf.' After a moment, she continued, 'Have you any idea how long you want to stay if Mrs P. really isn't here?'

'If she wasn't here I hadn't actually intended to cross the threshold, but the woman who is currently making us tea didn't really give us any choice did she?'

'I wonder who she is.'

'At the very least that is something I intend to find out, and why she has the right to invite people into Domaine Parmentier and pour her tea into them.'

'My name is Arifa Akbar, and my family works for the Parmentier

105

family, especially at vintage time, when everyone comes over to work,' said a voice from the door from over the top of a tray with a teapot, a small jug, a couple of slices of lemon on a saucer, and two cups stacked on it. Her arrival, up till the moment she spoke, was absolutely silent. 'The tea was already made, all I had to do was put it on a tray.'

'You have work permits?' asked Truchaud, wearing his municipal police hat.

'I do,' she said, and added after a moment, 'somewhere. Do you want me to go and look for it?'

'I wouldn't bother at the moment,' said Truchaud affably, 'But when you next come across it I would put it somewhere where you know where to find it. I am sure that Constable Montbard here will want to see it before this investigation is over.'

'You're here about the bomb in the vineyard,' Arifa said. It was more a statement of fact than a question, but Truchaud treated it as such anyway.

'Yes,' he said. 'Do you know anything about it?'

'No, apart from the fact that I heard it. Everyone in Vosne must have heard it.'

'Funny,' said Truchaud, 'Nobody appeared after it went off. The first person who turned up was the medical examiner, and she had to come down from Dijon. I assumed that everybody was too involved in their lunch break to notice that had been a very large bang nearby.'

'I heard it,' she said, 'but I was serving lunch to the pickers and sorters. That is what I do at this time of year for the Parmentiers.'

'And they were all here?'

'No, Mr Parmentier wasn't, but Mrs Parmentier said serve it anyway, he would only be a few minutes.' A large tear appeared at the corner of her left eye, and she brushed it away angrily, as if it was betraying an emotion that she felt she had no business feeling. She stopped for a moment.

Montbard looked at Truchaud and then asked, 'Was there anyone else missing?'

'My brother, Mehdi. He was due to be at lunch yesterday,' she said. 'He usually tells me if he isn't going to be there.'

'Mehdi? What does he do?'

'He drives tractors and cars and things. He's been here more or less full-time for the past few years. He drives one of the vans when they release the wine they're about to send to market. That wine is usually at least two years old, and some of the better wine is even older than that when my brother finally drives it to Beaune or Paris or wherever.'

'He's a good driver, then, to be trusted with expensive wines in the back of his van?'

'Oh yes, he drives like a midwife, very gentle.'

'And he has a work permit?' asked Mac drily.

'I would think so,' she said, 'I can't imagine how Mr Parmentier would keep him on long-term without one.'

'And how do the others get here?' the gendarme continued.

'My other brother, Walid, drives them all over in his bus.'

'How? Which route do they come?'

'They land in Spain and drive up along the coast. Walid says it's motorway all the way.'

'How many people does Walid bring in this way?'

'About twenty-five.'

'And they all work at Parmentier's?' said Montbard, her eyebrows going up in surprise.

'No, of course not, he leaves the motorway south of Beaune and starts dropping people off where they've been booked to work. He usually gets here about eleven at night, absolutely exhausted. That's his bus parked out in the yard. It stays there until it is time for him to leave and take them all home again.'

'And that will be?'

'Sometime in late November, early December.'

'And he'll have checked the tyres by then?' remarked Mac drily.

Arifa looked at her quizzically. 'I'll tell him that you think they need checking,' she replied. 'That is if you do actually think they need it.'

'Aha, tea!' came a male voice from outside the door. A face looked around it, saw Mac in uniform sitting on the sofa and muttered, 'Oh shit! What's happened now?' and disappeared back out of the door. I know that face, thought Truchaud.

'Walid,' said Arifa, and followed it with a cloud of excited Arabic that neither Truchaud nor Mac understood. She looked at them for a moment and reverted to French for their benefit, 'I'll go and get him.' She left the room, once again shouting out in Arabic.

Truchaud looked at the freckled gendarme for a moment and chuckled quietly. 'Never a dull moment in the Parmentier household,' he said quietly. 'Think about how much fun it must have been when *Le Patron* was still alive.'

'This is Walid, my brother,' said Arifa, who wasn't actually leading him by the ear, but sounded like she would have been if he hadn't behaved himself and come back of his own accord. 'He doesn't speak a lot of French, but he promises to try. I'll go and get him a cup of tea.'

Walid sat down nervously opposite the police, looking absolutely terrified. *That's where I have seen him before*, thought Truchaud, *the man with the bomb in the vineyard must have been his brother*. The faces look very similar, especially when they're both frightened. 'You found Mehdi?' asked Walid after a moment.

'I don't know Mehdi,' said Truchaud after a pause. 'What's he like?' he added, being very careful about tenses. At this stage, it was a complete guess that the other body in the vineyard belonged to Mehdi Akbar. They hadn't found anything at all to even suggest that. He certainly wasn't going to worsen Franco-Algerian relations by telling him that he had seen his brother explode before his very eyes the previous day. That isn't the sort of thing you say to anyone without a shred of proof to back it up.

'He's like —' Walid paused. 'My brother.'

'Does he look like you?' Mac asked him.

Walid nodded, smiling almost obsequiously, 'Yes, yes, look like, er, my brother.'

There was another very pregnant pause, and Truchaud was relieved when Arifa emerged from the kitchen stirring a mug, which she put down in front of Walid. 'Well?' she asked the room in general.

'We were trying to find out about your brother, Mehdi. Your other brother, Walid here, says he looks like him,' Mac explained.

'Why are you trying to find Mehdi?' she asked sharply.

'You said he was missing,' Mac explained.

'You weren't looking for him before you came in here?'

'I, for one,' Mac replied, 'had never even heard of him before five minutes ago. Should we have been looking for him already?'

'I don't know, should you?'

'Look,' Truchaud interrupted what looked like it might become a fairly interesting argument, 'there's no point in this. We know where to come if we find we need to find out more about Mehdi. We will list him as missing for you. If he reappears, can you ask him to pop into the gendarmerie in Nuits-Saint-Georges just so that we know we don't have to keep looking for him? I expect you ought to warn any members of your family that from here on in we'll be looking for a missing Algerian, and they might find themselves being asked. If any of them know where he is, tell them to tell him to report to us so we can cross him off our list of things to do. Can you do that?'

'Yes,' said Arifa, 'I think I can do that for you.'

'In which case,' said Truchaud swallowing the dregs of his tea, 'I think that's all we need to do for the moment. If we find your brother we'll send him back to you, telling him that he shouldn't go running off again without telling his sister first.'

Arifa smiled for a moment and said, 'Thank you.'

Truchaud and Mac made their way out of the house and back to the car. When they had got themselves sat in and belted up, Mac remarked, 'You know, that minibus really does need a new set of tyres before it ventures out on the highway again. They're almost down to the canvas in places.'

'I'm sure we'll be back here again before long,' said Truchaud. 'We didn't even get to see Mrs Parmentier, remember? You can tell him when we come back, and also where he can get his bus some new boots.'

'I get the feeling that you have some ideas about the meeting we've just had,' Mac said.

'Oh yes,' replied the commander, 'Back to the gendarmerie as fast as possible. We've got some information we need to get up to the lab PDQ.'

## CHAPTER 14

*Sunday, Nuits-Saint-Georges, then on the road to Meursault.*

Mac let them into the gendarmerie without bothering to ring the bell, and Savioli looked up from the desk with the slight expression of embarrassment he might have worn if they had caught him doing something either illegal, immoral or fattening.

'The captain still in?' she tossed at him.

'Yes, of course, shall I fix some coffee?' he replied going into automatic Truchaud mode.

'I shouldn't bother, we're not going to be here very long,' she said and tapped on the connecting door.

Truchaud, following Mac into the captain's office, was fascinated by the pecking order between constables, of which he really hadn't been aware before. There was Mac, who was obviously a 'senior' constable, then Savioli, who he could tell was middle ranked because at least everyone knew his name, and then right at the bottom of the tree was the young woman who wasn't senior enough for anyone to remember her name, assuming she had yet been allocated one.

Truchaud followed Mac through the door into the captain's office, but he was the one who spoke first. 'Mehdi Akbar,' he said, getting the expected rise of the eyebrows from the other side of the captain's desk.

'Who?' came back the expected reply.

'Mehdi Akbar. He's missing, used to work for the Parmentier family, and his brother, Walid, who is not missing, bears more than a passing resemblance to the fellow with the bomb tied to his chest. I think we ought to ask the people sifting through the human remains to look for an Algerian called Mehdi Akbar.'

'I can certainly toss that up the wire to Mrs. Clermont's team in Dijon. Does he have a record at all? Does he have any DNA on file?'

'Well, his sister didn't think so,' replied Mac from behind Truchaud's shoulder. 'Do they put DNA markers on work permits?'

'Not that I know of. He's got a work permit you say?'

'That's what his sister said.'

'Well the interior ministry in Paris will have that on record. I'll ask them, or better still, Commander, why not ask that delightful divisional commander of yours to ask them? When questions are asked by divisional commanders they're more likely to get answered. If a question is posed by a mere captain of the gendarmes from somewhere out in the sticks, they tend to be put on a spike marked 'pending', and then forgotten about altogether. Heaven knows, Paris may not even know the existence of Nuits-Saint-Georges.'

'Oh, I imagine Paris will know the existence of Nuits-Saint-Georges all right, they don't make fine wine in Paris, only the petrochemical imitation they make from imported freeze-dried grape juice, but they sure have a taste for the good stuff. After all, it isn't that far from the great vineyards by road, and there is plenty of cellar space in Paris for great wine to ripen at its own speed. However, I take your point about the old man, may I use your phone?'

'Go for it,' said the captain pushing the phone across the desk.

Truchaud tapped in the number he carried in his head, and a familiar voice grunted into the earpiece.

'Truchaud here, in Nuits-Saint-Georges,' he started.

'Truchaud, hmm, Truchaud, eh? I knew someone called Truchaud once, strange fellow, escaped from the police nationale and went off to hibernate near the river Styx. You any relation?'

'It's me, sir,' the commander chuckled. 'I was wondering if you could brandish a little muscle with the home office. We're looking for a copy of a work permit for one Mehdi Akbar who works at least six months in every year at Domaine Parmentier in Chambolle-Musigny as a general factotum and driver. He's of Algerian extraction.'

'Any idea of date of birth?'

Truchaud looked at Mac to pass the question on. Mac shrugged but didn't say anything, so Truchaud continued, 'I would imagine in his early thirties.'

'Not really enough information to wake up the bureaucracy,' said the divisional commander down the phone, 'But seeing as it's you, I'll lean on them a little. Maybe I'll trample on them like you do to persuade the juice out of your grapes. Anyway, if anyone knows if they've got a work permit for a Mehdi Akbar, Algerian, early thirties, working as a driver in Chambolle-Musigny, I'll find it. After all, there can't be very many people who answer to all that.'

'Thank you sir, I'll get you the date of birth by tomorrow if that's any help, I've got to go back to speak to Mrs Parmentier later. She wasn't there when I was around a few minutes ago. Mr Akbar just came up in the conversation, and it seemed to be just so right that I came back here to the gendarmerie to pose the questions.'

'Rather than going into your own bijou little office I spent so much time and effort setting up for you ...'

'Eh?' Truchaud was not sure where he was going with this.

'In the town hall, your municipal police office. I can tell that you're sitting in the captain's office at the gendarmerie at the moment. I've got one of these new-fangled call identifier widgets on my phone, so I can't tell if you're standing or sitting, but knowing you, you're sitting, but if you call me up and threaten me, I know where you are.'

'But I'm not threatening you.'

'You know that, and I know that, but my telephone has no intellectual capacity whatsoever, and thus it keeps telling me who I'm talking to and where you are.'

'We must get one of those things down here,' Truchaud replied, 'One of the phones on my desk in that office still has a circular dial.'

'Does it work?'

'Haven't the faintest idea, I'll give it a whirl next time I'm in there. It might even confuse your bit of high-tech on your desk.'

They both chuckled, and then the DC observed, 'You haven't asked about her.'

'Who?' Truchaud asked, knowing exactly who the old man was talking about.

'Sergeant Dutoit,' came back down the phone.

'Oh her,' said Truchaud trying to sound nonchalant. 'She's not here you know. Didn't she get back to you? She left here a couple of months ago, soon after we sorted the conundrum of the missing German boy.'

'I know, she's been up to her eyeballs in it in Paris here. There are all sorts of things going on up here that I could tell you about if it wasn't embargoed.'

'Well, I'm glad she's enjoying herself,' Truchaud replied, 'meanwhile I, too, have things to do, so remember: Algerian, Mehdi Akbar,

Domaine Parmentier, Vosne-Romanée, work permit.'

'I wrote that down when you first said it, and my widget recorded it. I'll get the results to you or your captain as soon as I have it to hand. He doesn't mind being called your captain, does he?'

'I expect he will cope with it, provided you come up with the information,' Truchaud replied drily and, after a pause, added the respectful, 'sir.'

'Good, good, well, goodbye for now then,' and the phone went dead.

'I take it that went okay,' said the captain from his side of the desk.

'I think so. Anyway,' said Truchaud, standing up and pushing his chair backwards, 'I think I need to go to Meursault. Is Mac cleared to go there, out of her jurisdiction?'

'I don't see why not, after all, all she is doing is being your driver. Can you provide a driver from your municipal police lot in the town hall?' Duquesne didn't let him answer before carrying on, 'No, I didn't think so, so of course the gendarmerie would be willing to help out the local municipal police.'

'Thank you. To be honest, I have no idea how Fauquet or, indeed, any of the other members of my team drive. For all I know, they all qualified from the same school as your wonderful Lenoir did.'

'May I remind you, Commander, that Lenoir has never had an accident.'

'I can understand that, even other accidents keep out of his way.'

A youngish face poked itself round the door. 'Somebody mention my name?' it asked.

'No, it's all right Sergeant,' said Truchaud. 'How are things going with Mrs. Clermont?' he added to prevent Duquesne suggesting that Lenoir take him for a spin down to Meursault.

'Scary woman,' he said thoughtfully, 'She's had us collecting trophies from the crime scene; she hasn't made any comment on them yet. It's slightly bizarre just standing around being given plastic baggies of meat and vegetables and carrying them down to the car. We don't get a lot of these sort of events in Nuits-Saint-Georges, you know.'

'Quite,' said Truchaud and nodded at Mac, who was standing behind him. 'We're off to see the other side of the Parmentier family then, perhaps we will find the widow there.' He led her back out to the main office and, nodding at Savioli, they walked out of the front door and out though the wrought iron gates to the car park.

Back on the seventy-four, they headed south past the quarry where Comblanchien limestone was hewn out and worked into fine Burgundian marble. Then they went through various villages to the impressive Corton Hill, which always reminded Truchaud of a monk, although a monk's tonsure was, in fact, exactly the opposite, as the tuft of trees on the top of Corton Hill was exactly how a monk's tonsure wasn't. Just below the copse was the only area in the whole of Burgundy where they made both red and white Grand Cru wines. Moreover, there were no Grand Cru reds south of Aloxe Corton, and no Grand Cru whites to the north. One day, he mused, the Count de Vogüé will produce his fabled white Grand Cru Musigny in Chambolle to the North of Nuits-Saint-Georges, but at the moment, they are just ordinary white Bourgognes with a very expensive price tag and the good count's name on the label.

He looked at the activity among the vineyards, yes, the pickers were out in force in the Corton Clos du Roi red wine vineyard just below the copse, and as they travelled further south, he could see activity in the Corton Charlemagne south-facing slopes. His father had christened him after those vines. He supposed his parents must have liked that wine, though he couldn't remember ever having seen his father drink white wine. Even with a plateful of the whitest fish in front of him, his father chose to drink red. Maybe it had been his mother's idea. It was one of the many things he now regretted that he and his parents had not discussed when they were still alive.

They drove over the motorway from Paris to the south and motored into Beaune. The traffic was slowed down by traffic lights as Mac drove into the small town, well, small by Paris or Dijon standards. Beaune was, in fact, the second ranked town in the whole department of the Côte d'Or. It has a population of around eleven thousand, though Truchaud was never sure whether the count was taken during term time or during the holiday. There were a lot of students at the viticultural university who were not in Beaune right at this moment. One or two of them were employed at Truchaud's. You couldn't tell that from the number of feet on the street.

Once they reached the inner ring road, he was concerned that

Mac might be having a quick cogitate as to whether she was going to follow the inner ring road, which went counter-clockwise around the old town centre, or whether she was going to plough straight through the middle of it over the cobbles and round the twisting narrow streets of the historic centre. In the end, he was relieved to see that she took the ring. It would have potentially have cost a lot of time if they had come upon a white van unloading grapes at any of the wineries in the town centre.

Heading south from Beaune, the next villages were Pommard and Volnay, and the vineyards that surrounded them told their own tragedies. There was very little activity in either of those villages, which had been ravaged by hail at just the wrong time earlier in the year. The grapes that had managed somehow to stay on the vines might yet make some wine, but there won't be that much of it for sure. He was more than partial to the light fragrant wines from Volnay without really knowing an inordinate amount about it. Twenty kilometres south of Nuits-Saint-Georges, he was already in another world, a world he really knew very little about.

One thing they both knew, though, was how to use a satnav, and it took them directly to the door of Domaine Parmentier (South) or, in other words, René Parmentier's place. It had an impressively large black painted steel gate, at least three metres tall, which stood wide open so that Mac could drive straight into the large yard. It was somewhat more impressive than his brother's place, and considerably larger than Truchaud's, though somehow it felt like place of work rather than a home. Across the yard from the gate was a large double door in the wall which, had it been open, one could have driven a large van through. It was shut. There was a very modern black plastic bell push screwed into the wall beside the door. The bell push was mounted on a white disk hand painted on the wall, with a sign that said 'ring'. Somehow, it all looked rather amateurish. There was certainly no old-fashioned bell pull you pulled out of the wall like he had outside the gates at Domaine Truchaud. Mind you, like Domaine Truchaud, the main gates were open, which did offer an open invitation to enter.

Truchaud offered Mac the opportunity to press the button. Faintly in the distance, an electric bell sounded, and they waited patiently for someone to come. They were both looking at the double door still when they heard a polite cough behind them. 'Can I help you?' reached them even before they had turned around. It was Mrs René, and as they both recognised her, she recognised both of them, although Mac's uniform was a fairly large hint.

'Ah!' she said as she recognised them. 'I was expecting you, won't you come in?'

## CHAPTER 15

*Sunday, Meursault*

Truchaud followed the women through the door that, from the out-side, looked like it should be a door into a workshop. Once through the door, he realised it couldn't have been further from the truth. The outside face of the door looked weathered and a little tatty. Its inside face looked new and fitted flush with the frame. Interestingly enough, it opened outwards like a Swedish front door, and Truchaud won-dered how, despite being intermittently exposed to the elements, the inside face managed to keep its youthful elegance.

'What can I offer you?' she asked, 'It's a little early for an apéro for me, but I suppose it has to be that sort of time somewhere. There are some ex-pat Bourguignons out in Oregon making some very nice wine out on the Pacific Northwest. They'll be sitting down to an apéro about now. Maybe you'd like some juice? Tea? Coffee? A soda perhaps?' She was making it abundantly clear that she had not been planning on lubricating herself at all at the moment, so Truchaud and Mac politely declined. 'Well then,' she said, 'What can I do for you?'

'We were looking for your sister-in-law, and as she wasn't at home, we thought she might be here.'

'How odd,' she said, and then clarified her thoughts, 'Not that she wasn't at home. At this time of day at this time of year, you will invariably find her in a vineyard somewhere picking grapes. What puzzles me is that Arifa wasn't there to tell you. Arifa hardly ever goes out, you see, there's always something in the house for her to do.'

'That was the Algerian lady we met, I take it,' said Mac, perhaps with a faint question mark at the end of it.

'Yes, her name is Arifa. She would know where Yvonne is at most times of the day.'

"Well, she didn't earlier on today. We were there about half an hour ago and met your Arifa and her brother, and neither of them had any idea where your sister-in-law was.'

'How odd. I suppose they must have been playing at "being loyal".' She even did the 'air quotes' thing with her fingers. 'Well, you do look like policemen — even you, Inspector, despite your not being in uniform — and where they come from, it doesn't do to be particularly helpful to the police, especially where your nearest and dearest are concerned. You never know whether you will ever see them again if you do that.'

'Ah!' said Truchaud noncommittally.

'So, do you know where she will be this morning?'

'Not off-hand, but I do know that Pierre had already written down the order to pick the grapes this vintage. He was very organised, Pierre, and compiled a schedule for the vintage each year. Yvonne told me yesterday that the picking would go ahead just as Pierre planned. She said that it would help her cope, and the grapes weren't going to stay good on the vine for very long if she and the crew did nothing about them. She and the rest of the family will need the money from that wine the year after next, so it's got to be picked and fermented whatever happens.'

'Will your husband help out?' Truchaud asked her.

'As much as he can, but remember, he has our own vintage to sort out as well. This is a very busy time of year, you know. That's why Arifa is there; she prepares all the meals for everyone, so that the family and team can work from dawn till after dark at the sorting tables and just collapse in a rumpled heap at the end of the day, preparing to be up with the cock's crow on the following morning. The vintage is very intensive work for everyone.'

Truchaud looked round at Mac for a moment. 'Got that?' he asked.

'Not completely,' she replied, scribbling in her notebook.

'The intensiveness of the labour during these six weeks or so is what guides the family's income in twelve to eighteen months' time,' Truchaud carried on. Mac could see he was getting into his stride. 'Last year's vintage will go onto the market as an *en primeur* wine in a couple of months or so. Soon after, this wine is doing its fermentation in its various tanks, and the wine makers will be contemplating putting their feet up. Out of the blue there will come a sudden buzz of wine merchants hovering around like hornets with their little tastevins round their necks to see what they think of the product of last year's labours. Whatever Burghound and Jasper Morris think of the wine will have a great deal to say about how the winemakers live next year!'

'You know a lot about this, Inspector,' said Jeanette Parmentier with just a drop of respect in her voice. 'Though I am trying to picture a hornet wearing a tastevin and having trouble,' she added with a smile.

'Commander,' he replied without undue force, but she might as well know how high up the ladder the plain-clothes detective in front of her actually was. 'My family is a wine family too, I'm its black sheep doing something else.'

She chuckled for a moment. 'I'm just thinking about that, how someone becomes the black sheep of their family by being a policeman.'

'We're only a little winery, and my parents had more children than could be supported long-term by the winery. My elder brother was given the choice as to which kid should stay and which should go, and he stayed. I have no regrets, and I still get to taste the best of the family's wine, so I'm not bothered really.'

At that moment, there was a squeal and a tornado of hair, arms, and legs hurtled into the room howling, 'Mummy, Mummy, Mummy, there's a p'lice car outside.' After a moment, the owner of the powerhouse lungs realised that her mother was not alone, and a moment later, she spotted Mac's uniform and said, 'Oops!' and crept round the table and grabbed a hold of her mother's arm.

'This is Marine, my daughter,' said Mrs Parmentier.

The little girl looked at Truchaud and Mac coyly through her fringe as she tried to get herself back under some sort of control. She knew, after all, even at her age, that you didn't misbehave when the p'lice were watching.

'Hello, Marine,' said Mac. 'And how old are you, then?'

'I'm nearly nine,' she said, and after a moment's pause, she continued, 'and I didn't do it.'

'What didn't you do, dear?' Mac asked.

'Whatever it is you're here about.' Pause. 'Honest.'

Truchaud smiled inwardly, and if it had been Bruno, he would no doubt have ruffled the child's hair, but as it was not his child, even by proxy, that would have been inappropriate.

It was the girl who broke the slightly uncomfortable silence that followed. 'Are you here about Uncle Pierre?' she asked.

'Yes,' said Mac, 'very sad, isn't it?'

The girl shrugged. 'S'pose so,' she replied noncommittally. 'Do you know who did it?'

'Not yet,' replied the gendarme, 'but we will catch them.' Pause. 'Promise.'

The girl looked at them both for a moment, walked over to the old stand-up piano in the corner, opened up the lid, sat down on the stool, hit a C major chord and then stopped.

'Do you play?' asked Mac.

The girl wriggled on the seat for a moment and then shut the lid of the piano, looking at them through her fringe. That wasn't a shy look, thought Truchaud, that was full-on coy. This child obviously could play the piano, and knew it. 'Play us something,' he said.

The girl got off the stool and walked round to her mother, and having grasped hold of her left hand, she turned, cocked her head, and looked, wide-eyed, at Truchaud and said firmly, 'No.'

'Please yourself,' he replied drily, deciding he was not going to be dragged into an unnecessary battle of wills with a nine-year-old. He had better things to do with today. He looked back directly at Mrs. Parmentier. 'As I was saying, have you any idea where we might find your sis …'

'I could do,' interrupted the child, 'if you really, really want me to.'

Truchaud looked back down at the child with some annoyance now. This was one spoilt brat who was determined to be the centre of the conversation.

'Just a little one,' said her mother. 'Play that "In Dreams" piece that we like so much.'

The child walked back to the piano and lifted the lid to the keyboard. She hadn't needed to adjust the seat, Truchaud noted. She was obviously the only person in the house who played it.

He couldn't believe his ears. The sound that came out of the piano was unlike anything he had ever heard before. It was a soft, gentle, and innocent piece, and yet was embellished with trills especially in the upper register. He found himself being soothed and excited at the same time. As it came to its ending, and it couldn't have lasted more than a minute, tops, the girl suddenly played a loud discord and giggled.

Truchaud jerked back to his senses. 'What?' he spluttered.

'That's just how it was written,' said the girl, 'right with the crash at the end. I think that was the composer's attempt at showing how we suddenly wake up, and it isn't so peaceful after all. Me, I just think it's funny the faces people pull because they don't expect it. You were funny too, Mr. P'liceman.'

'That was exquisite playing,' said Truchaud, as much to the mother as to the child. 'What was it? I've never heard anything like that before.' Mind you, he wasn't really surprised, he didn't listen to a lot of piano miniatures.

'That was "In Dreams", written by Alkan.'

'Who?'

'Alkan,' replied the girl, 'Don't you know who Alkan is?'

'I don't believe I do, where did he come from?'

'Paris,' interjected the girl's mother, 'Like all good pianists in the nineteenth century, he was based in Paris. However, unlike all the others, like Chopin and Liszt, he had the good luck to be born there.'

'And yet, I've never heard of him. Did he write lots of music?'

'A fair bit.' Marine rejoined the conversation, not willing to be left out. 'But it isn't played very often; it's really, really difficult. When I'm grown up and my hands are big enough, I'm going to play his solo concerto to the grapes. Aubert de Villaine plays Beethoven sonatas to La Tâche just before the vintage.'

'I didn't know Mr. de Villaine played the piano.' Truchaud had heard many things said about the great wine maker of Domaine de la Romanée-Conti, but being a gifted musician was not one of them.

'I think it is pre-recorded music,' said Mrs. Parmentier, 'but I have heard it said that it is his secret ingredient. I can't personally see the old gentleman getting up at silly o'clock with a boom box loaded with "Sunrise Sonata" to awaken his vines, but there you go.'

Truchaud ignored the apocryphal tale of one of Burgundy's finest, but he did know what a concerto was, and he knew it was a piece of music with a solo instrument on one side and an orchestra on the other, so what was this about a solo concerto? He asked her that very question.

'Well, he wrote his solo concerto so that the man behind the piano played the piano parts, but he also played the orchestra at the same time.'

'But that sounds impossible,' he expostulated.

'Pretty much,' she agreed, 'but one day, when I'm bigger, I'm going to give it a go.' He looked at her hands at the same time that she did and realised that she didn't have delicate little hands like he expected, but that they were already far larger than they had any right to be at her age. She had long fingers that she waggled at them 'Goodbye Mr P'liceman, must go,' she said and bounced out of the room. And bounced was exactly the right word. She moved like a tennis ball.

'I'm so sorry about that,' said Mrs. Parmentier. 'There are times when we find it very difficult to keep her under control, and it's usually easier to let her have her way for a moment or two. It doesn't last for long, and as you can see, it is often worth the interruption.'

'Don't apologise for that,' he replied, 'that was one of the most extraordinary experiences of my life. I have to find some more of that music. How do you spell his name again?'

He copied down the name 'Alkan' in his notebook and resolved to find a recording of the solo concerto as soon as possible, as well as a recording of 'In Dreams', though he doubted that any recording would have that little giggle that followed the final discord that made that particular performance so special.

'Do you play the piano at all, or your husband perhaps?' he asked, looking up from his notebook.

'No, just Marine. She's the only one of us who has the Gift.'

'Because it's not a new piano,' he said, rubbing its finely polished woodwork.

'Oh no, the piano's been in the family forever. My father-in-law used to play it. He played a little jazz and a little Debussy, but I think he was just a natural player. He would sit down and play. I think the only music he ever read was Debussy, and then after a while he would sit and improvise around what Debussy wrote.'

'Did he ever play in public?'

'Not that I know of. He would quite often stop if he realised any one of us was listening, so we had to pretend to be doing something else. My husband says that he read about half the textbooks he had for Beaune pretending not to listen to his father play.'

'He went to the Beaune University for viticulture?'

'Yes, both the boys did. I think you've got to do that, go and learn the basics before you call yourself a winemaker round here. You have to learn the law and the bureaucracy. The art of making the vines behave how you want them to behave, well, that's the gift on top, and maybe it really does involve playing tunes to the vines.'

'You mentioned her having the gift just now …' he started.

'The gift of music, yes.'

'When we first met you also were talking about the Gift as being naturally able to make wine.'

'Ah, that Gift, yes. It's the Gift to make fine wine. Anybody can make good wine round here, that's what they call *terroir*, but the ability to create great wine is a mixture of *terroir* and the Gift. I have no idea whether Marine has that Gift yet; that we will find out in the fullness of time. Her grandfather who played the piano also had the Gift, you know, so we are hopeful.'

'What would happen if she turned out to have the winemaker's Gift too?'

'Lucky girl, and just think what might happen to her if she turned into a great beauty as well.'

They all looked at each other thoughtfully. Nobody should be too talented, should they?

# CHAPTER 16

*Sunday Lunch at Domaine Truchaud*

Truchaud glanced at Mac and asked as they drove out of the gate and headed back north up the seventy-four towards Beaune, 'Satisfy my curiosity, where exactly where does one buy records round here?'

'The hypermarkets have CD browsers,' she said, and continued, 'I think the Athenaeum in Beaune has a rack of CDs too, but I don't think it's very big.'

'Do you ever buy records?' he asked her, realising that the last record he had bought, he had bought in Paris, and specialist record shops were two a penny up there. When he came to think about it, he could remember finding a shop in Paris that specialised in Russian pressings of LPs recorded by left-handed flautists, or so the man behind the counter told him. Mind you, it may have been a riposte to being asked whether he had a copy of an obscure Grateful Dead concert in stock.

'Yes,' she replied, and realising that wasn't enough, she added 'I buy online'.

'You mean you listen to music on your telephone with those horrid earplugs.' He shuddered, remembering sitting next to someone on the métro who was wearing one, and all he could hear was a repetitive treble 'tink' and nothing else. He remembered the whole journey, looking for a reason to arrest the man just so he could rip the damnable machine off his head and fling it through the doors at the next station.

'No, of course not,' she replied, 'I have a CD player just like everyone else, although we have to keep it turned down in the barracks, and I've also got a pair of proper headphones. Nobody ever likes listening to other people's music, especially when it's coming through the wall.'

'So, you can find any music you want online?'

'Pretty much, so long as somebody's actually recorded it and the recording's still in print. Come to think of it, there are sites on the internet where will find you a secondhand copy of pretty much anything, even if it's not currently in print.'

'I'm impressed, when we're not working can you show me?'

'Well, by the time we get back to Nuits-Saint-Georges, it will probably time for lunch, and I can show you while we stop at the gendarmerie.'

The traffic round the inner ring road at Beaune was as frenetic as ever, but Mac coped with it fine, and Truchaud was really relieved it was her doing the driving and not Lenoir. Duquesne may have been being truthful when he said that Lenoir had never had a crash, but there was always a first time, wasn't there? He wondered about all the lorries in Beaune too. The signs had stated that it was illegal to drive one through the middle of Beaune or even round the inner ring, and all large through traffic had to travel on the motorway. It wasn't quite the right time of year for artics to be collecting cases from individual *domaines* to take to the international markets, not yet.

He followed her in through the office, nodding at Savioli on the desk. He supposed that poor Savioli was bored; he always seemed to be at the same desk when Truchaud had walked through. Maybe that was just a trick of the eye. Mac sat down at the computer and let herself in. Truchaud wasn't quick enough to note her password. He was getting sloppy since the incident. 'Here it is,' she said, 'I typed in "Alkan" and "En Songe", and it has brought up all sorts of alternatives. Oh look, and here's a CD that also has that *Concerto for Solo Piano* on it as well.'

Truchaud looked at it; it wasn't cheap, oh hang on, it was two CDs in a box. Without further ado, he took over from Mac and bought it online, making sure it was delivered directly to his address at the *domaine*, hoping that Mac hadn't spotted his card number. Wasn't that the point of the card number, that they were too long for people to remember having seen it only once? 'You must show me how you got in there some time,' he added.

'Ask Bruno,' she grinned, 'every kid of his age will know exactly how to buy anything online, and in all probability he'll know how to charge it to you, as well. It's only your generation that doesn't know how to do stuff like that.' She looked slightly embarrassed for a moment and prepared to apologise for being impudent to a senior officer, but he didn't bat an eyelid. He had, after all, successfully made the purchase.

'So,' came the voice of Captain Duquesne through the door, followed by the man himself. 'What are you two doing back here?'

'Well, it's like this,' replied Truchaud, 'I've just been introduced to some very interesting music that I'd never heard before, and Constable Montbard here was just showing me how to buy a copy to listen to at home. Apparently various winemakers play music to their vines to encourage them to produce better wine. It could be evidence, you see?'

'I think if anybody started playing Johnny Hallyday in the vineyards it would probably be more likely to confuse the vines that aren't theirs,' Duquesne replied icily. 'If I were making wine in a neighbouring plot, I might get a little upset about that. I would be on the lookout to see if your mate Jean Parnault had also shot up a boom box as well as that wild boar you were telling me about.'

'May I go and grab some lunch, sir?' asked Mac, emitting a discreet cough from behind them. 'And will you want me to drive this afternoon?'

Duquesne looked at Truchaud and raised an eyebrow.

'If you can spare her it will be appreciated; we still haven't talked to the grieving widow today.'

'Be my guest. So, Constable, report back here in an hour, and meanwhile Truchaud and I will wander off and bite something too. Coming?'

Truchaud followed him out of the door. 'Do you want to come round to mine?' he asked. 'I'm pretty sure they will have some lunch on the go at the *domaine* for the pickers and sorters. It will probably be some bread and pâté.'

'And your sister in law won't mind?'

'I doubt it. After all, she got a free hunk of that wild boar you were talking about that Jean Parnault shot the other day, and she only got that because her brother-in-law's the local municipal chief; well, temporarily anyway.'

'So, how's the case going?' Duquesne asked as the lights stopped the traffic and allowed them to cross the road and walk down to the central square.

'Well, I think we've identified the second victim, although if the magistrate were to ask if proof of his identity would stand up in court,

I would have to say not yet. That will have to come out of the forensics lab in the fullness of time. The only other thing we've discovered today is that Parmentier's nine-year-old niece, Marine, can play the piano.'

'Is there any significance in that?'

'Not that I know of yet, though it was an interesting interlude. It appears that she and her grandfather were musically gifted. Of course, you need to use the present tense if you're talking about Marine. Apparently, neither of her parents can play a note. Shows how these things can skip a generation.'

'It will be interesting to see if we have a talented Burgundian musician in the future, it's not something that the locals are famous for.'

'Like cycling skill too, Bernard Thevenet won the Tour de France back in the day, and I have no idea where that came from. I can remember him cycling through here, and us all cheering the local hero. I was quite a small child at the time. It never occurred to me that this was a rarity, a real local hero winning the Tour. Mind you, the Tour doesn't come this way very often, it's not as if we're near the Pyrenees or the Alps.'

'Or Paris,' added the gendarme with amusement. 'Did you ever get to see the final on the Champs-Elysées?'

'Only once, and I was on duty that day. We were on the lookout for a criminal. We didn't catch him, but I wasn't far from the place when Abdoujaparov crashed at the front of the peloton. It was terrifying, I thought we were going to get the whole Tour around our ears at that moment.'

'It's the sort of thing one never forgets, the Tour de France,' said Duquesne wistfully. 'I suppose every nation has their own national sporting moment that they hold close to their hearts. I always try to get to be somewhere on the Tour each year; I was halfway up Alpe d'Huez last year, cheering on with the loudest of them despite the rain. We camped the previous night nearby, me and my very bedraggled son. I don't think my wife forgave me when he went down with a cold just after we got home. It was completely the wrong time of year to get a cold, she told me.'

They walked through the main gate of Domaine Truchaud, and everyone was seated around the table outside in the shade of the wall and the fig tree. Eddie looked alarmed for a moment as he recognized Duquesne's uniform before he recognized Truchaud himself. Michelle spotted them and told Truchaud to go and find a couple of folding chairs and a bottle of nice wine from the cellar as a payment to the crew if they were going to invade their lunch.

When Truchaud reappeared from the cellar door with a couple of dusty bottles of Nuits-Saint-Georges, a few years old, in his hands, Duquesne was already parked at the table next to Suzette and another student whose name he couldn't remember, munching on some bread and Époisses cheese. The detective pulled the corks on the wine and put them on the table. There was an almost indecent rush to get hold of the bottles and pour the contents into their tumblers.

'We've just picked this,' said Suzette when the bottle got to her, and she looked at the label. 'It's nice to know how it will turn out in the fullness of time.'

'How did they look?' he asked her.

'Very nice and very healthy,' she said. 'I even bit into one of the grapes. It was very ripe, with plenty of sugar and nice thick skins too.'

'So, you're now in training to be a winemaker on the sly then,' he chuckled.

'Well, I have to be prepared in case this university course doesn't pay off. There are a fair number of unemployed university graduates wandering about nowadays, clipping tickets and the like, and I have no urge ever to become one of those.'

'Why not join the gendarmes?' chuckled Duquesne from her other side.

She looked at him quizzically for a moment and then shook her head at him in disbelief. There was obviously no way she was considering a career in law enforcement. She was probably more likely to follow her father into health care.

'What was it like being driven around today?' asked Michelle, probably testing whether he had actually been behaving himself and following doctor's orders.

'Mac is a very good driver,' Truchaud replied, 'and hopefully she is going to continue to remain so this afternoon, that is, if we all ask the good captain, nicely.' He turned and threw a grin at Duquesne. Michelle was shrewd enough to be able to tell he had already asked that and got a positive answer.

'Do you think it is possible she could be a bad driver if I told her to be one?' mused Duquesne, momentarily drifting off on a tangent.

'Probably yes,' Truchaud replied, remembering that Mac had been perfectly relaxed riding shotgun when Lenoir was throwing the gendarmerie's own Mégane around bends at strange angles with squealing tyres, 'But that wasn't what I was meaning, and you know it.' He sniffed at the wine for a moment. Well, this bottle's all right anyway. And as no one was complaining about the other one, it was highly likely that the other one wasn't corked either. The Époisses was just about perfectly ripe, and the bread was fresh. For a perfect outdoor light lunch, it didn't get much better than that.

In the end, it was Suzette who addressed the elephant in the room. 'How are you feeling today Uncle Charlie? Any problems after last night?'

'Not that I'm aware of,' he replied. 'Certainly, Mac hasn't told me that I fell over at any time today, nor that I stopped making sense, but maybe she was just being polite. Anyway, she handed me over directly to Captain Duquesne here without comment while she went off to lunch.'

'And you've felt okay?'

'Are you reporting back to your father?'

'He hasn't asked me to. He will probably ask me whether I've seen you, and then I expect he will then ask how you are. I can tell him I haven't seen you if you like.'

"No, no. Tell him that as far as I can tell I'm fine. I haven't really got any closer to solving the case yet, though I think we've worked out who the other victim is, so that's a start. It appears that the logic centres are still working. Changing the subject for a moment, the captain here was wondering whether your uncle has shot up a personal stereo over the last few days.'

Suzette looked at him quizzically, and if she had been wearing glasses she would probably have looked over the top of them. 'What's that all about? Are you sure you're all right?'

Duquesne came to the rescue, 'I think, *mon cher*, it would be just as well if you didn't try to be funny at the moment, not when people are worried about you.' He looked at Suzette and added, 'We were talking earlier about how your uncle might react if someone put a boom box in the Chambertin vineyard playing Johnny Hallyday to encourage the grapes to ripen.'

Suzette smiled. 'Yes, I could imagine he might take exception to that, though, if it weren't within earshot of his own grapes; he might have been interested in the experiment. Does anybody play music to their vines?'

'Somebody says that Aubert de Villaine plays Beethoven to La Tâche shortly before the picking.'

'Well that sounds as if it might work then, doesn't it? I'm told it's not a bad drop of wallop, though I've never had the opportunity — or money, come to think of it — to actually try some myself. I'll ask my uncle what he might play to his vines to encourage them.' She sat and thought for a moment. 'I'm just picturing in my mind the cacophony if this whole idea took off. Can you imagine it, every winemaker in the Clos de Vougeot playing their own favourite tunes across the vineyard, all fifty of them. I think at that point one of several things might happen to the Clos de Vougeot, and I'm not sure it would all be positive.'

Truchaud took a thoughtful munch on his bread and cheese. Would he play them the Grateful Dead, he wondered, or slink back into classical sounds like the Grand Master, and if he played them classical piano music, what? What arrived in the post over the next few days might answer that.

## CHAPTER 17

*Morey-Saint-Denis, Sunday afternoon*

Suddenly, there came a sound of squealing tyres at the gate, and everyone looked round, Truchaud expecting to see a Mégane with the word 'Gendarmerie' along its flank and Lenoir at the wheel. He was wrong; from the driver's seat of the van at the gates Maréchale emerged, waving his fist down the road and howling a stream of invective at what everyone now assumed was a dog, slinking away with its tail between its legs. He calmed down and walked through the gate. Everyone was still watching him.

'Have you all finished?' he asked.

It was Suzette who spoke first, perhaps a little uncertainly. Truchaud was always interested to watch the interactions between these two. During the spring, you would have needed a crowbar to prise them apart, and then at the height of the summer Dagmar had appeared from eastern Germany, and ever since then she and Maréchale had become an item, and it was as if his relationship with Suzette had never been, from either side of the relationship. It wasn't as though the girls were so different to look at; they were both dark-haired, slender and, in their own individual ways, pretty. No doubt it was on the inside that the differences lay. He was not sure how intelligent Dagmar was on paper, but she was certainly learning conversational French remarkably quickly, and with her Osti accent, it was all rather charming, but Suzette... He thought for a moment, well, there was no choice, Suzette could have been his daughter, and she was now, in several people's eyes, his unofficial niece anyway. Of course, if he and her mother, back in the day, had realised what was happening, and had got together, the offspring of such a union would have been completely different. She might have been plain, dim, and probably male. He chuckled to himself at that thought and wondered what her father, the doctor, thought about all this. Maybe he wasn't that interested; it was perhaps the presence of carbuncles or scrofula that really floated his boat, and as long as no one had dragged his wife off into the sunset and beyond, what was there to worry about? He was jerked back to reality with Simon Maréchale's opening statement.

'How much of the Truchaud Nuits-Saint-Georges is there still to pick?'

'The one thing I didn't do before lunch was walk round the plot just to check we haven't missed any,' she replied.

'And that will take?'

'Ten minutes, tops.'

'Right, we do that first. I then want to take everybody to finish picking the Laforge Chambolle-Musigny, which I understand will take no more than half an hour. Then I have been given an offer I couldn't refuse.'

Everybody looked at him smilingly and expectantly. Who was the Mafioso in Nuits-Saint-Georges? 'Jean Parnault, Suzette here's uncle, has asked for our help.'

Jean had been an old school friend of Truchaud's brother Bertin, and they had been very close friends right up until Bertin's sudden death that spring. Since then, he had struck up a good friendship with the detective himself, built at least partly round Charlemagne Truchaud's affection for his sister, which also dated back to school days, even though only Parnault himself had understood the hormones that were active at the time, and he had kept his own counsel and done nothing at all about it. Such is life.

'There is going to be a storm this evening,' he continued. Everybody instinctively looked upwards. The sky was a wash of pale blue without a puff of cloud to be seen anywhere between the trees or the buildings. The sun was in the shadow of the house next door, but its warmth was very evident. 'A big one,' he added with emphasis. 'So when we have finished picking the Chambolle, everyone will go straight down to his Bonnes-Mares and help the Parnault crew pick that, and then to go on with them to pick his Clos de la Roche after that.'

'Who's predicted this storm?' asked Truchaud, looking sceptically upwards again.

'Well, I did,' he replied, 'so I picked up the phone and asked Jean, and he agreed with me. I think he wanted someone with a similar feeling in his waters to make the jump too.'

'He's a class act, my uncle,' agreed Suzette. 'When was he planning to pick his Bonnes Mares?'

'Tomorrow morning,' replied Maréchale. 'But he felt that picking the surviving twenty-five per cent of a Grand Cru vineyard that was perfectly ripe wasn't the sensible choice over picking all the grapes that were near as dammit ready to be picked. The trouble was, he hadn't got the crew to pick them, but we do. So as I said, we made a deal.'

Suzette leapt to her feet, 'Right, team,' she said, 'shall we get on with it?' She turned back to face Simon Maréchale. 'Our bit of this deal you talk about is another of those wonderful German evenings by that Dagmar girl of yours, is she up for it?'

Oh, there it is, Truchaud thought, some nice little bits of sexual tension.

'I'll ask her. She may not be able to come up with the goods tonight …' He broke off, suddenly aware of a wolf-like grin on Suzette's face that Truchaud had never seen before and thought looked completely out of character. She didn't even need to say 'But we may not be able to come up with the goods this afternoon' in reply. Whether or not she would play that game with her uncle's vineyard Truchaud was not sure, but she was playing Maréchale at his own game. 'I'll see what I can do,' he said, and then added, 'I'm not sure how big are your uncle's shares of those two Grand Crus are.'

'Big enough,' Suzette replied, 'but if I promise we'll all be picking until the last grape is picked or the heavens open, then there will be another Dagmar German dinner as soon as possible. Let's go for it.' And like a squad leader leading her troops, she opened the back of the van and loaded everyone up, including some of the Truchaud sorters who had thought they were going to be working at the tables that afternoon.

After the sudden exodus, Truchaud looked at Michelle. 'Are you all right about that?' he asked her.

'If Simon has arranged a deal, it will be an okay deal for us all, that I can guarantee; every last one of the Nuits-Saint-Georges will be in the vat by nightfall tomorrow. We picked the Clos de Vougeot yesterday morning and started the Vosne in the afternoon. That got finished this morning, and we were sorting those today while Suzette and her team got on with the Nuits-Saint-Georges. The Clos de Vougeot is already fermenting in its vat, so we're up to date. We may have a reduced yield of the *vin ordinaire*, but that's not an enormous problem for us, as they are now mechanically picked by the Laforge machinery anyhow. Anyway, if Simon has come to a deal with Jean Parnault, you can rest assured that it will be mutually beneficial. You can see, however, he wasn't going to go into any details in front of Suzette.'

'No,' he said, 'I got that. Won't it be obvious that there is increased activity in the vineyards this afternoon?'

'It isn't a competitive sport, the vintage,' she replied drily. 'If anyone were to ask, we would tell them that we think a storm's brewing for this evening. It'll be up to them whether they believe us or not.'

'So you knew about this storm before just now?' he asked his sister-in-law.

'No, as a matter of fact I didn't, but I do know Simon, and I know he is one of the sharpest arrows in the quiver, and right now, I know he believes there is a storm on the way, and he is trying to get all of the top grapes in from both our *domaines* and those belonging to his friend and ours in under cover before it arrives. Do you want to put a bet on as to when the storm might hit?'

Truchaud shook his head. He knew never to make a bet with his sister-in-law. That was a guaranteed way to empty your pockets. What he did think was that it might be about time to get off and see the widow Parmentier. If she had got wind of the impending storm, then she would be seriously busy this afternoon.

He walked fairly briskly back to the gendarmerie with the captain, and they didn't talk much. They were both slightly puffed by their speed walking and weren't going to waste the breath they still had on small talk. They had got back to the gendarmerie before Mac got back from wherever it was she had gone, so Duquesne made them both the inevitable cup of coffee, which they were two thirds of the way through when there came a knock at the inner door, and Constable Montbard let herself in.

'Where are we going, my *Chefs*?' she asked lightly.

'Back to the *domaine* at Chambolle,' Truchaud replied. 'Mrs Parmentier is almost certainly picking her major vineyards that haven't already been picked. So, first stop is to talk to Mrs Akhbar and find out what remains unpicked. She should at least know that.'

There was little traffic moving on the seventy-four that afternoon, but he lost count of all the white vans parked up that they drove past on their way to the Parmentiers' *domaine* in Chambolle. Mac and Truchaud pulled up in the courtyard and knocked on the front door. There was no reply, but much to his surprise, when he pushed at the door, it opened. They looked at each other, shrugged for a moment, and walked in. 'It's not breaking and entering, the door's already open,' Mac reassured him.

They heard a crash of dishes in the back of the building and followed the sound. They entered what they assumed was the kitchen and came face-to-face with Arifa Akhbar, piled high with plates. 'Sorry officers, did you knock? I can't have heard you,' she said.

'But the door was open so we came in.'

'So I can see,' came the dry reply.

'Madame will be picking her main vineyards today; you don't happen to know what she is working on at the moment?'

'I'll have a look on her husband's planner, it's in the front office.'

'Did she talk about a storm that's supposed to be coming tonight? Certainly my family's pickers have all been reorganised because of it,' Truchaud replied.

Arifa Akhbar thought for a moment. 'If she was aware of anything, she didn't mention it to me, not that she necessarily would.'

Truchaud thought for a moment. Looking at the list would help a little, at least it would tell him what had already been picked and what was left to be picked. 'Can we have a quick look at that planner?' he asked.

'Sure,' she replied, 'follow me,' and she led them through into what passed as an office.

It was soon obvious where she would be. She too had some Bonnes Mares that were listed to be picked tomorrow, and likewise some Premier Cru Morey-Saint-Denis, also for tomorrow. Well, it was those two villages that were in Simon Maréchale's high-risk zone, so if she wasn't where she was supposed to be, looking at the planner, then it was there that they were going to start looking. 'But first we're going to see if she's working in the Combottes, where she is listed to be this afternoon, and then we'll be looking in the two we mentioned. If she comes in between time, can you tell her that's where we've gone to look for her?'

'Yes sirs,' Arifa replied, and, feeling very gender-neutral, they left.

The Gevrey-Chambertin Premier Cru vineyard aux Combottes is an interesting place. It is surrounded on all sides by vineyards, which are most definitely Grands Crus, and yet all it lays claim to is Premier Village Cru status. Jean Parnault had a theory that it was because, at the time of the handing out of the status symbols in the 1930s, Combottes was in the parish of Gevrey-Chambertin, as it still is, but all its owners lived just to the south in the village of Morey-Saint-Denis, so the owners had plots that were closer to their own hearts in their own village to distract them from fighting for its status. They were far more determined to make sure that the Clos Saint Denis, the Clos du Tart, and the others in Morey-Saint-Denis got their Grand Cru badges, and at the same time the good burghers of Gevrey-Chambertin weren't particularly bothered about poor old Combottes either, as none of them had any plots in the vineyard. A little later on, various excuses were made about it being in a bit of a dip and the microclimate being just slightly wrong, but Parnault wasn't convinced by that; after all, the vineyard just below it on the other side of the Route of the Grands Crus, the Charmes-Chambertin, had got its Grand Cru badge even though it lay in the same coombe. 'There are rumblings of upgrading a few vineyards from their Premier Cru status into full Grand Cru, and Combottes is one of them,' Parnault had muttered on one occasion, 'but the counter-argument is that if all these Premier Cru vineyards are upgraded, then there have to be some of the Grand Cru wines that will have to lose their status to pay the system back. The jury, as they say, is out.' Parnault was very interested in the outcome.

There was nobody in the Combottes at all, they noted as they drove north from Morey-Saint-Denis, so Mac did a quick U-turn in the little road junction just beyond the vineyard and drove back into Morey, slowly enough that Truchaud could look carefully between the vines. Nope, no one there, and it had to be said, most of the vines looked as if they had already been picked. They drove back into the village to the junction where the main gate to the Clos du Tart stood, and at that junction Mac turned left, and then fifty yards down the hill she turned right into a tiny little street just wide enough to fit the Mégane, but certainly nothing wider. 'This is why they still use Deux Chevaux vans,' she said, 'You'd never get a Renault Trafic down here.' Just past the wall between the houses, the tiny little road turned into what was little more than a path, and on their right there were people picking grapes. Truchaud and Montbard got out of the car and walked up the hill.

Truchaud was aware of the woman he had met the previous day walking down the hill towards him. She was holding out her hand in front of her. 'Inspector,' she was saying, and he realised just how completely had recovered as he caught every syllable of his demotion.

'Mrs Parmentier,' he said, extending his hand as if he were an Englishman. 'We've found you.'

'You have, what can I do for you?'

'Well, the first thing we need to clear up is what we should call you. We spent a lot of this morning with Jeanette, and a little of it listening to Marine play the piano.'

'Isn't she a dear? I'm Yvonne,' she said, 'and you're the famous Charlemagne Truchaud, but there are those who shorten it to Shammang.'

'Yes, my nephew had real trouble with the whole word when he was little, and his solution to the problem unfortunately stuck. I am, however, a commander and not an inspector.'

'Are you really?' He wasn't sure whether she was being sarcastic or not and decided to let it pass.

'You're not quite sticking to your husbands planner, are you?' he asked.

'Well, as our Romanée isn't there any more, everything has moved forward a bit, and as there is a rumour of a cloudburst tonight, everybody's out picking. Have you heard about the storm that's coming?'

'Oh yes,' said Truchaud, 'and like you, we have all our pickers and sorters out in the vineyards picking grapes to make sure that none of them get damaged.' All three of them looked up at the sky. It was still clear blue and looked totally innocent.

Yvonne looked Mac directly in the eye and said, 'You don't believe us, do you?'

Mac shrugged, 'I'm not a winemaker,' she replied, 'but if it depended on the weather for me to catch a criminal, then I'm sure my basic training would have contained a lot more elementary meteorology. I am, however, very interested to see how it all turns out. I personally would be quite happy if the *Chef* here took a day off police work to go picking, but he isn't going to do that despite being well aware how important this all is to the local economy.'

Yvonne Parmentier raised an eyebrow but didn't say anything.

'Can you tell me a little about Mehdi Akhbar?' asked Truchaud, changing the subject and hoping to relieve the tension.

'Well yes, he came over about ten years ago in the winter and met my husband. It was perfect timing as far as he was concerned; the vintage was all in the barrels, and the previous vintage had all been tasted and sold on to the dealers. Sometime soon that wine would need to be labelled and bottled, but we were in the sort of time when nothing much needed doing. It was too cold to be out in the vineyards anyway. It was at that point that Pierre turned up with Mehdi and said that he would be a perfect general factotum to do all the useful jobs around the *domaine*. I never quite worked out how he thought that might be true, but during all the time that Mehdi has been here, I never once saw any reason to doubt my husband's decision. He drives well, and you never had to tell him what needed doing more than once. He never goes back to Tunisia as far as I know, and during the next vintage one or two other members of his family also came for the season, and before you ever began to think that they were outstaying their welcome, they were already gone. Right now, I can't think I would have got on without Arifa and Walid to help me through what's going on at the moment.'

'Is he involved in politics or anything?'

'Who, Mehdi? I doubt it. If anything, he has come here to get away from local politics.'

'Was he religious?'

'Not fanatically, no. I did spot him facing east and praying occasionally, but he never stopped to pray if he was doing something. He would wait until he had finished a job. It was if he had thought "Well, that's that finished, I'll have a quick prayer before I get on with what I've got to do next". We don't have any minarets round here or anyone up in them calling the faithful to prayer.'

'I fully understand. Did he drink wine?'

'Not in excess, no, but he certainly understood the ranking of vineyards. That, he learned from Pierre. So if you're asking if he was an Islamist, the answer is no, but if you were to ask him to what religion he belonged he would have said he was a Muslim. He would also add that there were some very good Muslims who enjoyed a little glass of wine. As far as food was concerned, he was particularly partial to boeuf bourguignon or coq-au-vin, provided it was made without the use of bacon lardons. I have no idea what he thought about snails or frogs' legs, I never asked him. Was that the sort of thing you were looking for?'

'I suppose so,' replied Truchaud thoughtfully.

'What are you looking for anyway? Have you seen him recently? You know he hasn't been seen over the last couple of days, and that isn't like him during the vintage.'

'Yes, I think I've seen him,' Truchaud replied gravely. 'I have a shrewd idea that he was the other victim of the bombing.'

Yvonne Parmentier took in a very deep breath and the corner of her eyes glistened. Truchaud wasn't exactly sure what she said in reply, but he was fairly sure that it was a word that a good Christian woman had no business knowing.

# CHAPTER 18

*Nuits-Saint-Georges, later that Sunday*

About half an hour later, Truchaud and Mac found themselves back in the gendarmerie. Sergeant Lenoir was sitting in the back room looking bored. He had the air of a man who seriously wanted to go out and abuse a gendarmerie Renault Mégane once more. Truchaud felt strangely dissatisfied with his day's work. He had technically achieved everything he had set out to do and somewhat more besides, and yet at the same time he felt he had actually advanced the case very little. Yes, he knew who the second victim was, but he had been fairly sure who it was when he woke up that morning. He had found out the widowed Mrs Parmentier's forename, but that would have cropped up sometime, and it wasn't critical anyway, and he had heard some Alkan for the first time, but talented and amusing as she was, Marine had nothing to do with the case apart from being the niece of one of the victims.

The captain was out, but it was apparent that all the other gendarmes were permitted access to his precious coffee machine, and Mac made Truchaud and Lenoir a cup each. Lenoir, in the middle of the afternoon, drank a real French cup of black espresso so strong that it should have peeled the backs off his eyeballs. No wonder he could drive like he did, he would have been seriously alert after one of those. The sergeant listened to the two of them carefully while they bounced ideas off him concerning what they had unravelled from the case so far, just to see if he could spot if they were missing anything.

'There's only one question mark that immediately springs to mind,' Lenoir said after they had finished. 'You know Tangier's in Morocco, don't you, not Algeria?'

Truchaud looked at him, feeling slightly embarrassed. He knew Tangier was at the northern tip of North Africa and pointed towards Gibraltar, which was the pointy thing on the southern coast of the Iberian Peninsula. He also knew that it was that pair of cities straddling the Straits of Gibraltar that made the entrance into the Mediterranean from the Atlantic Ocean so narrow. If it were not for that gap, the Med would be by far the largest true inland sea of them all. His thoughts took him to the Caspian Sea in Russia and the Dead Sea, which were by comparison quite tiny. However, he had to admit that, for a Frenchman, his knowledge of the exact locations of the state borders on the African continent was embarrassingly poor.

'So the Akhbars are Moroccan then?' he said.

'Not that I know of,' said Mac, 'I'm pretty sure they're Algerian.'

'But Parmentier brought Mehdi over from Tangier…' continued Truchaud uncertainly.

'No, I think they met up in Corsica. Whether they had first met in Tangier, I don't know,' Mac corrected him.

'There are no longer any iron curtains between Algeria and Morocco, and anyway Tangier has the reputation of being a "free city".' Lenoir paused for a moment to take a breath and then carried on with his dissertation. 'It really was a free city, until 1956 anyway. It was annexed by Spain in 1940, but they had some sort of agreement with the British not to fortify it and to allow the Brits to be there. Very strange behaviour considering the Gibraltar situation, and anyway, being a fascist, if he was on any side, it was surprising that General Franco would have come to any sort of agreement with the British. Tangier must have been a very surreal place during the Second World War. If your country was not officially on speaking terms with another country, as most of the European nations weren't at that time, and you wanted to have a surreptitious chat with one of the opposition, they would arrange for you to meet up in Tangier and have that chat. Apparently, you could often see Germans and Allies in surreptitious huddles in the back rooms of cafés near the Souk throughout the forties. It must have been quite an entertaining experience for the locals. Must have been where Hollywood got the concept for the film Casablanca.'

'America wasn't even in the war when they made Casablanca,' said Truchaud thoughtfully.

'I wonder whether they used Tangier to have surreptitious chats during the Algerian conflict in the fifties too. Can you imagine de Gaulle and assorted sinister Berbers sipping coffee in a darkened back room? But actually, there was an electrified Iron Curtain between Algeria and Morocco in the fifties.'

'Really?' said Truchaud in surprise. 'You know a lot about this period, Sergeant.'

'My grandfather did his National Service in Algeria at the end of the conflict, and there were times when I was a kid that he didn't stop talking about it.'

Truchaud looked up at Mac, expecting her to make a comment, but she had already moved to the sink and was giving the mugs previously abandoned in it the treatment. He looked back at Lenoir and suggested that he go on.

'Well, it was one of those Pyrrhic wars; you know France won all the battles and yet somehow contrived to lose the war. My grandfather was in Algeria in 1961 when they called the referendum, and he says he felt really stupid when the results of the referendum massively supported Algerian independence. It wasn't just Algeria that voted in that referendum, it was the whole of France. There he was in Algeria, under fire, and nobody back home apparently wanted anything to do with what he was fighting for. He was mighty relieved when they repatriated him home at the end of it all. The government was in a complete mess, and there was a cabal in the army that was trying to take power to prevent the planned Algerian Independence from actually taking place. Were the orders he was getting from one day to the next coming from that cabal, or was it coming from the Fourth Republic? He didn't know, why should he? He was only a foot soldier after all.'

'So what did he do?' Truchaud asked. He knew what had actually happened — de Gaulle overthrew the Fourth Republic himself, taking increased presidential power, and granted Algeria complete independence. That was the global picture, but he sensed that the sergeant had a more interesting tale to tell. What was Grandpère Lenoir's role in the whole thing?

'He had a number of friends who were Pieds-Noirs.'

'Pieds-Noirs? They had black feet?'

'They were the French Algerians who served as auxiliaries with the French Army during the war, which was a very unpleasant conflict with both sides committing atrocities that would have made

Genghis Khan shudder. After they were granted independence, the new Algerian government and the outgoing French had come to an agreement that there would be no reprisals against those Algerians who had sided with the colonists. That, of course, didn't happen, and over a hundred thousand refugees arrived on the south coast of France over the coming months, and at least as many of the men, women, and children who didn't get out were murdered by the Algerian government or simply by unofficial lynch mobs. My grandfather knew and trusted his immediate superior officers, and so when they ordered him to help extract the Pieds-Noirs that they knew, those were orders he could follow without question.'

'It sounds an alarming time,' remarked Truchaud to keep his place in the conversation. He couldn't remember in all the time he had known him for Lenoir to string so many words together at one time. The young man who had been recently promoted to sergeant was slender, almost thin and wiry. He wasn't particularly tall either, which was probably why he fitted in the 'cockpit' of the gendarmerie Mégane when he threw it all over the road. Truchaud chuckled to himself; Lenoir was lean enough to be a Tour de France cyclist. He imagined him steaming up the Alpe d'Huez in a yellow jersey ahead of the peloton. Actually, his thoughts took him on to more like Vuelta d'España with that rather swarthy colouring, but he didn't know the name of any famous stages of the Vuelta so he couldn't actually follow that version of the thought through it its natural conclusion. He realised that Lenoir had started talking again and that he wasn't listening, so he tuned back in.

'... but they landed safely in Toulon and many of them simply disappeared into the French countryside.'

'Mugs,' said Mac reappearing out of the blue and holding out her hand.

Lenoir looked thrown for a moment, as if he thought Mac was calling him a mug. Then he realised what she was on about and passed his empty cup to her and picked up the empty mug from in front of Truchaud and passed that to her as well. Truchaud was fascinated that Mac could be so domestic. It was not a thing he would ever have thought of doing, asking her to do the washing up. He doubted she would have refused to do so, he did outrank her considerably, but somehow her expression while she did it would have been interesting. But there were things that senior officers didn't ask of juniors, and treating them like a skivvy was one of them. His mind was full of stray thoughts that day. Of course, he may have completely missed the point, not being very skilled in the ballet that was human relationships, but the previous summer, he had rather assumed that Mac and Lenoir were an item, and he wondered whether Lenoir's promotion has put a spanner in those works.

'So are you saying that the Akhbars are Pieds-Noirs?' he asked.

'Not as such, no, they're all much too young, but they may be first or second generation descendants of those original French Algerians.'

'No, that's not so. Arifa, the sister, says that she comes over each autumn to run the house at picking time. So presumably she and Walid are still Algerian citizens. I wonder if they have work permits.' He remembered that Yvonne Parmentier had said that she assumed that Mehdi had one, but if he was here all the year round, being a real French Algerian or a descendent of one since the fifties, he would have full French citizenship and therefore wouldn't need a work permit. The commander was becoming increasingly puzzled.

'They could be Pieds-Noirs who went back to Algeria when it all calmed down,' remarked Mac, coming back into the conversation.

'It has never "all calmed down" in Algeria,' replied Lenoir drily. 'They had their own personal civil war throughout the nineties. I doubt that anyone would have chosen to relocate there at that time, especially if they were erstwhile refugees. Didn't you hear about "The Dirty War"?'

'Oh, is that what they were talking about when I was at school?' she replied airily. 'I did wonder. What was it all about?'

'Well, it was started when a new Islamist political party, The Islamic Salvation Front, appeared likely to win the December '91 election and the ruling National Liberation Front party didn't like the sound of that, so they cancelled the result of the election. Then the army — the Algerian army that is — took over and banned the Islamic Salvation Front outright. They arrested and no doubt killed many thousands of its supporters. Those they couldn't catch took to the hills and took up arms against the army and anyone else they thought supported them. It was a bloodbath. At least the Moroccan border was open by then, and a lot of refugees fled to Morocco and Tunisia. They either hid there, or once again found their way to France. Meanwhile, the Muslim Brotherhood re-emerged from the debris of the civil war, claiming to have had no links with either side in the carnage, to try to achieve power for itself.'

'So your Grandfather and you kept a close eye on Algeria all that time even though it had become fully independent. Why so?'

'One of the families of Pieds-Noirs my grandfather brought out of Algeria sort of broke up shortly after they arrived in France. The adults disappeared into the French urban undergrowth and the children were left behind at my great-grandparents' house, under the watch of their eldest sister. My grandfather and that eldest sister formed a relationship, and in time she became my grandmother.'

'So you're a quarter Pied-Noir then?'

'Yes, I suppose I am; who knows, maybe more than a quarter, maybe less, I never really knew my grandmother, she became ill when my parents were still quite young, and grandfather brought the younger kids up with his mother's assistance.'

'Didn't he marry again?'

'No, he always said he had never intended to get married the first time, it was just that somehow he couldn't resist it.'

'Do you ever get to see the kids nowadays?'

'Once upon a time I did, but I haven't seen any of them for ages. They probably remember I'm a gendarme, and they feel it is better that nobody in their current community has any idea they have links with the gendarmerie.'

Truchaud thought about that. 'So they're in Paris then?' he asked.

'To be honest, I really don't know, but if they were, that would explain why they're not talking to me anymore.'

Mac looked at them both, 'Am I missing something here?'

'There are *arrondissements* in Paris where a gendarme would not walk alone in uniform. If a uniform presence is needed in those places, they go in mob-handed.'

'I knew there were bits of your past I didn't know anything about,' she said thoughtfully after a moment.

'Is that a problem?' Lenoir asked, and Truchaud was now pretty sure that his earlier diagnosis of their relationship had been a good call.

'Not at all. It's just funny how one finds things out. It's like detecting, there are two ways of investigating something: one way is to ask and push and the other way is to wait and let them tell you under their own steam. You're more likely to get the right answer if you use the second method, but everyone involved may grow old in the process.'

'And the crime may have proceeded to its next phase without you,' added Truchaud, reminding them that he was still there to prevent it all getting too sugary for his own comfort. He then pulled them both back to the case and continued, 'If Mehdi was driving taxis in Tangier when Parmentier met him, how did he get to Corsica and why? Furthermore, what was it that drew him away from there to come to Burgundy to be the *domaine's* factotum, I wonder?'

'It's usually the case that two people just get on, and the financial and social package seems to work for the both of them,' said Mac. 'From what the sergeant here was saying, I don't think I would have wanted to be a gendarme in some of those Paris *arrondissements* for very long, and I suspect I would have been looking for something alternative to do fairly quickly.' Truchaud looked at her and tried to imagine her dressed in something that wasn't a gendarme's uniform and failed. There are subtle differences even between the gendarmerie uniform and that of the municipal police, and he couldn't even imagine her crossing that street and becoming a traffic cop.

The day was slowly moving onward and something was niggling at him to go home. Partly, he suspected that it was the grapes. He was aware that it wasn't Truchaud grapes that Maréchale had come in about earlier on that day, and that pretty much everyone had rushed out to pick 'because there was a storm coming.' He looked out of the window for a moment. It was a still clear blue sky without even a wisp of cloud to be seen. He was also aware that Mac and Lenoir wanted a little time together and that he felt a little like a third wheel. He had no will to get in their way, and if they were still trying to sort out what their relationship should be, they certainly didn't want a man who outranked their boss hanging around looking down his nose at them, even if he wasn't.

'I'm pottering off home now,' he said, taking his mobile out of his pocket, 'if anything comes through here, you know how to get hold of me. I'm top whack ten to fifteen minutes' walk away even if I'm round at Laforge's at the sorting table.'

'See you commander,' they replied in two-part harmony, and he walked out into the street.

# CHAPTER 19

*Nuits-Saint-Georges, even later that Sunday*

Truchaud looked at the phone for a moment before picking it up. He suddenly felt as excited as a child on the cusp of adolescence. He was about to call his office in Paris, and who would be there but Sergeant Natalie Dutoit. She might even answer his call herself. He could hear her voice in his imagination, smooth as liquid cream with just the tang of Cointreau in the background. He knew he shouldn't think about a junior officer in those terms. In fact, he had never had such thoughts until last summer. He knew she had a voice like cream and hair that lit a room without needing help from the sun or artificial lighting, of course. When she had worked with him down in Paris he had known she was attractive, of course, but he had never found her so for himself. His colleagues had told him so often enough, and indeed she had herself, saying that she was quite happy to be the 'distraction' in a 'take-down' and understanding how that worked. However, sometime during that case last summer, surrounded by the aromas of the flowering vines of the Côte de Nuits, he had suddenly found himself unable to take his eyes off her. And now, three months after she had gone back to Paris to resume her duties in the capital, he had still caught her intruding on his thoughts at times when she was singularly inappropriate.

It would probably be one of the others of his team who would answer the phone anyway. What were the odds that it would be Natalie herself who would pick up the receiver in his bullpen when he rang? A little over seventeen per cent, he replied to his own question. Well, maybe slightly higher than that, it wouldn't be Inspector Leclerc, he thought. He couldn't imagine his erstwhile sidekick getting up to answer any phone, even if it was right under his nose, if there was a sergeant or a detective constable somewhere in the room. He could picture him picking out a policeman with a piercing gaze and tossing a commanding nod at the phone, his expression getting slowly more fierce until the constable got up or the phone itself rang off in fright or perhaps despair.

It was therefore that it was with some considerable surprise that it was the voice of Commander Lucas that he heard. He was the leader of a different team altogether and had a team room of his own just down the corridor. 'This is Commander Truchaud's room, I'm afraid he isn't here at the moment. I'm Commander Lucas, do you want to leave a message?'

'I know I'm not there,' Truchaud replied acidly, 'I'm here at this end.' *What the hell's Lucas doing in my room? He hasn't been allocated my team has he?* He quietly shuddered, thinking that Lucas, whose urbane smoothness really irritated him, would have taken over his old team only over his dead body. With his other hand, he took the pulse of the wrist that was holding the receiver and was reassured he was still alive. Were they all assuming that he wasn't going back and that he was quite happy running the municipal police in Nuits-Saint-Georges?

'Truchaud old boy!' came the oily voice down the wire at him, with all the sincerity of a 'yours sincerely'. 'How are the sticks? And what's more important, what's this year's wine going to be like? Any good? Should I be buying up some in advance as an investment?'

'Wine from Bourgogne is always the nonpareil, so it's bound to be superb,' Truchaud replied stiffly, knowing that he had tasted more ordinary bottles of Burgundy than Lucas had tasted good ones. He couldn't quite see Lucas investing in wine; buying top quality stuff to lay down and let grow and improve in the bottle, that way he could sell it on in a few years for a much higher price. He doubted that Lucas had ever bought anything better than industrial fermented grape juice of uncertain provenance. Which sometimes isn't that bad, Truchaud's inner voice chipped in, though that was not a comment he would have made out loud in the little town where he was sitting.

'Anyway,' said Lucas, 'I can't sit here shooting the breeze all day, what can we do for you?'

'Well, I was hoping to get one of my crew to look into a man called Mehdi Akhbar, an Algerian who used to work here in Nuits-Saint-Georges, and see whether there was anything on our central record file.'

'Haven't you got access to it down there?'

'They probably have in Dijon, but they don't know me there, whereas you know exactly who I am and if there are any sensitive links then you know I can be trusted with them.'

'What was that name again, let me fish around here for a biro — ah, here's one.'

Truchaud repeated the name and presumably Lucas wrote it down.

'Where was he from again?'

'He was thought to have come in via Tangier around ten years ago.'

'Tangier, got it.'

'How are the rest of the crew?' Truchaud asked carelessly, although in himself he felt anything but careless inside.

'Fine, fine.'

That wasn't enough, Truchaud thought, he had to know more. 'Inspector Leclerc?' he asked; it was only politic to start at the top of the food chain.

'He's fine, the general consensus is that he'll make commander soon.'

'And Sergeant Dutoit?' There, that was what he wanted to really know about.

'Absolutely delicious as ever, promotion certainly suits her.' Well, that didn't tell him very much, apart from the fact that she was well.

'And the constables?'

'Fine. Look, I'll get one of them to look into this Akhbar fellow and one of them will get back to you soon. Was that all?'

'Very soon,' said Truchaud with emphasis on the 'very'. 'It could be the nub of the case I'm working on at the moment.'

'Yes, I heard you were working on something municipal down there. Has he been parking his tractor somewhere where he shouldn't?'

Truchaud couldn't cope with being patronised by this arrogant oaf any longer. 'No, he's been blown to bits,' he snapped and slammed the receiver back into its cradle. That was unnecessary, he criticised himself. He should not have lost his temper like that. He could imagine the arrogant Parisian the other end chuckling to himself and marking up another point he had scored off 'the peasant'.

He glared at the phone angrily for a moment and then wandered outside. He kicked a pebble that shot off and bounced off the garage door with a clang. If someone hadn't shut that garage door he would have scored a goal, and that thought made him smile again.

It was still very warm, he thought. And, oh look, there's a puff of cloud up by the cockerel-shaped lightning conductor on top of the church. There was nobody else at home, so he walked into the sorting room. There were still grapes on the sorting table waiting for the work to restart after the panic picking in the afternoon. He picked up a pair of secateurs and walked along the conveyor belt. He didn't turn it on, he supposed he felt somewhat naughty as if no one should really be in there, but his near miss in talking to Natalie had made him feel he wanted to do something constructive. There was a bunch of grapes that was furry at the bottom but beautiful near the stalk. He put the secateurs between the join and separated the grapes. The furry grapes went into the hopper at his feet, and the good grapes went back on the table. He picked up another bunch. On that one there was a single berry that had not ripened. How very odd, he thought, and pulled it out. He bit into it and shuddered and spat it back into his hand. That was really sour, and yes, the only polite way to describe it was unripe. That went into the hopper too. The rest of the bunch went back onto the conveyor belt. That one very sour unripe grape probably wouldn't have made much of a difference in a whole *cuvée,* but he would have known that a bottle he tasted, say, half a dozen years later could have been just that little bit better. Why a bunch of ripe grapes might contain just one unripe berry was one of the mysteries to which certainly Truchaud had no answer. He had asked his father and brother once, back in the mists of time, and they had each come up with an explanation that was totally different from the other's, and neither of them made any sense to the policeman, so they probably never knew either.

Oh, that's interesting, this bunch has already been trimmed. It must have been Suzette. She was the only one he knew who might trim bunches while she was out picking in the fields. He looked at it closely; it appeared to have had the mouldy berries dug out to the middle of the bunch, but above and below there were healthy berries. She was leaving as much wood as she could. From what he understood, his father had liked to leave some of the stems to go into the must, so not all the bunches would go into the destemmer so that just the grapes went into the fermentation tank. Simon had said that he was going to try to make the wine like Philibert Truchaud had this year. He had been very laconic when Truchaud had tried to discuss it with him.

'So you're going to put some stems into the must, like Dad did.'

'Yes, I think this year I'm going to make the same wine that he did last year so that there will appear to be continuity in the product.'

'So how many full bunches are you going to put in this year?'

'The same number as your father did last year.'

'But how many is that?'

'The right amount.'

'But how will you know what the right number is?'

'By tasting last year's wine and working backwards from there.' Simon's taste buds were apparently so refined that he could tell how many whole bunches of grapes had made up a bottle of wine. That was the difference between the professional winemaker and the simple amateur like Truchaud. He doubted that he would ever be able to train his taste buds like that, and he wondered if he would have ever been able to do so, if it had been Bertin who had decided to become a policeman, thus leaving it to his little brother to cultivate the grapes. Maybe that explained exactly the nature of the 'Gift'. He also wondered whether he would get anywhere near as much pleasure out of a glass of wine if his sensory input was answering him in mathematical equations.

He completed a circuit of the conveyor belt and he couldn't see any grapes that needed to be separated from those he had left behind, but he didn't turn any machinery on. He had no idea whether Simon would want to put those grapes into the destemmer or straight into the must, and he felt that whatever he, Truchaud, decided was bound to be wrong. He picked one particularly nice-looking grape off the conveyor belt and popped it into his mouth.

The skin was quite thick and almost leathery, not like an eating grape at all, whose skins are very thin. Once he got through the skin, the juice was thick and sugary-sweet. All the various tastes came from the skin, which was quite tangy, and the pips, which reminded him a little of the taste of a walnut. No, it didn't taste anything like the final product, but then, all the tastes were different and not blended together for a while, and then separated when the time was right. What he was tasting there was pure nature, the time would come when the hand of man would take over, with the skills of the sorters, the winemaker, the coopers and the cellarman, all of whom had a role to play in the creation of a fine wine. And yes, the role of the pickers and sorters had already started. He had once asked his father what would happen if a furry, mouldy bunch got into the wine, and his father's face had just puckered up in a way he had never forgotten. So much so that when he was asked that same question, he pulled the same face. He had no idea what it meant in words, but everyone seemed to understand.

As there was still nobody to see, he walked out into the yard again. He looked up. The puff of cloud had moved away from the church tower now, but there still weren't any more of them. He went into the kitchen and put on a kettle. He would decide what he was going to make with it once it had boiled.

## CHAPTER 20

*Nuits-Saint-Georges, Monday in the early hours*

The discord crashed into his consciousness. Marine hadn't played a discord as loud as that or as long when she was playing to him. He was aware there was light behind his eyelids, had he overslept? He never overslept; that wasn't likely. His eyes jerked open. It was dark. Had he gone blind? He certainly wasn't deaf. The racket on the other side of the shutters was a deafening percussion. A sudden explosion and a flash of light he could see through the slats in the shutters explained everything. Either Nuits-Saint-Georges was under a military attack or there was a thunderstorm and it was overhead, not nearby, but right overhead. The thunder and the lightning were as near as dammit simultaneous.

He got up and opened a shutter carefully. A cataract of water was cascading down in front of him. Some of it was, no doubt, running off the roof, but the lion's share of it was coming down directly from the sky. He looked down into the courtyard, and there were large puddles forming. He had no idea that the yard surface was so uneven. There were parts of the yard that were totally underwater, other parts that still stood proud above the water level. He realised that the original designer of his cellar had been a wise man, having built steps that went up before they finally descended into the bowels of the earth. The underground stream that flowed under Nuits-Saint-Georges did not pass anywhere near the Truchaud cellar, as far as he knew, and therefore if the cellar got flooded it would have to be pumped out by hand or the extra humidity that would have been the result would do no good at all to the young wine down there, sleeping in their barrels. He thought of the Laforges' cellar, which did open into the underground stream at its lowest point. He assumed that stream made them lucky. Of course, it might have been exactly the opposite. Maybe the water would rush down from the hills like a rampant Assyrian horde, straight into the underground stream, and swamp any cellars to which it had access.

The thought of Laforges' then led to a thought about Maréchale. Well, he certainly got that one right. The rain was as heavy as he had seen for a long time. Where did it come from? The last time he had looked up, as night had fallen, there were a few puffs of cloud but the sky had been predominantly clear. Ah yes, but the air was indeed becoming distinctly muggy. It had felt like the sort of evening that brought on the thought that 'it could do with a spot of rain, just to clear the air.'

The next lighting flash had already faded by the time the thunder reached his ears. The light was reflected off the building on the other side of the road, and the *domaine* yard was lit by reflection rather than the storm overhead. The storm was moving off to the north. It was probably over Vosne at that moment. He hoped that the grapes from which they made the Grand Cru wines in that illustrious village had all been picked. He couldn't bear the thought of those wonderful wines never actually being made because of one storm. This sort of drenching did not require hailstones to do its damage, the sheer volume of the water would be enough. In fact, as he looked down, he couldn't see any hailstones bouncing in the yard.

He had never had the pleasure of even a mouthful of Romanée-Conti, but knowing that that famous wine even existed was something that made all Burgundians proud of their heritage, even though most of them would never even see a bottle on a shelf somewhere. No, surely if Maréchale, Parnault, and Yvonne Parmentier had all predicted that storm independently of each other, then surely it would have been a piece of cake for the great Aubert de Villaine, and he and his team would have got all his grapes in under cover well before the storm struck.

Truchaud stood at the window and took in a deep breath. The storm had indeed washed the dust and mugginess out of the air. It felt cool and clean over his mucous membranes already, and he also noticed that the intensity of the rainfall was dropping. Within a further five minutes it was all over. It was no longer raining over Nuits-Saint-Georges. There was still lightning about, but there was a distinct time lag now between flashes and thunderclaps, the difference between the speed of light and the speed of sound. Ten seconds was the last gap. The storm, if it was following the escarpment of the Côte, would be over Gevrey-Chambertin now. Parnault would be relieved that he managed to borrow some pickers. He had some very nice Chambertin, Truchaud knew that, he had tasted it in one of those 'you have a glass of mine and I'll gave a glass of yours' affairs earlier that month. Those particular evenings were fairly common between the two families while Bertin was alive, as he and Jean had been friends since school. There were occasions when they had even happened when Bertin's little brother was home from Paris or wherever he was billeted at the time. He remembered one particular evening for reasons other than the wine. It was going to be the first time he had seen Parnault's sister, who had been the light of Truchaud's teenaged years. However, she had gone into labour that morning, so he never got to see her. That baby was now all grown up and part of the picking crew who had rescued her uncle's grapes the previous day. He remembered that the Truchauds had produced a bottle of their Clos de Vougeot and Parnault had produced a bottle of his Chambertin. Both wines remained in his memory, and at this moment as he pulled the shutters and climbed back into bed, the general memory of that evening came back to him, as well as those two great mouthfuls of wine from long ago, one of which had been made by his father and brother, both of who had now gone.

The next thing he remembered was light again. Had the storm come back? No, it was quiet outside, and anyway the light wasn't guttering, it was steady. He caught his bedside clock in the corner of his eye, it was morning already. He was a little concerned about that. Had he gone back to sleep when the rain stopped or had he lost consciousness again? What was the difference anyway? His concern was only if he lost consciousness while he was driving, and he wasn't behind the wheel at the moment, doctor's orders. And when that doctor was also the lucky devil who had got to marry Parnault's sister, you followed his commands, at least for the time being. When would he override that decision? When he had to, he supposed, when he needed to go somewhere in a hurry and Mac wasn't available. That would have left him with the choice of Lenoir or himself. He was fairly sure that driving himself, with the risk of losing consciousness at the wheel, was a less frightening prospect than being driven by Lenoir, despite the captain's reassurance that Lenoir was a completely accident-free zone. Well, there was always the first time, and sod's law said that that would happen when Truchaud was riding shotgun. For reasons that never seemed to occur to him, he never even thought about the municipal crew whose boss he seemingly was.

He visited the ablution department of the house and scrubbed away the grime from the previous day and then got dressed. It was still early enough for Bruno not to have left for school yet, and he was very excited about the previous night's storm. It appeared that it had woken the whole house up, apart from Michelle. She could sleep through anything, even her husband's death in bed beside her. Truchaud was not really in the mood for Bruno to be worshipping at the temple of Saint Simon Maréchale the Storm Prophet at that time in the morning. Bruno was still a little unhappy when the postman tapped on the window in the back door. He was holding a small package. Maybe Bruno was expecting a parcel too, as he leapt up and opened the door. They mumbled at each other for a moment, and it was a slightly crestfallen Bruno who walked back in brandishing the package. 'It's for you, Uncle Shammang,' he said. 'Are the police sending you data files on CD?' he asked.

'Data files?' said the detective slightly bewildered.

'Feels like a CD,' replied the boy, 'or is it another of your Grateful Dead recordings that your landlady in Paris thought you just had to have?'

Truchaud took the package off the boy and opened it. Heavens that was quick; it was the two CD set of Alkan piano music he had ordered just the day before. 'Remember my telling you about Marine Parmentier playing the piano to me yesterday?' he said.

Everyone in the room looked bewildered at him. Words like 'who?' and 'when?' were the general responses to his question. Oh well, maybe he hadn't mentioned the music to his family after all, so he started again.

'You know Pierre Parmentier who was killed the other day?'

'The chap whose case you are working on?' Bruno clarified.

'That's the one. Now, I went round to his brother's house yesterday, but he wasn't in. Practically nobody is at this time. However, his brother's daughter, Marine, was. And this Marine can play the piano.

She was there, and she played me a piano piece I had never heard before, written by someone I had never heard of, and it's on this record.'

'She must have impressed you a lot for you to go out straight away to buy the record.' Bruno wasn't giving up in a hurry. 'Is she hot?' He grinned for a moment and then continued mischievously, 'How old is she anyway?'

'She's nine years old,' replied Truchaud starchily.

'Really?' replied Bruno changing tack. 'Oh well, you win some, you lose some. It doesn't mean I'm not still on the lookout for an aunt,' he said, sounding slightly miffed again.

'Anyway,' Truchaud continued his narrative, ignoring his nephew's interruptions, 'here it is. I only ordered it yesterday afternoon and here it is already.'

'It's a double CD,' said Bruno, looking at the blue jewel case, 'She played you enough music that needs a double CD? I'm impressed.'

'No, she only played one little piece that's on this record, but her mother talked quite a lot about Alkan, and there were other pieces I wanted to hear after that, and they're all in this set.'

'All right,' said Bruno, 'let's hear it before I have to go off to school.'

Truchaud ran his eye down the track listing on the back and took out the first CD of the set and slotted it into Michelle's sound system, on which she usually listened to the radio when she was being domestic. 'En Songe' was listed as being a little over a minute long. Michelle looked impressed with its gentleness, Bruno not so much, but they both jumped at the crashing discord at the end. 'I didn't expect that,' said Michelle, probably the first thing she had said all morning.

'Okay, sweet little tune with a twist,' remarked Bruno drily. 'What else does this fellow have to offer?'

'I have no idea, that was all I have ever heard, but they were talking about the *Concerto for Solo Piano* and that's on the other CD.'

'Put it on then,' Bruno said. 'I've still got a few minutes before the bus comes.'

So Truchaud did, and momentarily the room went silent. Then some rapid descending chords came out of the speaker, which, although were played on a piano, they sounded as if they could have been played by a full orchestra. Truchaud wondered whether the appropriate word was 'should'. The melody built over the next half minute and morphed into a lilting little tune in waltz time, which built up to a series of crashing chords, which certainly demanded a whole orchestra playing in unison. That didn't last very long, and the melody split again, slowly building to a climbing run of notes which, for the first time, sounded as if it should have been played on a piano on its own. Within two minutes, Truchaud was totally mesmerised. Perhaps Bruno was too, but his mother reminded him he had a bus to catch, and that moment had gone. Truchaud stopped the record and took it out of the machine's maw. He was about to be collected too. He wondered whether the police Mégane had a CD player in it. He knew his old BX had one, but he wasn't sure whether Mac was insured to drive it. He certainly hadn't got his old car insured on an 'anyone can drive it' basis. Maybe Mac wouldn't like the Alkan anyway, or, come to think of it, the BX either. It was a quirky sort of car which required a driver to wait after starting the engine, for it to pump the suspension up to the required setting, from open road to rough ground to changing the tyres. Mac might not like that very much, and being too polite to say, she'd suffer in silence. Truchaud would feel guilty, and…. he had certainly never heard her listening to music when she drove. In fact, he hadn't the slightest idea what Mac actually listened to out of choice. He would ask her, and if she was happy to listen to some Alkan, then he would take it with him next time. No, on second thought, he wanted to experience it through in its entirety in the privacy of his own room. If the two bits he had heard already were the general standard, all well and good. However, he knew from past experience that there were many one-hit wonders out there, who had had their fleeting moment of brilliance and then faded into banality when they tried again. He also bore in mind that if the first movement was over half an hour long, he didn't want to be stopping and starting it while they got out and interviewed suspects. He also felt that if the first couple of minutes were anything to go by, he was not going to be very keen on doing the interviews; he would be in a hurry to get back to the car and have another fix of the music.

He left the record on the slab beside Michelle's CD player and told her if she wanted to listen to it, fine, but when he got back not to tell him about it. He didn't want any spoilers.

He walked out into the yard and there was Mac, pulling in through the gates in the Mégane.

'Quite a storm last night, wasn't it sir?' was her greeting as he picked his way through the busily evaporating puddles to the car.

CHAPTER 21

*Chenôve-en-Garde, Monday morning*

Mac spotted a useful looking place, pulled over and turned the engine off. The café from which Truchaud had chosen to watch the mosque wasn't quite in her eye line, nor was the mosque itself, but the route from one to the other was straight in front of her, so if Truchaud lost the plot and went charging into the service, she could probably be there in time to safely redirect him.

Muslim funerals are generally required, even in France, to take place as soon as possible after death, and Mehdi's funeral was taking place now. Truchaud had drily remarked to her already that he was not at all sure how much of Mehdi Akhbar was actually in that coffin, probably not a lot. Much of him was probably still in the vineyard, and some of the bits they had found were no doubt being pored over by technicians in the forensics lab, but as long as some essence of him was buried facing east, that would have to do.

Mac settled herself comfortably and looked out of the windscreen, where a young man on the other side of the junction looked straight back at her. It was no big deal, the car was in uniform with 'Gendarmerie' painted on the side, and it had a globe on its roof which might shine blue if it were inclined to be woken up; in much the same way the siren that often accompanied those lights would wake up the whole neighbourhood. She, again in uniform, sat behind the wheel. This was not an unmarked car on a stakeout, trying to look inconspicuous. This was a police car on duty. Had no one drummed into the young man at school that you very rarely saw one gendarme on their own? If you did see a solitary gendarme in uniform, all that meant was that you just hadn't seen the others, but sure enough they were there, and they had probably seen you. In point of fact, at this moment, the gendarme's associate was in *mufti* and was sitting in the café round the corner, watching the mosque and nursing the inevitable cup of creamy coffee. The young man realised that the gendarme in the car was watching him. They locked eyes for a moment and he shambled off directly away from the square. She chuckled quietly to herself as she imagined a conversation. "Gaw, mum, there she was, right outside Old Guillaume's gaff. Bold as you like. I think they must have finally got the old swine, after all, there was just one of 'em in the car, therefore, stands to reason that the others were in his office, banging 'im to rights and all. Mind you, I never did trust Old Guillaume, never since …"

She reclined her seat slightly to maintain a watchful readiness while at the same time trying to look marginally less conspicuous, and wondered why they had left Truchaud's own unmarked BX back at his *domaine* in Nuits and come up here in the Mégane. Maybe he wanted to show a police presence at the funeral of the murdered man.

She rummaged in her pocket and got her phone out. At least she got a signal here. Considering there was a massive telephone mast at Corcelles-les-Monts high up above Marsannay at the top of the Côte, there was no reason why she shouldn't get a signal, but she was surprised how often her phone didn't work. Maybe she just needed a new phone. She tapped it and asked it to take her into the police database and tapped in her password. That would block her phone if someone tried to summon her the fifteen clicks south back to Nuits-Saint-Georges before Commander Truchaud had finished his spot of curtain twitching. She didn't think it was very likely that she'd be called back, after all, she had been allocated to Truchaud, but that didn't mean that someone didn't need access to the official car.

The screen of her phone lit up brightly. The symbols along the top told her that the signal was strong and the battery was fully charged. She always stuck it in the charger by her bed every night, however much she had or hadn't used it the previous day. She did remember once or twice when the woman she was allocated to share a room with had turned off Mac's charger to 'save electricity', and thus Mac's phone was still moribund the following morning. Still, that obsessive-compulsive roomie had moved on, probably to the relief of both of them. The new girl, Solange, was fresh out of college on her first posting and had yet to say 'boo' to anyone. She wondered how she had got Nuits-Saint-Georges as her first posting. It's a very quiet job in a pretty small town with minimal criminal activity. She chuckled to herself as an addendum to that thought came to her: that is, unless Commander Truchaud's in town, then all the natives go stark staring bonkers, presumably just to keep him busy.

Still chuckling, she noticed that her phone had reacted to being ignored for a moment and switched itself off, so she gave it another tap. She might as well be doing something interesting while she was waiting for something to happen. It was Mehdi Akhbar's funeral, so it would be informative to see if he had anything on his police record. She logged in on to the National Judicial Record website and clicked through until she got to the right page. Well, that was something, he hadn't got a police record, at least not under that name. So she flicked over to the Ministry of Labour DIRECCTE site and then made her way over to OFII. Yes, he did have a permanent residency permit, and a current work permit as well. He seemed genuine enough. Interestingly, his work permit for Gevrey-Chambertin (Chambolle-Musigny) had been transferred from Patrimonio (Nonza) . Well, neither of those sounded French. She grinned to herself, Nonza sounded like it would appeal to Lenoir. It sounded very like the place in Italy where cars got driven very fast. She tapped in 'Nonza' into her phone, and with the spellchecker still on, it took her straight to the Autodromo di Monza, with an 'm'. Her phone even thought like Lenoir, she thought as she turned the spellchecker off and tried again. Her phone had to think for a moment or two, so it obviously wasn't that smart. Finally, it took her to the north-eastern tip of Corsica. Once she was there, she found Nonza, and the word Patrimonio appeared off the screen at her as well. She tapped the second word, which sounded like it had something to do with native lands, but she understood very little Italian. It led her to an article about wine; well naturally, everything in her life was about wine at the moment, even though she wasn't a great fan of the stuff, truth be told. But don't tell Commander Truchaud, whatever you do. The phone then produced a slew of words she didn't recognise at all like 'sciaccarellu'. How did one pronounce that, she wondered idly. She replied back to herself that it rather depended on what language it was. As it ended in a 'u', was it Rumanian? She remembered back from school geography that the Rumanians originally came from Rome, hence the name. And as the inexhaustible Wikipedia then told her, Corsica had been ceded to

France by the Italian principality, later called The Republic of Genoa, as recently as the 1760s. That didn't explain what 'sciaccarellu' was, but at least she had a start.

She stopped browsing. That was the trouble with the addictiveness of the phone. She had started looking for Mehdi Akhbar and various tangents had taken her to an unpronounceable word, the meaning of which she had no idea. Was she going to click on 'sciaccarellu'? She drifted off the point for a moment as Lenoir snuck back into her thoughts. He had a habit of doing that. She had hoped during the summer that they might well be building a relationship there, and then the silly bugger goes and gets himself promoted. She knew she was in France, so those things about officers of different ranks getting together shouldn't matter unduly, but it was in the regulations and had never been rescinded. It required a change of law to rescind those regulations, and she tried to imagine the prime minister trying to explain to the first lady just exactly why he had chosen to rescind that particular law on that particular day. Lenoir knew the regulations, come to think of it so did she, and interestingly so did Truchaud. It was fairly obvious, to her anyway, that Truchaud had a thing about that sergeant down from Paris during the summer, and he did absolutely nothing about it. I think everyone was a little disappointed about that, probably most of all the sergeant in question, but there you go. Who drafted the regulations for the point of what in the first place? she wondered. And with that philosophical question still ringing in her ears, she forced her thoughts back to Nonza in the locality of Patrimonio and the something called 'sciaccarellu'.

She was amused to notice that the first few entries in her phone were indeed how to pronounce the word, and it was only further down the page that she was even told what it was. Oh right, it's a variety of grape, of course it is. As if it would ever be anything else. She was about to take it further when she noticed she had received a missed call notification. She tapped on the number and Truchaud's voice came back to her. 'Oh there you are,' he said. 'I think I'm all finished here.'

'You want me to come round and pick you up?'

'That's what I had in mind, yes.'

'I'll be with you in a minute,' she replied, and started the car.

Within a minute, she was outside the café with the engine running and the door open. Truchaud climbed in and they set off. She noticed in the mirror as she reached the end of the road that there was a man outside the café brandishing a tea towel at them.

'Did you forget to pay them?' she asked. 'Do you want me to drive round again and you can sort out the bill?'

'Would you mind?'

She rolled her eyes to herself and turned the car round, and a further minute later, she was again outside the café with the door open and the engine running.

They didn't say much to each other on the way back to Nuits-Saint-Georges. Part of it was no doubt embarrassment on Truchaud's part, and part of it was because Mac wasn't sure she wanted to discuss what she had found on her phone, not quite yet anyway.

She pulled up outside the *domaine* and Truchaud got out, and then she drove down the lane back to the seventy-four and turned left at the traffic lights taking her to the back entrance of the gendarmerie to park the car.

# CHAPTER 22

*Nuits-Saint-Georges and Épernay, Monday before lunch*

Truchaud acknowledged the departing Mégane as it set off down the street. There was a low key buzz of activity in the sorting room. He vaguely acknowledged the people at work in there with a lazy wave. No doubt the sorters were glad to see the Mégane disappear down the road. Nobody wants a uniformed policeman to be watching over your shoulder. You may have done nothing wrong, but their presence always seems to leave that uncomfortable feeling that good intentions won't stop them finding something if they really look for it.

Truchaud walked through the door into the house and called out a variant of 'Hey!' but there was no reply. He wandered into the kitchen, and there was his CD in exactly the same place as he had left it. No one had even picked it up to look at the cover. He grunted to himself, picked it up, and took it up to his room. He slotted it into the CD player and pressed the button marked 'play'. The CD player swallowed and the CD vanished into its innards. The device started to whir and Truchaud lay down on the top of his bed just as the first notes began. The opening chords sounded of the *8th Etude* or perhaps the first movement of the *Concerto for Solo Piano*, it was both depending how you looked at it. He didn't think Alkan would mind as long as you played it. He would probably be impressed if you actually could, on a piano that is. Truchaud realised what a leveller recorded music had become: even the least deft of musicians could hear the works of musical geniuses. A little over a hundred years ago, no one would have heard this. Actually, until Ronald Smith recorded it in the sixties, he doubted if many people had any idea that this music was even out there.

The crashing chords that heralded the arrival of the second theme made him tingle, and then his phone rang in his pocket. He swore, certainly a word that he would never have used in public, but one of the wrong'uns he had arrested in Paris had aimed it at him some time ago, so he tried it out to see how it felt: nasty. Especially when he looked at the screen on his phone and saw who it was calling him. He leapt up off the bed and rushed to the CD player and turned it off. He pressed the green button on the phone and heard the voice like liquid cream purring down the phone at him. 'Morning *Chef*, I'm not disturbing you, am I?' As if that was possible.

'No, no, not at all, doing a spot of paperwork, that's all, glad of the distraction.' Why did he lie, he asked himself. 'What can I do for you?' he added, already aware of at least one answer, along the lines of 'just about anything actually'. The angel on his right shoulder then chipped in, *Behave! You're a middle-aged man for Christ's sake, not a half-witted teenager.*

He was so involved with his internal response to the shock of Natalie actually calling him that he missed her answer to his question and had to ask her to repeat it, lying that he was resitting the phone on his other ear.

'As I said, I have been allocated across to the team in Épernay which is investigating the bomb scare there, and I wondered whether you had any findings about your bombing. You know, maybe we could help each other,' she hesitated, almost as if she was awkwardly shuffling her feet, 'if you see what I mean.'

'As it's only a phone I can't see anything …'

'Oh, if you had one of those really spiffy new ones you could actually see me while we talk,' she interrupted.

'I will see if my lad in the shop down the road has got one in stock,' he replied, wondering how he was going to explain to him that he now wanted a phone that was so clever it could help him look at Natalie from two hundred kilometres and change away, especially as he had turned down such an offer so strongly when he was recovering from his hard landing on its predecessor not so very long ago. 'Anyway, what happened up your end?' he added.

'Well, it's been kept out of the papers because it was only a scare and nothing actually went bang here in Épernay. There was quite a large quantity of explosive here which would have made the ground shake if it had actually gone off, at least in part because it was actually underground in the cellar. And of course, once it had gone off, it would have then shaken a few bottles, and you don't do that with

174

champagne unless you've just won a motor race or are in the process of launching a ship.'

'Quite,' murmured Truchaud, contemplating that voice and a bottle of champagne in the same place. The devil on the other shoulder then chipped in and suggested that instead of a bottle of champagne, perhaps a Crémant de Bourgogne would be more appropriate. And then a voice from the logic part of his brain reminded him that Crémant was only a general AC, and while it could be gorgeous, it didn't have to be so to be awarded its AC certificate, whereas the champagne Dom Pérignon, for example, got its AC at least in part from being totally gorgeous, and thus it would be utterly appropriate for Natalie who was also uniquely gorgeous. And then from yet another wight in Truchaud's head came the comment that he had never actually tried Dom Pérignon, so how would he know? Yet another voice drily added that he hadn't actually 'tried' Natalie either.

He realised that Natalie had started talking again, and he reminded himself that there was content in the voice that was purring in his ear as well as texture, and if he was going to continue to enjoy being massaged by that texture, he was duty bound to listen to the content.

'… it was military grade C4 explosive.'

Truchaud didn't need to know anything about what she had said before to know that there was a ready-made line to bring him back in there. 'Where the hell did they get that from?' he spluttered down the line.

'My question exactly,' came the reply. 'It would help if we knew who "they" were. If "they" were actually members of the French army, aside from it being an alarming thought, then there would be a reason for them having access to the stuff.'

'But if they weren't?' Truchaud added, encouraging her to keep her talking and massaging his senses. *You really are a disgraceful old fool*, chipped in one of his inner voices, *as if you didn't actually know the answer to that already*. And the other voice replied tersely that it should let him be and allow him his moment in the sun.

'Huh?'

'Are you listening to me, *Chef*? I asked you a question.'

*Gotcha!* came a throaty cackle in the back of his head, *Get out of that one with her and her Cointreau Double Cream voice.*

'Er, yes, and I was looking for an answer and couldn't find one off the cuff,' he replied cautiously, hoping that would fit the bill and prevent her from slamming down the receiver in a huff. He also swore to himself that he would listen to what she was actually saying and not just how she said it. Whatever, it worked, and so she carried on.

'Fascinating place, Épernay, the cellars just go on and on and on. Everywhere you go there are chaps walking along rows and rows of bottles, giving each bottle a sharp half twist, to free any sediment that has stuck to the glass. Each bottle is not just lying on its side like they do in Burgundy, they are racked with the cork pointing downwards so the sediment slowly drifts towards the bung end. That's how they found the bomb so easily, because there are always a lot of people in the cellars there titivating the champagne. The thing that puzzles everyone is how someone got down there with a bomb without being seen.'

'I suppose the bomber was someone who actually had a right to be down there anyway,' Truchaud replied thoughtfully, 'You know, one of the vintners themselves.'

'But why should someone want to blow up his own wine?'

'Ah, find an answer to that one and you'll be one step closer to finding who actually did it in the first place.'

'Mmm,' she purred. There she goes again, there's a fluffy kitten on the other end of that phone.

*Oh, be quiet the pair of you. The commander is a senior police officer, and it is singularly inappropriate for him to have these sort of thoughts about a mere sergeant, whatever she looks and sounds like.* That was a new voice in Truchaud's head with a rather more aristocratic sound than the others, and that one, he thought, should be coming from the top of a lamppost.

'Shut up the lot of you,' he stormed, 'I'm trying to have a conversation on the telephone, and I can't hear a damned thing with you lot jabbering incessantly.'

There was silence.

After a moment, a soft voice like *crème anglaise* appeared in his left ear. 'Sorry *Chef*, did I call at the wrong moment? Are you busy?'

He looked round the empty room, suddenly feeling very relieved that his phone was not one of those spiffy new ones that would allow her to look around his room.

'No, no,' he wriggled for a moment, 'I'm in the edge of the sorting room, and sometimes the sorters get very excited.'

'Oh, is this year's wine any good?'

'I very much hope so. Can the people in Champagne tell already how good their wine is going to be?'

'A young man I was talking to this morning was blowing his own trumpet, telling me how fabulous his vintage is going to be this year. Mind you, there was an old boy out the back who just rolled his eyes at us. I don't know how much of that was real. In Burgundy?'

'Well, we have some idea about the quantity, and the grapes seem to be of uniform quality. I certainly have little idea, although Simon has a rather smug air about him at the moment.'

'Or is that the Dagmar effect?' she chuckled, but the voices in Truchaud's head didn't risk his flying off the handle again. 'Anyway *Chef*, I shouldn't be keeping you,' she added gaily, and there was a click and she was gone.

He immediately pressed the recall button and the number came up, but what else was he to say? Well the number was there in his phone. So if something came to mind he could call her, couldn't he?

He climbed off the bed and restarted the music again from the beginning.

## CHAPTER 23

*Late Monday Morning in Chambolle-Musigny*

Mac pulled up in the yard outside Domaine Parmentier in Chambolle and both of them got out. The sad face of Yvonne Parmentier looked out at them from the glass door from her office and she painted on a welcoming smile. 'Morning,' she said. 'Would you like to water your throats?' Oh, that was a wonderful throwback to his past, Truchaud thought. It took him back to his youth when it was a common use of the word to 'water' as in 'water the flowers,' perhaps even using the rose of a watering can. If you were going to water yourself, it could be with a lemonade, or a hot drink, or you could go down the alcoholic direction, like a kir or a pastis. Even a whisky would pass if you wanted to *'t'arroser'*.

On this occasion, Truchaud replied as was his wont, 'Well, if there's a milky coffee flying about, I'll try to catch it, but please don't put yourself out for me.'

'Constable?' Mrs Parmentier cocked an eye at Mac, standing at ease at Truchaud's right shoulder.

'No thank you,' replied Mac. 'I've just had one.' It was a slight discouragement to the civilian policeman to pursue anything any further.

'Never mind,' she said and cleared her throat, 'Well what can I do for you today?'

'Well as part of our ongoing investigations we have to try to work out who gains from any crime, and as you were very close to the two victims, we were wondering if you could help us in any way with that?'

'Well, poor Mehdi's brother and sister are about at the moment. I don't know what their inheritance laws are like in North Africa. Mind you, I think Mehdi has French citizenship, so I suspect that his brother and sister will probably inherit what little he owns anyway. I can certainly state that we wouldn't be likely to put in a bid for any of his stuff.

'And presumably, madame, you will be the beneficiary of your husband's estate.'

'I hadn't really thought about that. At this moment in time, I have been almost completely distracted by the logistics of getting the harvest in and getting the juice into the tanks. As you know, you have to make sure that the fermenting mustn't be allowed to get too excited, it can destroy the wine before it's even started.'

'How would you calm it down if it does start getting excited, madame?' Mac's voice chopped in from behind Truchaud's ear. He could understand that this was really her first opportunity to understand the industry of the area to which she had been posted.

'We chill it,' replied Mrs Parmentier, 'but we have to be careful even there; if we over-chill it, it won't do very well either.'

'I thought that people paid a lot of money for ice wine,' replied the constable, diving in with both feet.

'Ah, ice wine.' Yvonne Parmentier let out perhaps the first chuckle that had escaped from her lips for the past few days. 'That's a different kettle of fish completely. We don't do ice wine in Burgundy, but the Germans do, and the Canadians do, and even the Alsatians have been tempted from time to time when they aren't thinking too clearly. They leave selected grapes on the vine to continue to ripen and wither until December, and they wait till the first frost. And then all the villagers, every kid and grandparent, rush out before dawn onto the hillside and pick the frozen grapes. They rush them down to the wineries and pick all the spicules of ice out of those grapes and ferment the concentrated juice. It's all very labour-intensive, and there's not very much of it, so that's why it's so expensive. Chardonnay doesn't like that sort of treatment, so we don't do it. It does need a Riesling grape to make ice wine, and the rules state we aren't allowed to use the Riesling variety to make Burgundy. I would love to watch that frozen harvest, though, from behind a window on the other side of the river. I can picture all those little German children with their blue frozen knees scrabbling up the hillside on the Rhine, making sure they got every last frozen grape down to their aunts who are pulling spicules of ice out of the *Reben* with tweezers, wearing perhaps an eyepiece in one eye to make aunty look even more like a witch.'

Truchaud could hear Mac almost giggle behind him as she conjured an image of the crone with the warts on her pointed chin in her mind's eye. It was time to get the discussion back on track. 'Have you thought who would benefit if something unpleasant were to happen to you, madame? The value of some of your vineyards must be immense, the Bonnes Mares and the Musigny are both highly rated Grands Crus. We have a parcel of Clos de Vougeot, and it is always the main topic of conversation at the annual visit of the insurance assessor, and it is not in the same rank of Grand Cru as the Musigny.'

'But it is your leading wine, so you can't blame them,' replied Yvonne slightly tersely, 'although personally I prefer your Vosne village cru.'

'Me too,' replied Truchaud with a grin, 'I see you have been doing your homework on me too.'

'I am fascinated by the concept of being investigated by a policeman who understands all the little twiddly bits of my life.'

Truchaud smiled and made sure that she noticed it, and returned to his original question. 'So, who would benefit if something untoward were to happen to you, madame? I would hate for it to be inherited by some Parisian plutocrat who knows nothing about the poetry of wine and cares even less.'

'Don't worry about that,' Yvonne replied. 'Long before it gets into the grubby mitts of my relations — one or two of whom are, as you so rightly surmised, mucky plutocrats in Paris — they would have to get rid of Pierre's children.'

There was a moment's silence, and then Truchaud said softly and very slowly, 'I didn't think you had any children, madame.'

'I don't, but Pierre had.'

'Had?' asked Truchaud, alarmed, 'What happened to them?'

'Oh, they're still alive, the past tense was for poor Pierre.'

'I think you had better tell me the whole story, madame.' Truchaud's voice was soft but definitely had an edge to it. He wasn't going to let that get away before he had got an answer he was satisfied with.

'Well, the story went something like this. Once we had been married a couple of years, Pierre and I decided that as his elder brother was showing no inkling to add heirs to the family dynasty, we had better start. René isn't the sort of person you can talk to on subjects like copulation and procreation,' she said with a rather wan smile, 'He's a little dry, you know? Anyway, Pierre and I stopped trying to be careful and went for it, like you do. You know how it is.' She grinned at Truchaud and Mac without probably realising that, in fact, that they might not. 'It was not long before I was late and feeling sick in the mornings. But I was suddenly aware that I was also in a bit of abdominal discomfort. I hadn't yet seen the midwife when I collapsed and was rushed into the Bocage Hospital in Dijon. They told me that the baby had not got far enough down my tube into the womb and had implanted in my tube and had burst it. Apparently, there were blood and bits everywhere, and they tell me it was touch and go for a while.'

She stopped for a moment and got up and poured herself a small glass of Pastis from a bottle on the sideboard. She then got a bottle of mineral water from the fridge and poured a splash into the glass. The example of 'chemical change' that Truchaud had first seen when he was at school always amused him, when the clear yellow liquid that was pure pastis had water added to it, it turned a milky white. She returned the mineral water to the fridge and took an ice cube from the icebox and plopped it into her glass.

'Well,' she continued, taking a long satisfied pull at the pastis, 'I took a little time to get better after that, but after a while I did. We also noted that, despite the horrific thing that had happened to me, it hadn't persuaded René and Yvonne to do their bit. You can see this was becoming more like the business of keeping the Parmentier dynasty going for the future rather than anything particularly romantic. As you have rightly pointed out, there is quite a lot of wealth and history built up in grandpa's vineyards, both up here in the Côtes de Nuits, as well as down south in the Beaunoise Vineyards that René is looking after in Meursault, and if René wasn't going to produce an heir...' She paused for a moment thoughtfully and then added, 'But as I said, René isn't the sort of person you can talk to about things like that. So, rather gingerly, we approached the doctor, and he set up a set of scans and stuff. It turned out that I had a number of fibroids in my uterus and unless they were removed, they could almost guarantee me another tubal pregnancy. If they shelled out the fibroids, then that would improve the odds. So that's what we did. I went in for a myomectomy, as they called it, warning me that there was a risk of that procedure too. It might be impossible to stop the bleeding, and if that was the case, they would have to take the whole uterus out as a life-saving procedure, and that would be that. Well, it took us all of five minutes to decide to give it a go despite all the risks and, of course needless to say, the disaster happened, and I very nearly died on the table and hadn't got a uterus either when I woke up.

'So what happened then?'

'Well, we had a counsel of war at home which interestingly enough Yvonne came to, as well as Dr Girand, you do know the local GP, don't you?' Truchaud knew Dr Girand, he was Suzette's father and husband to the woman who was Truchaud's "One That Got Away".

'Firstly, Dr G suggested that we might do a surrogate baby. Firstly, we would need to recruit some likely woman who was willing to carry someone else's baby to term and then give it back to them. We knew that Pierre's mechanicals were all in fine working order, and we knew I could make some half decent eggs, but it was my transport system that had been iffy when it was still on board, as Dr Girand put it, and now it wasn't there anymore. So, what we could do was take an egg from my ovary, pop it in a test tube with some of Pierre's man juice, give it a good shake, and pop it into a cooker and see what happened. If an embryo formed, they could then put said embryo into the woman's uterus and see whether it would cook to term in there. It would be fairly intensive and wouldn't be cheap, but it would be genetically a Parmentier child, and so yes, a true heir to the estate.'

She cleared her throat and took another mouthful of pastis. 'Well that was out there on the table. Pierre felt that it would be a fairly intrusive thing for me or that unfortunate woman to put up with during that year or so and remarked that it was a shame that René and Jeanette hadn't had a crack at it, just the once, as the inheritance laws would work just as well with either brother. The doc and Jeanette exchanged a glance, and Pierre said rather loudly "What aren't you telling me?"'

'Well, the doc asked Pierre whether he remembered whether he had had any illnesses when he was a child. Pierre thought for a while and said he had had the odd runny nose and the chickenpox when he was about six or seven, and the doc said "yes", oh, and he had a mild dose of the mumps when he was ten. It was no big deal. So the doc said yes, not for him, but for René, who was thirteen at the time, it was rather less of a "no big deal". The doc had looked in René's notes and had spotted that René was quite poorly for a time. He did get better and that was that, but it was distinctly possible that the mumps had sterilised him while he was ill with it. Apparently it can do that if you're male and past puberty when you get the mumps.'

'So you're saying that René was also in the state that he couldn't sire any children,' Truchaud interjected.

'Well, it was possible; Jeanette had been watching what we'd been going through and said that she had had all her tests done and as far as she knew there wasn't any difficulty on her side about her having children. You must understand that Jeanette and I may not be related by blood, but we have become very good friends over the years. Becoming a Parmentier hasn't always been very easy, the family has quite a cachet locally, and we two incomers did stick together. You know, when the Parmentier family put on a show for the great and the good of the Côte d'Or, we always teamed up and ran it together.'

'And René?' Truchaud remarked drily, trying to get her back to the elephant in the room.

'Well, Jeanette had tried to talk to him about getting a test, but every time she did, a wall just went up. I suppose some men just can't cope with the idea that they've got problems in the manhood department. They are very different things you know, whether you can perform at night for the pleasure of both or to fertilise a woman's eggs. René's mind worked on plant stuff, not animal. So, Jeanette had no proof one way or the other as to whether René was firing blanks, but listening to her stories of their wild nights of frenetic activity, it sounded quite likely that he was. She wasn't taking any precautions and realised what a mess we were in on our side of the family tree. Anyway, by the end of that council of war, it did appear that there was now one other offer on the table. This was Jeanette's offer, needless to say, but was for the benefit of the whole family. Her offer was that Pierre should fertilise Jeanette's eggs by the traditional method.'

She sat back and slurped her pastis again.

'And?' said Truchaud, unable to wait for the punch line.

'Lucien and Marine. They did the deed twice, that's all it took.'

'Did René know?'

'To be honest, I haven't the faintest idea, as I said this wasn't the sort of thing you ever discussed with René. He did remark at one supper party recently when Marine was amusing everyone on the piano that you could see she had inherited her musical gifts from grandpa. It was one of the things that everyone knew about grandpa that he could play the keyboard off a piano. Jeanette was quite tense about that when we sat down to chat over the next couple of days. She had no idea how René would take the news that his brother was the biological father of his children. To be honest, we still don't.'

Truchaud looked thoughtfully at her. 'We may have to discuss this with him, madame,' he said.

'I know,' she replied, 'but can you do me a great favour?'

There was a thing, the wife of a victim asking the police for a favour. Mac looked at the pair of them; this would never happen in a gendarmerie investigation, she thought.

'Go on,' said Truchaud.

'Can I warn Jeanette that you're about to do this?' she asked.

'How long do you need?' Truchaud asked.

'I can contact her over lunch,' she replied.

'If René has disappeared into the undergrowth before I get there this afternoon, I shall not be amused, madame.'

'After all he has put me through over the years, neither will I,' she replied.

Truchaud looked over his shoulder at the gendarme standing there, 'Lunch?' he said.

## CHAPTER 24

*Nuits-Saint-Georges, Monday after lunch*

Truchaud caught Mac's slightly baleful expression as he put his hand on the handle of the left side door of the car and crept sheepishly round to the passenger side. She was smiling when they were both strapping themselves in. 'I have no idea how that would have played out,' she grinned across at him. 'I'd have had to report you to the municipal police if you'd actually started driving. Presumably you would then have had to have arrested yourself. That would have put me, for one, in a very uncomfortable position. I wonder if we could have seen that through, sir,' she mused.

'I haven't the faintest idea,' he replied. 'Good thing we didn't have to find out.'

She slipped it into gear and set off from Domaine Parmentier. 'Where to?' she asked.

'Do you want something to eat?' he asked. 'I'm sure I can rustle something up at the *domaine*.'

'I already have some fresh bread and some parsleyed ham from the charcuterie down the road sitting in the fridge in the gendarmerie,' she said. 'It would be a shame to let that go past its sell-by hour. I have been developing quite a taste for your local delicacies since I have been here. They all seem to have a very brief window for being just perfect for consumption. And I think that window will remain open for,' she looked at her watch, 'the next thirteen and a half minutes.'

'Okay,' said Truchaud. 'Tell you what, drop me off at my place now and I'll have a bite anyway. I have some cheese whose perfection window has just opened. Can you come and pick me up again in an hour and a half, and we'll go down to Meursault and see if we can run this René Parmentier to ground. Is that acceptable to you?'

'Yes sir.'

'And do you think Captain Duquesne would be okay with that?'

'Can't see why not.'

'One thing though,' Truchaud added, 'at this moment in time, can you keep stumm about the conversation we've just had at the Parmentier's? That topic may be a complete red herring, but if it is a lead then we don't want to lose the suspect.'

'But if that's the case, why did you say she could tell her sister-in-law that we were on the way down there?'

'Do you think we could have stopped her from giving her friend a call without formally arresting her and locking her up in your little gaol? At least playing it that way, she's aware how careful she has to be if she's on the side of the angels. If she's a devil in disguise, she already knows we are watching. So, for the time being, please don't discuss that conversation in the gendarmerie either. Not even with the captain. I will almost certainly be able to brief him this evening once we have the results of the meeting with Monsieur René.'

'Very good sir,' she replied as she pulled into the gate of the Truchaud Domaine. She looked around the small quadrangle. 'Where is everybody?' she asked. There was no sign of movement anywhere. They both got out of the car and, having opened the door to the sorting room, they peered round the door. The tanks at the back of the room were showing signs of activity, but the temperature was just fine. 'That's our Vosne,' he said proudly, pointing at one of the steel tanks at the back of the room with all sorts of dials and manometers on the front.

Mac looked at him quizzically. 'I thought you used oak barrels to make wine,' she said uncertainly.

'Further down the line that is the case, but this early in the first fermentation process we use steel tanks. Some people use concrete tanks and people occasionally use glass for fermentation, though I've never seen a big glass tank. There are people who use wooden fermentation tanks, but my father always found that it was easier to control the temperature and the rate of fermentation if he used steel tanks.'

She looked around. 'Sir, aren't you afraid that without anyone here at all, somebody will just walk through the gate and nick the lot? There's no security here at all.'

'Why would they do that? It's hardly in any state to be fit for consumption, and if you start shaking it about and putting it on a lorry, it'll never be any good. It will remain at its best in the future if you leave it alone right now.'

'But they could sabotage it …'

'But why would they want to do a thing like that? That would be just spiteful.' But Truchaud did see the point. The crew had probably gone off to Maison Laforge to sort the basic Bourgogne, which traditionally was a mixture of Laforge's wine from the east side of the seventy-four and grapes from Truchaud's vines from the same location. Still, it probably deserved a comment when they all got together in the evening. After all, it was possible to walk off with kit, like sorting tables and baskets. They weren't things you could share with other winemakers, as you would probably only get a few day's use each year out of them, it was the same few days every year for every winemaker, and so every *domaine* would have to have a complete vintage kit of their own.

'You're attached to that Vosne, aren't you?' she remarked. 'Come to think of it, Mrs Parmentier said that it was her favourite of your wines. Sometime I would like to try a glass.'

'And so you shall,' replied the commander, 'just not that version of it, not for several years yet. Once we've sorted out this mess, we'll have a bottle of something about ten years old. I know that's a cracking bottle of juice.'

'I think this will be a story to tell my grandchildren: me, a junior gendarme, being invited to share a bottle of fine wine with a commander of the national police. I didn't think life was supposed to pan out like that.'

'I don't think any of this case is exactly being played by the rules,' he replied drily, 'Look at it carefully after all, my role here is as municipal chief of police. But what am I doing? I am being a commander of the national police. But where are the rest of the national police? In their offices in Dijon, watching from afar. And who is my personal assistant in this case? You, mademoiselle, a local gendarme, and we are wandering all over the Côte d'Or starting in Chenôve this morning, and this afternoon we're going at least to Meursault, so I'm taking you well outside the area you are supposed to be policing. If we sort the case, I hope no one will have any problems with the ways we've been bending the regulations.' He grinned at her, 'Enjoy your *jambon persillé,* I'll see you in an hour or so.'

Mac climbed back into the car and disappeared out of the gate. She drove herself into the back entrance of the gendarmerie and walked though the back door.

'Is my car in one piece?' Lenoir greeted her when she walked in. No 'hello, how are you' or a peck on either ear, nothing friendly.

'Your car?' she replied tersely. 'And why might you think it wouldn't be?' she added, following no response from the newly promoted sergeant who was swinging his legs on the desk in the back room. 'Have you broken my computer?' she added, looking at the laptop folded shut beside him.

He grinned at her. 'I imagine it's in much the same condition as the car.'

'That's good then,' and parked herself in front of the computer and powered it up. She gave up trying to get a friendly response from him and decided to get back to strictly professional. 'What do you think of this?' She tapped at the keyboard, once again having to switch off the spellchecker, as the sergeant appeared to be getting quite excited as the screen displayed The Autodromo di Monza.

'I don't know how much we are supposed to be collecting information about the Vosne bombing,' she said, 'but following Truchaud around has rather got me investigating stuff on the internet. I don't think the old boy is very internet savvy.'

'That's the problem of getting old. We're all going to start getting old one day, you know. I wonder what colour your hair will become.'

How her hair would age had never crossed her mind, ever. 'Just because you've just been promoted doesn't mean you're getting old, it just means that people will say we oughtn't be playing around together until I get promoted too.'

'I don't believe that for a minute, but if it is true, arise Sergeant Montbard.'

Mac looked at him for a moment, wondering whether they had actually been flirting again. When they had both been constables, that sort of thing had not been an issue. She closed her eyes for a moment. She could just picture her promotion interview. 'Tell us, Constable Montbard, exactly why is it that you want to be promoted to sergeant?'

'Well Commander, it's like this, ever since Sergeant Lenoir was promoted to sergeant, it appears that, for protocol reasons, I have not been permitted to snog him silly, and I would like to be permitted to do that again.' No, she really didn't think that that would cut the mustard, even if his intermittent daft behaviour, especially behind the wheel of a car, had ever been due to her having kissed him into such a state. Not that she ever had, but it would be nice for it not to be a disciplinary issue if her libido were to get carried away with itself. Anyway, knowing her luck, she would end up being promoted directly to lieutenant and transferred to Martinique, or somewhere else hot, steamy and humid, without the presence of a Lenoir to entertain her.

She cleared her head of the unwelcome thoughts and went to the fridge. Out came the *jambon persillé* and the butter. She ripped off the end of the baguette, and with the table knife that was handily lying around and looked clean enough, she spread some butter in the bread. She then hacked off a hunk of ham and put it in the bread and took a munch.

Lenoir was watching the performance with interest. 'Any of that going spare?' he asked after he saw her swallow. He was too much of a gentleman to encourage her to talk with her mouth full.

'Help yourself,' she replied, handing him the knife and trying hard not to smile. She took another munch of her own ham sandwich.

For a while the only sound that was heard was that of young teeth on crusty bread. In the end, Lenoir broke the silence, 'What we really need is a bottle of red to wash this down with.'

'Can't do that,' she said, 'I'm driving again this afternoon.'

'Truchaud again?' he asked.

'The same.'

'Why does he always pick you?' he asked. 'You don't think he's having iffy thoughts about you, do you? Don't forget he had quite a thing about that sergeant he brought down from Paris last summer.'

'Don't be silly, just remember that the only other choice as a driver here is you, and your driving simply terrifies the wits out of him.'

Lenoir opened his eyes as wide as he could, giving her the full-on innocence. '*Moi*? Scary? I haven't crashed that Mégane once yet.'

'Quite, and he's quite convinced that he's going to be in the passenger seat when you finally get round to it.'

'So, what did you get up to this morning anyway?'

'I took him to Mehdi's funeral in Chenôve …'

'Oodles of fun with the civilian police,' Lenoir interrupted drily.

'Well, it wasn't as bad as all that. He sent me off to park up round the corner, and I did a little internet research.'

'What on?'

'How Mehdi got here. Apparently, he was of Algerian extraction, and his route to Bourgogne was via Tangier in Morocco and then to Nonza in Corsica, where he got involved in the wine business. I don't quite know what his involvement in the wine business there was, but one of the Parmentiers met him in Nonza and then brought him over here. I assume it was Pierre he met there because it was Pierre who took him on as his factotum in the Chambolle *domaine*.'

'You make it sound like Parmentier has more than one *domaine*.'

'Well there is another Domaine Parmentier run by brother René, in Meursault, where we are going this afternoon to interview him.'

'Who is still alive?'

'I bet both René and our Commander Truchaud would be rather disappointed if he wasn't. The two *domaines*, how I understand it, work together as a partnership of equals with the Meursault *domaine* being predominantly about white wine, and I think the Chambolle domaine is exclusively red.'

'Are the labels the same?'

'You know, I don't know the answer to that. I'll make a note to find out.'

'And I guess the main question everyone is asking is who will benefit from the death of Mr Chambolle-Parmentier,' Lenoir added to her mental note.

'I'm pretty damn sure that that is number one is on Commander Truchaud's agenda for this afternoon.'

Lenoir took a final mouthful of ham sandwich and swung himself off the desk. 'You know Mac, that was a very nice impromptu lunch. You could make a man I know very happy if you were to keep that up.'

'What, just by nipping down to the *charcutier* and picking up some cooked meat and fresh bread from the baker? He'd be awfully easy to please, that one. I don't think I would remain interested for very long.'

'Coffee?' Lenoir changed the subject, realising that the previous topic hadn't got legs.

'If you're making some. None of that thick milky stuff the commander drinks, just a cup of the real stuff.'

'An espresso to put hair on your chest, coming up,' he replied with a grin.

Why was he such an oaf, she wondered, and why did she like him so much despite that?

# CHAPTER 25

*Monday, early afternoon, Nuits-Saint-Georges*

Truchaud put the CD player on the sideboard and plugged it in. He fed the disc of Alkan's music into it and turned it on fairly quietly. He then spread the case papers all over the dining room table. There must be something in that lot that he'd missed, but what was it? Where was it? There was a musical crash from the CD player, and he found he was being distracted by the sounds. Right now, he knew he should be working rather than listening to music, and it was painfully obvious he couldn't do both simultaneously. He walked over to the CD player and turned it off.

'Oh, don't do that for me,' came another male voice from the doorway, 'I was quite enjoying it.'

Truchaud spun around, almost dropping into a self-defence stance, wondering where he might have secreted a firearm. Oh yes, it was in his office in the town hall, but it wouldn't have mattered, he had never been much of a shot anyway. He looked up at the man who had walked into his dining room and relaxed. He knew that face, and the expression on the front of it was friendly, perhaps even amused at having made Truchaud jump.

'*Monsieur le Juge*,' Truchaud said, mock-severely, 'Haven't people warned you about making policemen jump?'

Mr de Castaigne, the examining magistrate, dressed in a suit that had outgrown him several years ago, grinned at him. 'I just came round to see how you are. I heard that you had been declared unfit to drive and were being driven round by a gendarme.'

Truchaud wandered up to the magistrate, shook his outstretched hand, and invited him to sit down. 'Coffee? Tea? Something a little stronger?' he enquired.

"Not while I'm on duty,' replied the magistrate.

'What? Not even coffee?'

'Oh, I'm allowed coffee,' he replied, 'We'd be having to sort you and

Captain Duquesne out big time if that wasn't permitted, the amount of coffee you two put away during the working day.'

'Would you like a cup of coffee?' asked Truchaud, beginning to feel irritated, 'I've already got one on the go myself, and if you've taken the trouble to come down to Nuits-Saint-Georges from your office in the city, I imagine you've got stuff to talk about.'

'I'm told you fix a good cup of coffee, so I accept.'

Truchaud walked through into the kitchen, raising his eyebrows after he had passed the thin man. He emptied the grounds from the Bialetti, rinsed it out, and filled the reservoir with water. He poured some coffee beans into the grinder and whizzed them up into a fine powder, filled the funnel, and, having screwed on the top, he put the contraption on the stove and waited. 'Milk and sugar?' he asked.

'Look at me, do I look like a milk and sugar man? Anyway, no thanks, I like it just as it comes, direct from the pot.'

Truchaud nodded and wandered back into the dining room. 'Anyway,' he said, 'What can I do for you? Why have you come down to Nuits-Saint-Georges? You could have phoned me?'

'Well, I wanted to actually see for myself how you are, and having done that I was then going to ask you how the case was going?'

Truchaud looked at him and was then distracted by the sound like a child sucking through a straw from a nearly empty bottle. 'Hang on a moment,' he said. There was steam coming from the spout of the Bialetti. He picked a cup off the draining board and filled it from the steaming steel jug. The cup and the jug, calmer now, he put on a tin tray and placed the tray in front of the magistrate. 'There's more coffee in that machine if you want some,' he said and then went and sat down within reach of his own cup again. 'Bottom line is that as far as I can see, I'm fine, and slightly irritated about not being allowed to drive myself. The case? I suppose less so, we don't seem to be getting very far.'

The magistrate sipped his cup. 'Hmm,' he murmured, 'your reputation for coffee is well deserved.' He cleared his throat and began, 'So what have you found out so far?'

'Well we know who the victims were: Pierre Parmentier, a vintner from Chambolle-Musigny who owned that plot in Vosne-Romanée where it all happened, and the man tied to the chair with the bomb strapped to him was Mehdi Akhbar, who was a general factotum at Parmentier's *domaine*.'

'Mehdi Akhbar, that's an interesting name, what's his history?'

'His father's Algerian, but Mehdi got here in a fairly roundabout way, via Morocco and Corsica.'

'If you look at a map of North Africa, you will see that you go left from Algeria to Morocco and you go up and to the right to get to Corsica.' He smiled gently at Truchaud.

'Oh quite,' replied the policeman, 'I think it was a long journey. I understand that he was still a teenager when he left Algeria during the civil war and got a job driving taxis in Tangier for a while. I have not quite worked out why he left Tangier or how he got to Corsica, though we'll get answers to that, as his brother and sister are here at the moment, but it was in Corsica that he met Mr Parmentier, and our Mr Parmentier offered him a job here at his winery, and apparently Akhbar decided that it was a step up from what he was doing at the time.'

'When did he come over?'

'He must have been here in the Côte d'Or for the best part of the last ten years or so.'

'So he may have been a political refugee from Algeria?'

'His brother and sister only come here for the vintage, and as far as I know, they still live in Algeria most of the year.'

'Well, they're not political refugees, are they? Hmm, and the third victim? How did he fit into all this?'

'The third victim?' Truchaud looked at de Castaigne quizzically. 'I don't know anything about a third victim.'

'You.'

'Me?'

'Yes, you. How did you actually get to be at the scene of the incident when it went off? You weren't summoned by a telephone call that told you that there had been an incident, which is how you usually get to the scene of a crime; you were summoned by a telephone call that told you there was going to be a bombing, and exactly where it was going to be.'

Truchaud thought for a moment and said, 'Yes, I see what you mean.'

'Do you know whether Parmentier also received a similar phone call?'

'What, asking him to come up to the vineyard? Well, he certainly looked cross about something on his way up to us. I assumed it was the chair in the middle of the vineyard that was annoying him. I'd have been pretty miffed if I'd come across someone playing silly buggers in one of my vineyards too.'

'So you don't know whether he received a call telling him something was going to go down in his vineyard?'

'No, not as such, but I also don't know whether he didn't either. Was his phone found in the wreckage by the CSI's?'

'There was a phone found there, but it's completely toasted. We know it wasn't yours, so it might have been Parmentier's or it might have been Akhbar's.'

'But they only found one phone?'

'They only found one phone.'

'Well, that's one question I am going to have to ask his widow when I next see her, has she got his phone?'

'Where would his widow be now?'

'Well, I saw her last within the past half hour, and she was completing the vintage without him. The rest of us are helping her wherever we can, but it's her business now, and if the grapes don't get harvested at the right time, then the wine doesn't get made, that's a year's income down the pan. The employees don't get paid and you won't find anybody willing to help with next year's vintage.'

'And who decides the right time to harvest the grapes?'

'The grapes and the calendar make that decision. She had a close enough call with that storm. Fortunately, she got her Bonnes Mares in before it hit. There were those that didn't, and there were the grapes strewn all over the turf the following morning.'

'Can't you use those grapes once they have fallen? After all, they are ripe and ready to go.'

'You might be able to make Marc or vinegar out of them, I suppose, but Bonnes Mares is a Grand Cru wine, and if it's found to be damaged at one of the early tastings, questions will be asked. If the critics then find that the grapes spent time on the ground after a storm, not only will that wine have a bad reputation, but the whole wine house that made it will have the reputation of one who tries to sell damaged substandard wine, and that will be something talked about for years to come. So the answer to that is "no". But she got her grapes in, and our man Simon Maréchale made sure of that himself. I think some of our kids were in there helping her with her harvest.'

'Somehow, I wish I was a Burgundian winemaker, I do get the feeling you all look out for each other.'

'I suppose we do, although to be honest, I am really on the outside looking in.'

'Your family is a winemaking family though, and you've had your troubles this year.'

'Yes, we've lost both our winemakers, and yet Simon and Michele have got all our grapes in at the right place and time. Quite what will happen this time next year, only time will tell.'

'And someone attempted to take you out as well.' Castaigne said that far more slowly and more carefully. He was making an important point. 'Any idea why?'

'Well, I don't know much about the fine tuning of making wine. It was my father and brother who were the gifted winemakers in my family.'

'And you are simply a policeman, though you don't get to being a commander without being fairly good at it.'

'Thank you, monsieur, I don't think we need to be paying each other lots of unnecessary compliments.'

'I wasn't trying to do that, what I was doing was trying to tease out of you someone who might pay you a grudge.'

'I've put a fair number of felons behind bars in my time. It has to be said that we don't go out of our way to make friends with the criminal community.'

'Anything that might spring to mind, especially recently?'

Truchaud couldn't help thinking of the 'barbecue' at the end of May that spring. He had only just got back to Paris when that case had been slapped on his desk. A kid had been locked in the boot of a car that had then been torched. The case itself had been rapidly sorted, with the perpetrators locked up and presumably a key had been thrown away. They claimed they were innocent of the charge of murder on the grounds that they didn't know the kid was hiding in the car. They claimed they were guilty of arson, and admitted torching the car, but they had no knowledge that the kid had been spying on them for the rival gangster whose car it was. It had not been a difficult case to sort out, but one that remained in his mind for all the wrong reasons, not the least the smell of baked victim. Somehow, the snarl on the face in the dock was what he remembered most of all. That was a face of pure hatred that he would remember till the end of his days. He could not understand how, let alone why, it was possible to do that to a child. The bottom line was that there was a great deal of unpleasantness in the Arab quarter of Paris. The relationship between those Arabs and the police was rock bottom. So yes, he supposed that it was possible that there were people in the *arrondissements* who might bear him a grudge. That went with the territory being a policeman, didn't it?

He explained the case to de Castaigne who sat opposite, sipping his coffee, saying little apart from grunts of 'uh huh' to acknowledge he had got the point.

'But surely,' continued Truchaud, 'if gangs took that view, then every policeman would be living in permanent fear for his life.'

'Would that not be the point?' de Castaigne nodded sagely, 'I think that is the point. I wonder how many gang crimes go unreported, or at least unsolved, because of this sort of pressure being brought on the lead officer in question. They will try to sort him out *pour encourager les autres*.'

'I've heard that phrase before,' replied Truchaud, 'but I'm damned if I can remember where from.'

'In 1756, the English shot their one of their admirals, a chap called Byng, on the quarterdeck of his warship *'pour encourager les autres'*, as Voltaire wryly put it, to put some steel into the spine of the other commanders. If I remember rightly, it seemed to work, as by the time the following year was out, the English had captured Quebec from us.'

'You know your history, m'sieur.'

'It is a good thing to know and understand history. It should advise behaviour in contemporary events, but so rarely does.'

## CHAPTER 26

*Monday afternoon, Meursault*

'Just to keep you happy, I'll lock the gates as we leave,' Truchaud remarked as Mac drove into the quad.

'Why would that keep me happy? Won't they be unable to get in?' she asked.

'Depends who they come home with,' he replied drily. 'If they come home with Michelle or Bruno, not a problem, they've both got gate keys, and I would imagine Simon has a key too. He appears to be able to get into absolutely anywhere if he puts his mind to it. He's probably got keys to all the little crannies where you hide things in the gendarmerie if you look carefully enough.'

'I hope he hasn't,' she replied. 'The security implications ...' She paused, noting his very Gallic shrug. He was probably teasing.

Truchaud pulled the gates shut and locked them, putting his smallish bunch of keys back into his pocket. He then climbed into the car. 'The seventy-four, heading south,' he said as he buckled himself in.

Fifteen minutes later, they were approaching Beaune. 'How do you want to do this?' she asked. 'Round it on the motorway or straight through the middle?'

'Oh, I think we go through the middle until we get to the inner ring and then follow it round until we hit the seventy-four on its way out again heading towards Pommard and Meursault. I like Beaune, and even its ring road is picturesque. Also, the direct route is shorter, and we don't pay any motorway tolls.'

'Your wish is my command, sir,' she said, heading straight round the motorway roundabout and on into the town. It was an almost straight road until they hit the ring. There was a little arch in front of them, which you could drive round if you were minded to accept the challenge of the narrow cobbled streets of the town centre. They turned sharp right at the traffic lights onto the ring. Truchaud noted the various major wine businesses with premises on the Avenue Maréchal Foch, such as Bouchard Aîné. It was almost like a Bordeaux Château in style. Drive in through the gates and you can park in the gravelled courtyard. If you walk up the steps to the grand entrance door, it looks as though it should have a uniformed flunkey to show you in. The building has a grandeur that Truchaud's little *domaine* hasn't. Truchaud smiled to himself as he realised that the main difference was that Truchaud's *domaine* had their Vosne and Clos de Vougeot in its cellar, and Bouchard's didn't.

They followed the road round. 'Next right, D974,' chirped Mac from the driving seat.

'That's the one we want,' he replied, and she turned right past the shops on the corner, and the road was dead straight again, out of town. 'Follow the road to Pommard, leave delightful Volnay up the hill on the right, and drop down to the left into Meursault.

The turn to Volnay passed them on their left just before they drove into the village of Pommard itself. They had both scanned the devastation of the vines on either side of the road. Those vines hadn't just been picked, they had been stripped of their berries a couple of months ago by a hailstorm. The weather was an unkind master. They had just avoided a similar fate with their own vines in Chambolle. 'Interesting how localised those storms are,' he remarked to Mac. 'Almost as if it is fired like an automatic weapon at an individual site.'

'Or a bomb,' she replied drily from the driving seat, just spotting the sleeping policeman in the middle of the village before it launched them, out of control, into the busy market square. 'The storms they've been having serves them right for that stupid lump in the middle of the road.' She muttered to herself. 'We could have been warned about it in advance.'

'Maybe we were; we were looking out of the side windows.'

They headed on down into the next village, which was altogether calmer and more organised. They headed up to the *domaine* of Parmentier south, and she swung through the gate into the courtyard.

As they got out of the car, a recognisable figure walked over to them. This must be René Parmentier. He was leaner than his brother, whom Truchaud remembered tragically well. You don't forget people who have so recently died in front of you. This one was greying slightly at the temples. 'The police,' René said, acknowledging Mac's uniform, 'I have been expecting you.'

'Since when?' Truchaud asked.

'Since I heard what happened to my brother. Do you want to come through?' He led them through to the sitting room where, forty-eight hours earlier, Truchaud had been enchanted by Marine Parmentier playing the piano. 'Make yourselves comfortable. I suspect we both have a lot of questions for each other, would you like to start?'

'Well, the elephant in the room is to do with the children,' replied Truchaud. 'We were looking into the matter of who might benefit from your brother's death, and it occurred to us that the prime beneficiaries might be Lucien and Marine, your children.'

'Oh come on, you can't be accusing the kids of killing my brother?'

'No, of course not, but they will be the main beneficiaries of his estate.'

'In the long term, I suppose they will.'

'In the short term too, I suspect.'

Parmentier looked closely at Truchaud through hooded eyebrows. 'Ah,' he said, 'you know.'

'I know,' he replied. 'We weren't sure that you did.'

Parmentier got up and made sure the door was closed and that no one could walk in on them. He returned to his chair. 'Just to make sure that young ears don't find things out before they're old enough to handle that information. May I ask how you found out?'

'We asked your sister-in-law this morning and it all came out.'

'So she knows as well, does she?' He laughed ironically, and it wasn't a particularly pleasant sound. 'Aren't we a load of silly billies. Everyone knows the family secret, and yet everyone is too sensitive of everybody else's discomfort to talk about it. I wouldn't be in the least bit surprised if the kids know too.'

'Can you fill me in with your side of the story then?'

'Sure. Well, you know that my sister-in-law Yvonne's first pregnancy ended in a burst tube?'

'Yes.'

'Well, that came as a bit of a blow to the whole family, not just to her but to our side of the family too. You see, we too had been trying to create a kid, without success. I hadn't realised that despite the tubal pregnancy, they were going to have another crack at it anyway. So they went through all that myomectomy stuff and her next emergency operation for nothing. I suppose after that first tubal pregnancy we ought to have had a family meeting, but we didn't. I guess you understand how important it is to maintain a dynasty. It keeps the land and the *domaine* together. Truchaud thought about his own family. Yes, he thought, the long-term future of Domaine Truchaud et fils depends entirely on Bruno.

'Once Yvonne had her second surgical disaster, I wandered down to the GP in Meursault and explained the problems that we were having. She — the doctor that is — did a whole slew of tests on me and found that I was not producing any live sperm. We also went through my medical history and it didn't take a great deal of intelligence to work out what was going on. I had just passed puberty when I got mumps. I can still remember the big swollen balls I got as a result. It wasn't funny having to walk like a cowboy whose horse had just been stolen. Well, it turned out that those viruses also killed all the sperm I was making and had in store. My brother, Pierre, also caught the mumps at that time, but he was just that bit younger and didn't get sterilised by the Mumps Orchitis, so he was still firing live rounds. I was still trying to work out what to do when Jeanette fell pregnant. Well, I knew it couldn't be mine.' He paused for a moment, took a thoughtful breath, and continued. 'Anyway, soon after Lucien was born, Jeanette and I had a fairly firm and frank discussion about the lie of the land, so to speak, and we both decided that it would be good for the family if she was to have a second child, just in case Lucien didn't have the Gift. Hence Marine's arrival. Now, at this stage the only Gift we know either kid has is Marine's musical talent, which she has obviously inherited that from my father, who regularly used to play the piano for the amusement for all sorts of people. I don't think Pierre had any musical talent. Well, he showed no interest in that old piano, which is why it remained here for Marine to tinkle on. My father occasionally used to record himself playing the piano, and he played those tapes to the vines at the flowering and as the vintage approached. He swore that it helped them ripen in just the right way, especially the Bonnes Mares. None of the other people who have parcels in that estate have ever objected, not even the curmudgeonly old general who owns quite a lot of the Bonnes Mares. He used to say that if our vines could stand that racket and thrive on it, then so could his. He went on to say that if ever his vines actually complained, he would let us know.'

'Does the general actually make his wine himself?' asked Truchaud, drifting off topic for a moment.

'Good lord no, but from what I understand his son has the Gift, and has been known to make a fairly decent bottle. The general just marches up to the top of the hill, harrumphs a bit, and marches down again. He did actually see action somewhere I believe, though quite where I couldn't tell you. He is certainly too young to have served in the Second World War. He has been spotted wearing a kepi, so perhaps he was in the Foreign Legion, but then so did de Gaulle.'

'So did de Gaulle what?' Truchaud was having increasing difficulty following this conversation.

'Wear a kepi.'

'He wasn't in the Foreign Legion, was he?'

'Maybe not, but he wore the square cap. Mind you, his was rather more elaborately decorated than the plain white one that is part of the Foreign Legion uniform, and it didn't have the piece of linen dangling off the back to keep the sun off his neck.'

'Going back to the point in hand, did you talk to your brother about the kids and where they came from?'

'Often.'

'And was he happy about their living arrangements?'

'Quite. He thought it was important that they lived with their mother, certainly in these early stages of their lives. When they started to learn about growing and vinifying grapes, then no doubt they would need to spend more time at his place. After all, all the great red wine that the family makes is at Pierre's and all the white is with us. They already know they effectively have four parents, the red ones and the white ones. Sooner or later they will find out that they are the results of a combination of the two.'

'How will they take that?'

'I have no idea, we haven't got round to discussing it with them yet, but they certainly won't be the only kids round here who have been created by a family committee.'

'Yes? Would you care to elaborate on that?'

Parmentier shuffled his feet and looked uncomfortable for a moment. 'Only if I have to. You'll probably need to get the examining magistrate to explain to me why I actually have to. Sorry I even mentioned it. You know, you're very good at persuading people to say things that they really oughtn't be saying.'

Truchaud smiled. 'It's my job. But I won't push it. I can't see how that piece of information affects this case, and if it turns out that it does, I am sure the Mr de Castaigne will be on your doorstep before I am. He's the examining magistrate in charge of this case.'

Truchaud thought for a moment, and then decided that there wasn't anything further he could think of to ask. He looked up at the silent Mac, who had been standing easy by the door just in case one of the kids came barrelling in. 'Anything?' he asked.

Mac shook her head. 'No sir,' she replied.

'In which case, Mr Parmentier, we will take our leave of you. I don't have to tell you not to leave the country, do I?'

'You think I'd leave the country in the middle of a vintage?' he replied. 'You're lucky I took time out to talk to you this afternoon. I have wine to make and last year's wine to bottle before I even think about leaving Meursault. However, please find my brother's killer. You know where I am, and I will have my phone in my pocket if you need to talk to me at any time.'

# CHAPTER 27

*Monday afternoon, back to Nuits-Saint-Georges*

Mac pulled back onto the seventy-four, heading north again.

'Well,' said Truchaud, 'did you think he was telling the truth?'

She thought about it for a moment. 'Well, it's not really my place to make that sort of judgement,' she mused slowly.

'But if it were?'

'If it were, I would probably say yes,' she said slowly. She felt he was asking her to commit herself, and she also thought that was unfair.

'Good,' he replied. 'That makes both of us. Look, I'm sorry about asking you to commit yourself like that. No one wants me to drive in case I did something to my brain during the big bang the other day, and I'm now getting the uncertainties as a result. You're a good police officer, and I have come to respect your judgement.'

'In case you hadn't noticed, sir, I'm a gendarme. I have not been trained in any way to be a detective. For example, are there tells that you watch for to decide when someone is lying or not?'

'Sometimes individual people have tells that they are lying, but they are different for each person. You have to know that person to know whether that silly thing they do with their left hand is signalling that they're lying.'

'Damn!' she said. 'I didn't even notice his left hand. Do you see what I mean?'

'No, because he didn't do anything special with his left hand.'

'Sorry sir, then I'm afraid you've lost me.'

'It was just an example of a tell you might look for in a re-interrogation of a known suspect. It wasn't anything to do with our Mr Parmentier back there.'

Mac slowed down as they drove back through Pommard. She wasn't going to hit that sleeping policeman at speed this time. As they popped over it she remarked drily, 'You might consider having a word with the municipal police chief in Beaune about that one. Certainly if it was in Nuits-Saint-Georges, I would be having very strong words in your ear about making it safe and visible. I understand the need to slow traffic down, but I am sure how that is at the moment will cause an accident, which will stop traffic completely.'

'I will see to it when I get back to the office.' Truchaud felt appropriately chastised. 'So does that help us solving the crime in any way?' he added.

'Well,' she said, 'It excludes one perpetrator and a complete set of motives.'

He watched the world walking by without concentrating hard as Mac drove him round the other half of the Beaune ring, which continued its anticlockwise trip round the town centre. Maybe Natalie crossed his mind; she usually did when he wasn't thinking of anything else in particular. Maybe on this occasion he was hoping that her detective skills would come up with a solution. Unlike Mac sitting next to him, she was a trained and skilled detective, but she wasn't there either in reality or his reverie to cast her beautiful eyes over the case at the moment.

Mac was following a crowd of small cars, all using good lane discipline and keeping a sensible distance from the car in front. Truchaud, wearing his hat as a municipal police chief, was generally impressed at the standard of driving on the inner ring, this part of which was credited to the honour of Marshal Joffre, also a French general in the First World War. Well, driving standards were something he wouldn't have to discuss with his opposite number in the Beaune Town Hall.

He looked across the car at Mac and drove any thoughts about Natalie out of his mind. He was about to say something when he was aware of his phone buzzing in his pocket. He pulled it out. That's odd, it was Suzette on the other end. 'Hello?' he said.

'Oh hello Uncle Charlie, it's Suzette here. Are you anywhere nearby?'

'Why do you ask?'

'Well, I've just come back to the *domaine* to pick up my stuff, and somebody's locked the gates so I can't get in. I wondered whether you were nearby and have a key.'

'I could be there in about ten to fifteen minutes.'

'No, no, I can come to you, if you tell me where you are.'

Truchaud chuckled for a moment. 'I'm in a car on my way back from Beaune,' he replied. 'By the time you get to me, I will be where you are. Hang on and I'll be with you. Where are Michelle and Bruno?' he asked as an afterthought, but she had already disconnected.

Suzette, he thought, now there was someone who could — maybe should — have been his kid. He had been very fond of her mother in his teens. Still, he was seriously impressed that she had been working at Domaine Laforge and Truchaud that harvest rather than at the *domaine* owned by the Parnault family whose blood she shared. She had been romantically linked with Simon Maréchale at the early part of that year, but that had all gone to the wall during the summer, but still she was here. And she called him Uncle Charlie. The only person who ever called him Charlie before that year was her mother, and now Suzette was calling him Charlie too. What was going on here? Suzette's pleasant little face and bobbed hair were invading his thoughts in the just way that Natalie had done a few moments earlier. He really was old enough to be Suzette's father. Had he suffered some sort of brain damage when the bomb went off? Had he somehow disinhibited himself? Who else would invade his thoughts? Mac? Oh please not, he needed to trust Mac. At what inopportune moments would these invasive thoughts arrive? For example, he might be interrogating a suspect in the Quai d'Orfèvres, and suddenly the suspect's clothes all disappeared by magic and he was naked as the day he was born. He had no idea whether to laugh or scream.

'Take us back to the *domaine*,' he said. 'As you guessed we would, we locked someone out when we locked up, and Michelle and Bruno aren't back yet.'

They were passing over the motorway to the north of Beaune at the time, and she promised him they would be there in ten minutes or so. There were no trucks released onto the seventy-four at the Comblanchien quarry, and so she kept her promise. Mac pulled up in front of the gates, and standing there were Suzette and hairy Eddie.

He got out of the car, pulled his keys out of his pocket, and going straight up to the gates, he unlocked them. 'I'm so sorry for locking you out. We were afraid someone would have helped themselves to what is going on in the outhouse.'

'Not a problem,' replied Suzette, 'we were impressed that someone was thinking about security at the height of the season. I don't suppose anybody would have thought to lock the gates at Parnault's.'

'Is Parnault's ever left unmanned at this time of the year?' Truchaud asked, 'Surely there's always someone at the sorting tables or doing a little *pigeage* or something.'

Suzette chuckled, she was thinking of someone with his trousers rolled up to his knees, barefoot, stamping on grapes.

'Who?' the detective asked.

'Oh, probably you,' she replied. 'Either stamping on them or poking at them with a stick. How's the case going?' she asked, hardly taking a breath between ideas, while at the same time unlocking the doors of a small Peugeot parked behind the gates.

He looked at her, 'To be honest, I'm not at all sure. I have to say that if you or I are the guilty parties, then I'm way off beam.'

Mac heard that riposte and was stunned. She was sure in herself that neither Truchaud nor Suzette were the guilty parties, but to joke about it like that was inexcusable. And anyway who was that red headed man with them? Exactly where did he fit into the picture?

'Coffee anyone?' Truchaud offered.

'Er, no thanks,' replied Suzette, 'Eddie and I have to be off. Just because we are doing work for the vintage doesn't mean we haven't got academic stuff to put together too, and we both promised our essays a bit of attention tonight. Mac, can you move your car?' The last was aimed at the Mégane which had replaced the gates in blocking the entrance to the *domaine*.

Mac climbed into the car with 'Gendarmerie' painted in bold letters along its side, and having reversed it a few metres, she drove it into the courtyard and parked it near the door though which Truchaud had just passed. Suzette and Eddie waved thank you to her and drove out into the street.

Mac walked through the door, and there was Truchaud making coffee. 'Who was the red-haired man?' she asked, 'I could swear I smelled marijuana on him.'

'I expect you probably did,' was Truchaud's reply. 'Eddie's a student at the university like Suzette. I checked him out very carefully last spring when I first met him. He is strictly a buyer of pot and doesn't deal in the stuff at all. None of his flatmates, one of whom is Suzette, use the stuff, so I am inclined to let it pass.'

'If I catch him smoking the stuff in Nuits-Saint-Georges, I'll have him,' she said sourly.

'I'll let him know that you're on his case when I next see him.'

She snorted, probably a laugh, he thought and added, 'Cream?' about the coffee.

'No thanks, black.'

'I'm still at a loss about the case,' Truchaud said, stirring the cream into his cup. 'I have no idea why the bombing took place, and even who the intended target was. I have the feeling that we've got precisely nowhere.'

Mac thought for a moment. 'Suppose that was the intention.'

'What do you mean?'

'Well, just suppose that there wasn't a human target as such.'

'Go on, I'm listening.'

'Well, I was just wondering if the target really was the vineyard itself, you know, the grapes and the vines themselves. It certainly hit the target, and the people were just collateral damage, even you, sir.'

Truchaud thought for a moment. 'If we say just for the moment that you're right, who does that put in the frame as the guilty party?'

'Well, I guess that depends what you think of the wine. Is it any good?'

'Well, I understand it's a Grand Cru, so it should be truly excellent, especially as it's grown in Vosne-Romanée. I mean, our Vosne is only ranked as a Village Cru, but to tell you the truth, I prefer it to our more illustrious Grand Cru Vougeot. Somehow I find it friendlier. Am I making any sense?'

'So when are the next rankings going to be handed out?' asked Mac, following her own train of thought.

'You know, I've no idea. They were handed out in the 1930s and there have been very few changes since. La Grande Rue was given to its current owners as a wedding present at that time, but they didn't put in an application for Grand Cru status then. It wasn't until the fifties, after the Lamarche family swapped bits and pieces of vineyard with the owners of the next-door la Tâche, that they started looking at the status of the Grand Rue. Maybe it also involved the status of

Romanée-Conti too. After all, if they had added grapes from a lower pedigree than DRC to the mix then perhaps it shouldn't now be a Grand Cru either. One mouthful should have settled the issue once and for all. Anyway, there were three named vineyards lying side by side, the Super-Grands-Crus called La Tâche, La Romanée-Conti, and lying between them the narrow strip of land called La Grande Rue. When the Lamarche family belatedly asked for La Grande Rue to be upgraded to Grand Cru status in the fifties, the powers that be considered the *terroir* and the status of its neighbours on either side, and it was a no-brainer for it to be upgraded. It was finally awarded Grand Cru status in 1992'

'Is that the only time that has happened since the thirties?'

'Well, no, Clos de Lambrays was upgraded in 1981. But those are the only times, to my knowledge, that a vineyard actually was upgraded to Grand Cru status since the thirties. I know there was an attempt to get the Combottes Vineyard at the south end of Gevrey-Chambertin upgraded. The people who tried to get it upgraded used much the same logic: that if they had applied in the thirties, they would have been given the badge.'

'So why didn't they?'

'Aux Combottes is in the parish of Gevrey-Chambertin, but in the thirties all the winemakers who had a parcel in Combottes were in Morey-Saint-Denis and their main interest was getting the Grand Cru badge for the Morey vineyards, and very successful they were too. As far as I understand, nobody bothered putting in an application for Combottes at the time. However, in the period after the war, following La Grande Rue's upgrade, Combottes had some owners in Gevrey too. One of them even went so far as getting a label printed for 'Combottes-Chambertin Grand Cru'. However, that did not go through. There were many reasons given out for that, most of which I don't understand, but the fact remains, there is a very fine vineyard of Premier Cru Gevrey-Chambertin surrounded by Grand Cru sites which, in the right hands, produces wine that is every bit as good as its Grand Cru neighbours.'

'So are there any vineyards bordering on the Parmentier patch that may have an axe to grind? Do you know of any other applications to be upgraded?'

'Not that I know of, but then there is a limit to my knowledge.' He swallowed the last of his coffee. 'But I do know someone we can go and ask. Coming?'

# CHAPTER 28

*Monday, mid-afternoon, Chambolle-Musigny*

The Mégane rolled to a halt, almost as if it knew exactly where to park in the courtyard of Domaine Parmentier Père et Fils in Chambolle. Truchaud tapped on the front door of the office. The door opened and the friendly face of Walid Akhbar greeted them. 'Commander?'

'I wondered whether Mrs Parmentier was in?'

'I think she's in the sorting room, they've got the last of the Grand Cru in now that the forensics people have finished with the vineyard, and they're sorting out the grapes that were bomb-damaged from the rest.'

'Can I go through?'

'Can I stop you?' replied the Algerian drily.

'Probably not,' said Truchaud, and added, 'You're with me, Mac.'

All three of them walked through the office into the sorting room. There was a long table with a conveyor belt on it. It looked almost exactly the same as the device in Truchaud's own winery. He didn't suppose there were many different manufacturers of small sorting tables in France. One of the students was emptying white plastic baskets of grapes onto his end and then spreading the bunches out onto the conveyor belt. Once his end was covered with bunches, no more than one bunch thick, he said he was ready, and Mrs Parmentier picked up the controller and pressed the button on the top, and the grapes started to move down the line. She pressed the button again, stopping the process, once she spotted Mac's uniform.

'Officer,' she said loudly, 'Can I help you?'

'I think Commander Truchaud would like a word,' she replied. It was only after Mac's reply that that Yvonne spotted Truchaud standing on the other side of her Algerian assistant.

'Commander!' she said, 'Always a pleasure, what can I do for you this time?' Truchaud detected a fair amount of irony in her greeting.

'I was wondering if I might have a quick word with you about these little treasures,' he waved a hand over the sorting table.

'Of course,' she said.

'These are the grapes that survived the bombing?'

'They are. We were quite fortunate that actually the number destroyed in the blast was quite small. Blow a human up and you've killed him, blow a vineyard up and you may ruin a number of grapes, but you don't destroy the whole vineyard.'

Truchaud was quite surprised by her coldness. Her husband and Walid's brother had been killed in that blast. He looked at Walid, but couldn't read his expression either. 'Any idea how the wine's going to turn out?' Well, if they can be cold about it, so can he.

She plucked a grape from the bunch she was holding and tossed it at him. 'Try it and see,' she said. He looked at it, automatically triaging it as fit for human consumption. It passed the test, and he popped it into his mouth. It tasted very similar to that he had tried with Bruno the previous day. If that was an example of a good grape, then so was this. 'Well?' she said.

Truchaud shrugged. 'I don't know,' he replied cautiously. She cocked her head on one side, 'I don't know how that taste will turn itself into what will come out of a bottle a few years down the line.'

'I thought you were from a wine family,' she said ironically.

'I am, but I am the member of that wine family who is a policeman, not a winemaker.'

'We'll have to start educating you then, shan't we Mr Policeman?' she said with a smile. He wasn't sure how friendly it actually was. She then turned to face Mac and continued, 'And perhaps we will have to start giving some lessons to your gendarme here too.'

'Thank you, I would appreciate that,' said Mac.

'Walid, any chance of your taking Commander Truchaud here down to the cellars and introducing him to a bottle of our Grand Cru? Look for one about ten years old. There will be a few of those of a decent year way down among those we hang on to sell at the door. I'm sure one day soon he will return the favour and introduce you to one of his family's. You know, the Truchauds make a very good Clos de Vougeot, and their Village Vosne has a good reputation too.'

'Thank you for the compliment,' the detective replied.

'Meanwhile, Miss Gendarme — sorry, I don't know your name.'

'Everybody calls me Mac,' she said. 'It's a nickname that someone threw at me on my first day of training when nobody knew anything about me, and as is usual in those circumstances, it stuck.'

'Does it offend you?'

'Not at all, I quite like it really.'

'Good, then Mac it is. Follow me and I will introduce you to the delights of the sorting table.'

The two women walked back through the door into the winery. She was explaining to the gendarme exactly what she was looking for in a good wine.

'So you don't make large quantities of it, and you then sell on all that you make?' That was Mac's contribution.

'Pretty much, that's what we're in the business for.'

'Doesn't it — how do I put it — hurt to pass on the product of your labours to the, for the most part, ignorant rich who won't really understand what has gone into that bottle?'

'On the other hand, the ignorant rich pass on some of their wealth to us in exchange. We don't ask any questions as to how they got that money, we just put it in the bank. Tell you something else, the taxman doesn't follow the provenance of the money they take off us. It could be stolen, acquired fraudulently, the products of trafficking, or even money laundering, who's to say? The taxman doesn't ask any further than it was money drawn by us on the creation and sale of wine on the open market.'

Meanwhile, Truchaud followed Walid further into the building and into an archway, which led downwards.

'Follow me,' said the Algerian.

As he led Truchaud down the steps, the conversation upstairs became an unintelligible blur. Halfway down the steps the concrete became worn stone, just like most cellars. This cellar was the same as many he had been down into, his own included. The cellars predated the houses built above them by probably several centuries. The house above this one was a relatively recent creation. It had, at the very least, been rebuilt during the twentieth century sometime. Buildings in the Côte had not been systematically damaged during the war. It did not suffer from systematic shelling or bombing by the various combatants. The heaviest gunfire had been an exchange of small arms fire between individuals, probably different wings of the resistance squabbling among themselves as to the best way to kill a Boche. The buildings may not have been repaired properly after they suffered from the natural ravages of weather and the like during that time, but that was all. Anyway, that house may have been built during the thirties before the war broke out.

Once Walid reached the cellar floor he walked over to the switch on the left side of the tunnel, which stretched before them into darkness. 'Ready?' he asked, grinning at Truchaud in the gloom.

'Ready,' Truchaud grinned back.

Walid twisted the switch, and really quite slowly the lights came on in sequence as they revealed their treasures. There were four rows of 228 litre barrels, known as Burgundy *pièces*, made from French oak with occasional steel bands holding the whole thing together, disappearing off into the distance. Some of them looked very new, some of them, not so much. He remembered the *pièces* upstairs at his own *domaine*, which had just been delivered from the coopers. Those were paler still even than those nearest to him, so those in front of him would contain the wine from last year's vintage that was maturing quietly and minding its own business. He wandered down and looked at the end of a new barrel, which said 'Bonnes Mares' and a date on the end of it. 'So, you mature the Bonnes Mares in new oak?' he asked.

'Not all of it,' replied the man, 'some of it is matured in old barrels, come and see.' He wandered further down the row of barrels, and there was a dark old one, which had a recent label on it identical to that on the new one.

'How does that work?' asked Truchaud.

There was a much larger barrel standing upright, behaving like a table in the middle of the cellar. It had a box of tasting glasses on a smaller stool down by its side and a fairly large plastic funnel protruding from the middle of its top. The glasses were tall with a narrow stem and a rather bulbous round bowl, which slowly narrowed to a smaller tulip shape at the top.

Walid pulled a couple of glasses out of the box and, glancing at Truchaud to see if he was watching, as if he were about to perform a conjuring trick, he put them on the barrel. He then picked up a pipette and one of the glasses and walked back to the new *pièce*. He teased off the bung at the top of the barrel and dipped the pipette into it so that it was almost completely lost from view. He then put his finger on top of the pipette and withdrew it from the barrel. Once again, he looked Truchaud in the eye as he did it. Magic — there was now a column of red liquid in it. He held the other end of the pipette over the glass and released the column to allow the wine to flow into it. He pushed the bung back into the *pièce* and put the glass back onto the barrel. 'Hang on a moment,' he said, and repeated the performance with one of the older *pièces*, producing a different glass of red wine. 'Right,' he said, 'it's up to you to remember which is which. They are both last year's Bonnes Mares, but the first one was matured in a new oak barrel and the other in an old oak barrel.' So this was what his father had talked about, thought Truchaud. He had wondered what he meant.

'Now,' said Walid, still watching Truchaud like a hawk, 'taste the new oak wine.'

Truchaud picked up the new oak glass, and the first thing he did was hold it by the foot of the glass up to the light. The light shone clearly through it. It almost looked as if lots of tiny deep purple crystals were suspended in a very clear liquid. He then brought the glass down from his eye line, while still holding the foot, and sniffed it. After he took that first sniff, he then gave the glass a little swirl, and then took another sniff. It was heavenly. The heady aromas of cherry, blackcurrant, vanilla, and heaven knows what else, caressed the mucus membranes at the back of his nose. So, that was the scent of this *terroir*. Why would he want to taste it? He knew it was going to be far too young to drink. The scent was enough. He gave it another sniff, just in case he had missed something. There was a complete hubbub of conversation in that glass. He took a sip and sloshed it round his mouth for a moment, breathing in and out to also allow the aromas up the back of his nose. He then spat the wine out into the plastic funnel that protruded from the middle of the barrel. If it wasn't a spittoon then what the hell was it doing there? The wine was rather astringent in his mouth. It left his mouth feeling quite dry, and he wasn't sure he enjoyed that sensation. What a shame after the promise of the nose. He was obviously aware his face had puckered as he looked at Walid.

'Okay,' said Walid unperturbed, 'Now try this one.' He passed the other glass to Truchaud. Truchaud looked through the wine again at the light. It had the same purple crystalline look as the previous one. He took a sniff. The fruit flavours were very similar from glass to glass, but there was much less vanilla on the nose. The taste showed considerably less astringency than the first one, but somehow it tasted less. He spat again into the funnel.

'I assume that is a spittoon,' he said drily.

'It certainly is,' the Arab replied.

'Is that barrel a receptacle for everybody's spit over the years?' Truchaud asked quietly, shuddering at the thought of fifty-year-old spittle.

'No, of course not, the pipe on the end of the funnel goes straight down into the drain. That barrel covers the drain for this part of the cellar. When we wash the floor down, we move the barrel, and all the effluent goes down the drain and into the sewers.'

'You know, I'm quite relieved about that,' he replied, and then he continued, 'So, tell me about those wines. They're quite different.'

'Well, the first one is being raised in new oak and the second one is being raised in a barrel that has been used before.'

'For Bonnes Mares?'

'Of course. I think that one was a new barrel about three years ago, so this will be its third generation of Bonnes Mares that has grown up in it. There is very little vanillin left in it now to leak into the wine.'

'So what happens now?'

'That, I'm not sure. Last year it was Mr Parmentier's personal job to blend the old and the new to make his Prestige Cru of Bonnes Mares. The wines were blended together before bottling. He would hope that they would then lie down in the cellars of their buyers and develop in his own cellars for a further ten years or so before gracing his dining table at some grand occasion or another. All of those tannins will have softened by then, and the wine will be ready to be a polite but important guest at the dinner party.'

'You know a lot for a Muslim — I have to ask, do you actually drink the stuff? I didn't think you did that.'

'No, I think I am a good Muslim, but I do look at it, and I certainly sniff it, just like you did, and I have tasted it and then used the spittoon. I simply don't swallow. Allah watches over and protects me.' He grinned back. 'I need to know what I am talking about. You are not the only person I have ever brought down here to do a tasting, although, to be honest, bringing people down here to do a barrel tasting is not common. Those are usually limited to the people who are going to blend the wine, or perhaps a seriously important wine merchant from abroad.'

'So who is going to blend the old and new oaked wines now then?' Truchaud asked.

'Well, if Madame Parmentier isn't going to be asking you to do the blending, I am not sure. I had wondered why she asked me to bring you down to do this barrel tasting if it wasn't to introduce you to the wines. I assume therefore she is going to do it herself. She has the Gift, you know, Madame has.'

'So, following on from what you say about the blending. Say you have two barrels of wine maturing in new wood and four barrels maturing in old oak. And the boss decides that the perfect blend is in fact two new to three old, you have one barrel left over of the old oak stuff. What happens to that?'

'Well, I don't know what other winemakers do, but I know what we do here.'

'Do tell, I am learning fast. I don't even know what we do at our family *domaine*.'

'Well, here, we demote the wine that's left over. It's not usually as much as a barrel; Mr Pierre was pretty good at judging from the first fermentation how much to put in each type of barrel. He didn't usually get it very wrong.'

'You demote the wine? What does that mean?'

'Well, we don't just make the Bonnes Mares in a mixture of old and new barrels, all our Premier Cru wines we do the same way, and we've got four of them, as well. From the blending of each of those wines, we find that we may have some wine left over. Monsieur then pours all of them into a vat and lets them to get to know each other, and finally bottles a Chambolle-Musigny Premier Cru.' He walked out of sight around a corner, and Truchaud heard the chink of glass. Back came Walid, holding a bottle in each hand, by the waist and still horizontally. They had very similar, but not identical, labels. The one on the left, under the flamboyant Chambolle-Musigny Premier Cru heading, had, in smaller capitals underneath, *Les Amoureuses*. On the other, there was no vineyard named, just a blank space. 'It does tell you that all the wine in that bottle is at the very least up to the quality of Premier Cru status, and must all come from Chambolle-Musigny,' Walid explained.

'What sort of price does this command?' Truchaud asked.

'Well it's obviously cheaper than the Bonnes Mares and the Amoureuses …'

'The Amoureuses is as expensive as a good many Grands Crus,' remarked Truchaud drily, with an internal giggle about the name from back in his schooldays.

'Yes, there are a fair number of "Super-Premier-Crus" which would probably be ranked Grand Cru if they did a rebranding of all of them again today. And they do command similar prices in the marketplace. Les Amoureuses is certainly one of those.'

'And if they did, there would probably be some vineyards that would be downgraded from the Grand Cru list in exchange.'

'Yes,' said Walid, 'Probably the bigger Grands Crus with lots of owners of differing ability… Oh sorry.'

'Like the Clos de Vougeot, you mean?'

'Well, I wasn't actually thinking of Clos de Vougeot, but I see what you mean. Your family makes a Clos de Vougeot?'

'Yes, it's our flagship wine.'

'Being a Muslim, I really don't feel qualified to comment on this. All I can comment on is through loyalty to the Parmentier *domaines* which, as far as I am concerned, are the finest and best of all the wines throughout the world. Yay, go Parmentier.' They grinned at each other.

'Go Truchaud,' Truchaud replied in a slightly more uncertain voice.

'Well, I think I have done what I was told to do by my boss upstairs and introduced you to last year's Bonnes Mares. I must now do my duty by my brother.'

Truchaud heard a metallic click like a pistol being cocked.

He looked up at Walid, and that was exactly what it was, and he was looking straight down its barrel.

# CHAPTER 29

*Monday, mid-afternoon, under Chambolle-Musigny*

'What is this?' asked Truchaud coldly. He may have been appearing to play it very cool, but, truth be told, inside he was suddenly very frightened indeed. 'Is that thing loaded?'

'My brother failed to kill you, so it is my duty to succeed where he failed.'

'I'm afraid I still don't understand. Why would your brother want to kill me?'

'Because it was his duty to do so.'

'All right,' said Truchaud, realising that his only chance of surviving this was to keep the Akhbar in front of him talking. 'But why was it his duty to kill me? I don't think I ever laid eyes on him until that moment the bomb went off.'

'It had been decided by the North African Arab Brotherhood that you must die. As Mehdi, my brother, was the Brother in the area where you are, it fell to him to do the execution.'

'So your brother wasn't a refugee here? It was my understanding that he had escaped from Algeria during the Civil War and secretly escaped to Tangier.'

'He had gone to Tangier, but we always knew where he was. So, when the brotherhood decided he was needed to do more with his life than drive tourists round Northern Morocco, I went to find him and escorted him to Corsica into French territory. He always did speak French.'

'What did you want him to do in Corsica?'

'Work and become a French citizen. We didn't know what would happen after that. He struck lucky when he met a certain Mr Parmentier who wanted him to go to work for him in Burgundy; that met the brotherhood's approval. He would be buried deeper in the heartland of France, in an area where we really didn't have many members. In Paris, especially in the *banlieus*, yes, we have many Brothers, but in

Nuits-Saint-Georges, there aren't any of us.'

'What! You mean there are others like you in the Côte d'Or?'

'Well, I don't really know. This is not the area I am affiliated to, it is my brother's area. So, I don't know how it is organised round here. We want to keep your lot out of our business.' He waved his pistol at Truchaud, but too far away from him to reach.

'There are fewer people, period, in Nuits-Saint-Georges than there are in any of the *banlieus* and *arrondissements*,' replied Truchaud drily. 'What did you want him to do here?'

'Work, and become a visible and well-liked part of the community until such time as we might need him.'

Truchaud realised what he was being told: Mehdi Akhbar had been a sort of one man sleeper cell of a terrorist movement in Bourgogne, and Walid was, from a distance, his handler. 'So why did the brotherhood decide to kill me, may I ask?'

'Because you police have become a nuisance, and it was decided that an example should be made.'

'But why me exactly?'

'Because you were here in the countryside, and were thus more exposed than the police in Paris. Think about it — if you were in Paris, we would have had to kill a large number of police at once to have the same impact; we would probably have had to blow up the whole of the Quai d'Orsai as well. Have you any idea of the logistical problems that would have caused? Anyway, you had been part of the problem in Paris. Don't consider yourself in any way innocent.'

Truchaud watched him waving the gun around a bit while he talked, but so far, he was not yet being careless enough to point it away from the policeman's head. Truchaud was watching though, and inside his rumpled trousers, his muscles were tense and prepared for action.

'Anyway, it was considered that taking out one senior policeman in a vineyard in the middle of the vintage would send the sort of message we wanted to send to the Department of the Interior, and at the same time with one small bomb, it would be relatively simple and inexpensive to achieve.'

'What? You intended that your brother should kill himself in the process?'

'He has received his reward in the next life.'

'What? Even though he failed to kill me? Oh wait, he did kill himself and Pierre Parmentier, oh, and a few grapes.' Truchaud was aware he was now trying to annoy Walid Akhbar. Hopefully his aim with the brandished pistol would become sufficiently wild that it might be worthwhile taking a risk and attacking his potential assailant.

'Allah is merciful,' replied Walid with a beatific smile on his face, and his hand became steadier. Damn that didn't work.

'Not really to me,' Truchaud replied drily, 'not really to me.'

'No, not really to you, but you have been condemned to death by His court here on Earth, so his mercy is confined to rendering your death quick and painless.'

Truchaud thought about that for a moment. Yes, he supposed that was right, if the bomb had actually got him it would have been instant oblivion, and he supposed if Walid succeeded in putting a bullet between his eyes it would be a similarly brisk end. He needed to wind him up again. 'So why was I condemned to death by His court here on Earth? I feel that it is only fair that I should know this, and perhaps also that the Department of the Interior should know this too.'

'Oh, the Department will know, you can count on that. We will tell them when we accept responsibility for your death.'

'But nobody has accepted responsibility for Pierre Parmentier's death.'

'That was because it was not intended that Pierre Parmentier should die, it was intended that you would die. How would it look to everybody if the Muslim Brotherhood claimed responsibility for a particular action, but admitted that we had killed the wrong person?'

'Yes, I do understand your problem. Somehow your credibility as a competent terrorist would go completely down the crapper if it got about that you made a habit of blowing up the wrong person, to say nothing about the problems you might find with further recruitment.' There, that might upset him. He might, of course, just pull the trigger anyway.

Rather to Truchaud's pleasant surprise, Akhbar's response was a widening of his smile rather than anything more sinister. The gun was still out of Truchaud's reach and was still steady in Akhbar's hand. The hand itself seemed relaxed, and he didn't seem to be holding the gun hard. If he could get to it, he would probably be able to pull it free from that grip. However, if he jumped for it, he realised that the man would still have time to pull the trigger before he got there.

'So,' the detective continued, 'how are you going to explain my being shot in the Parmentier's cellar rather than being blown up in one of their vineyards? This will be a very public execution whichever way it plays out. One question I have to ask is, was your brother entirely happy with his role as a suicide executioner?'

'My brother has been well rewarded in the next life.'

'So the answer to that question is "no". He had no intention of being relieved of this life at that time or in that manner. When did he know what you were about to ask him to do? Or perhaps tell him what he was going to do, whether he liked it or not.'

'I don't know what you're talking about. My brother was a good Muslim and was dedicated to the cause. He would do whatever his faith told him to do.'

'That's what he told you, was it?' Truchaud was watching the man's eyes as well as his knuckles. He was trying to spot the moment when Walid lost his temper. That was the moment when Walid's aim would be off, and he might have a chance when he charged. He was also watching the knuckle of the hand holding the gun. The tell that he was about to pull the trigger would probably be short, but the skin on the knuckle would momentarily blanche. At this moment, Walid remained calm. The hand seemed steady despite the weight of the gun, which had been pointing at Truchaud for several minutes. Well, he supposed that it could have been all of thirty seconds; time passes at a strange rate when someone's pointing a gun at you and you know that it is only a matter of time before he fulfils his intention to kill you.

'He didn't need to tell me, I knew everything.'

'Pardon me asking, but how did you know everything?'

'Because I have faith. I need nothing else.'

'Oh right, because it's convenient for you to know something, then know it you do. I had no idea that Islam was such a convenient religion. You promise yourself you will have free access to all the virgins you can manage just by joining the gang and pointing its gun. I thought it was one of those clubs that excludes all alternatives. Satisfy my curiosity, what I don't understand is why it isn't possible to join all the different religious gangs at the same time, so that if, for example, there's a Muslim pointing a gun at your head, you can be a Muslim, and if you have a Jehovah's Witness door stepping you at home, you can be a Witness, and if you're sitting with an evangelical Christian, you can be one of their gang so that they'll just shut up. Hmm? Just a thought.' Truchaud saw the eyes narrow. He was getting through.

'Be quiet little man,' snapped Walid. Yes, Truchaud was definitely getting through. Now he was holding the gun in his right hand, so Truchaud needed to jink to his own right, being Walid's left, as the shot should go past Truchaud's left ear. Of course, Walid might have read the same manual, in which case it would have been a bad call.

'Getting up your nose, am I?' jeered Truchaud as he watched the knuckle blanche. He dived forward and to the right as he heard a very loud bang, and everything went black.

# CHAPTER 30

*Still Monday afternoon, still under Chambolle-Musigny*

Mac surveyed the carnage in front of her. At the foot of the stairs, prone, lay what looked like the form of the commander of civilian police with whom she had spent most of her recent waking hours. Beyond him, further down the cellar between the barrels, lay the supine body of the man she had just shot. Still wobbling on the spigot in the top of a barrel further down on his right was the pistol he had fired as he died. Between his eyes was a neat round hole, and behind his head a pool of blood was forming.

Mac was a crack shot. She knew it and the rest of the local gendarmerie knew it. The question was, where was the bullet that Walid fired at the moment that the bullet that Mac fired had killed him. She walked slowly down the steps to the cellar floor. She stood over Truchaud's body. Well, there was no obvious hole in the back of his head, so if Walid's bullet had gone into the commander's face, it hadn't come out the other side, so it wouldn't have been a high velocity round. She became aware of a sound somewhere nearby. It wasn't a threatening sort of sound, so she didn't automatically tense. No, it was a gentle soft sound. It was the sound of liquid making an occasional drip onto a stone floor, and that sound came from behind her. She turned to look where it came from. There were barrels stacked three high beside the stairs, and from near the top of the head of the third barrel was a neat round hole. The head is what coopers call the flat wooden piece at either end of a barrel. Mac found her mind fastening on these odd details obsessively. She also knew that the technical term for the rim that holds the head in place is the 'croze'. From that hole trickled red liquid, which rolled down the head until it collected in the croze. Interesting, the sort of useless information you pick up during the course of a day's work. Once the croze filled, the liquid dripped off the edge of the rim onto the floor below. It was the impact of that drop on the stone floor that made the sound that she heard. There was already a small puddle on the floor. She put her finger on the trickle and tasted the liquid. It tasted good. Pity, that barrel might be ruined.

She looked back at the bodies and tried to work it out. How had the bullet hit Truchaud and then changed direction to end up in the barrel over there with enough force to pierce the head to set up the leak she had just seen? A pistol? It wouldn't happen. She walked back to the commander's body and bent down and put her fingers on his neck. She felt a pulse, a strong pulse. She then checked her own pulse at the neck, just to make sure she was not sensing her own pulse at her fingertips. The pulses were not the same. She breathed a sigh of relief, Truchaud was alive. Finally, just to make sure that Walid was dead, she picked up his wrist and checked for his pulse, but felt none. She felt her eyes begin to water. She may have guaranteed to hit a static cardboard target ten times out of ten, but she had never actually killed anybody before, and the enormity of that understanding was beginning to create an emotional response.

She pulled out her phone and there was no signal, so she trotted up the steps again. At the top of the steps she found a signal, and her first thought was to call her commanding officer and fill him in on the situation. He told her to stay where she was and he would be right with her. He told her that he would arrange for an ambulance to attend, and the coroner. 'Meanwhile you stay there and make sure that nobody disturbs the scene. And don't you drink any more of that wine.'

'No sir.' She thought about going to find the owner, but then thought again. The best way of ensuring that nobody interfered with a crime scene was to make sure that nobody knew it was there in the first place. However, telling her not to interfere with the trickle of wine was a silly thing to do. She kept looking at the trickle, and even if she looked away there was the Chinese water torture of the drip drip drip that she could still hear. She walked over to the trickle and wiped her finger over it. And again, she licked her finger. Damn, that was good! Standing on a large barrel that was upended to form a table near where Truchaud lay, was a glass. She picked up the glass and put it on the floor to catch the drips. As the drips fell onto the side of the glass, it silenced their fall, at least it would until the glass started to fill up. She contemplated shaking Truchaud, or at least something, but people did not lie inert without there being a good reason, and she would hate to be damaging him further at this stage. She did not have paramedic skills, nor did she have any paramedic kit with her, so she left him alone. She walked back to the steps and sat down on them, and the tears just started to flow.

Captain Duquesne took very little time to get there. He and Mrs Parmentier walked down the stairs, both of them looking directly at the gendarme sitting at the bottom. When she got to the cellar floor, the winemaker surveyed the carnage with dismay. Mac was interested where she went first — the dead Arab, the prostrate detective, or the glass collecting the drips from the bullet hole in the barrel.

Yvonne Parmentier screwed up her face. She was not used to looking death in the eye. 'I take it Mr Akbar is dead,' she said.

'Yes,' sobbed Mac, 'I'm afraid so.'

'Commander Truchaud?' continued Yvonne.

'No, but he is unconscious, and I'm waiting for the paramedics to come and help him. I don't understand why he's unconscious, he just is.'

'So, the only thing that I can do anything about is that,' said Yvonne Parmentier, pointing behind her at the dripping barrel, still not looking at it. She reached up onto a shelf and picked up a spigot and a large wooden mallet. 'You don't mind if I do a little first aid on that barrel, do you Captain?' she asked. Without waiting for his answer, she tapped the spigot into the bullet hole. 'Hopefully that will stop any more air getting to it,' she said, and picked up the glass and sniffed it. She then passed the glass to Captain Duquesne. 'See what you think of that,' she said.

The gendarme sniffed it and then took a sip. 'That tasted rather good, how long will it take before the flavour of the bullet appears? How old is that wine?' he added.

'It's one of last year's barrels, so our next project was to be bottling those barrels over there. Will there be any delay because that barrel will be held in evidence?'

'I have no idea, but I will ask the examining magistrate to release the barrel as soon as possible. I take it the wine will need to be poured off as soon as possible to avoid contamination by the bullet. Forensics will also need access to the bullet anyway.'

'I'd not even thought about that,' she replied, 'I was thinking about contamination by air. Will they test the wine to analyse the degree of contamination by the residue from the bullet?'

'The least I can do is ask them.'

'Thank you for that.' She paused. 'Anyway, I must go back upstairs to wait for the paramedics to arrive. As there's no one up there to answer the bell, we don't want them to be breaking down my front door just because there's no one up there to answer it.'

'Or simply going away again,' remarked Duquesne drily.

'Or that,' replied Yvonne and, checking that the flow of precious red liquid had stopped from the head of the barrel, she climbed the stairs out of the cellar.

Captain Duquesne nodded at the floor. 'One round, Constable?' he asked.

She wiped her eyes and smiled faintly acknowledging with mute gratitude that the captain had not commented on her display of emotion. 'I fired the one between his eyes and he fired the one that ended up in the barrel. Neither of us hit Truchaud, so I'm not quite sure what he's doing down there.'

'I think that neither of you missed him by very much,' replied Duquesne drily, so he's probably down there to be safe in case the gunplay starts again. Maybe he just banged his head on the floor and knocked himself out. It has been known to happen.'

At that moment, the ambulance team arrived at the top of the stairs. 'He's down here lads,' Duquesne called out.

The paramedic glanced at Walid on the way down the stairs. 'I hope you aren't expecting us to work a miracle on him.'

'No,' replied the captain, 'He's waiting for the coroner's officer. She's due presently, but they don't get to travel under blue lights. By the time that the coroner gets involved, it's no longer an emergency. It's this fellow we need your help with.' As if on cue, Truchaud moved and groaned. 'His name is Truchaud, Commander Truchaud.'

Truchaud started to sit up and looked around at the variety of uniforms arrayed behind him. 'What happened?' he asked, 'Who shot me?' He then put his index fingers in both ears and gave them a waggle.

'That would have been me,' replied Mac.

'Oh, that's an embuggerance, I've gone deaf again. Can you speak louder and clearer?'

Mac pointed at herself, then pointed at him with her right index and middle fingers together. She flicked her wrist upwards and blew across the top of both fingers. She then pointed at Mehdi. Truchaud looked round at the supine Arab, jumped back a little, and then turned back to Mac, having now fully understood her mime. 'Thank you for that,' he replied verbally.

The paramedic helped him to his feet and said, 'Shall we get you up to the ambulance and take you down to the SAMU to get assessed?'

'What?' said Truchaud, pointing at his ears and shrugging.

The paramedic pointed upstairs and then rotated his finger, still pointing upwards, and mimed a running action. Truchaud got that one too, and allowed himself to be helped up the stairs.

At the end of it, Duquesne and Mac were left alone with Mehdi's body in the cellar. 'Take me through it, Constable,' said Duquesne.

'Well sir, I arrived at the top of the staircase, and those two were at the bottom. Walid had his gun out and it was pointing at the commander's head. I could see Walid's knuckle was tightening, so I drew my weapon and shot him between the eyes.'

'Over Truchaud's shoulder?'

'I didn't have any time to get to a textbook location, sir. It was shoot or lose the commander.'

Duquesne nodded, 'Good shooting, Constable.'

'Thank you sir.'

'He did have time to get a shot off though.'

'Yes sir.'

'Lucky it went into the barrel rather than into Truchaud or ricochet about the cellar.'

'Yes sir.'

Duquesne grinned at her. 'Not criticising you at all, Constable, good work.'

'Thank you sir.'

There was a squeal of tyres, and within a second a skinny gendarme with sergeant's stripes on his arm appeared at the top of the steps. Mac took one look at him and bolted up the steps as if someone had attached a rocket to her and lit the blue touch paper. She threw her arms round his neck and buried her face in it. Any last attempt at maintaining control was lost. Captain Duquesne looked up at his NCOs watching carefully to make sure they didn't overbalance back down the stairs into the cellar. He was relieved when they were swept aside by a booming contralto voice.

'Who's the idiot responsible for increasing my workload?' And standing with her legs apart with both fists on both hips, the proverbial double teapot, stood Mrs Clermont, the coroner's officer, glaring balefully down at the scene at the bottom of the stairs.

# CHAPTER 31

*Coda, a few days later*

Suddenly all is quiet. The vineyards are empty of people. White Van Man is conspicuous by his absence, and traffic is rolling along the seventy-four again at its regular pace, or to put it another way, a little faster than it ought to be. An occasional tall blue tractor can still be seen, but it is not moving, it is parked by the side of the road, and there is no one sitting on top of it.

If you were to cast a closer look at the vines, you would see very few of the dark purple clusters of berries hanging beneath their leaves, and in fact, those leaves are already taking on their autumn colours of red and brown. Phase One of the vintage, the harvest, is now over. The vines' role in creating this year's wine is now past. From here on in, it is down to the macerated grapes, the yeasts, the vats, and even the hand of man to take on their roles in the mystery of viticulture. The temperature is rapidly rising in those vats as the fermentation gets underway, and the winemakers try any number of tricks to keep it under control. It will do neither the yeasts nor the new wine any good whatsoever to boil the must.

Truchaud, looking over the tanks standing serenely side by side, remembered one way they had used in the past was to draw off wine from the bottom of the fermentation tank and pipe it through a refrigerated coil before allowing the cool, young wine back into the top. It re-entered the tank below the level of the must so it wasn't mixed with air at the same time though, at the moment, there wasn't a lot of air in that system anyway. The gas on the top of the must was all carbon dioxide bubbling up from within. Anyone standing in the must attempting to tread the juice from the grapes would suffocate very rapidly indeed.

Truchaud drew off a little of the roiling mixture into a glass from a tap set in the middle of the tank. He rolled it around the glass. It was very cloudy and middling pink, already the colour of a table rosé. He

235

sniffed at it and scented that it was beginning to take on the aroma of a very young Bourgogne, but there were other smells in there that he hoped would disappear long before the bottling took place a year down the line. He thought about tasting it and decided not to. It would only disappoint him. He took one more look through the liquid at the candle and dipped it untasted, but certainly not unloved, into the spittoon on the top of the upturned barrel which had, once upon a time, been full of young, maturing wine. Somehow, that barrel had never made the journey to Scotland, where most of the old Truchaud barrels, the ones for which they had no further use, ended up. An occasional bottle of the whisky aged in those barrels came back to its combined spiritual home in Nuits-Saint-Georges. It had been one of old Philibert Truchaud's pride and joy, his occasional tot of Rare Auld Malt Matured in Burgundy Barrels. He would swear he could sense just a little of his Clos de Vougeot on the nose. Neither of his sons could be so persuaded.

Simon Maréchale appeared from behind him. 'How's it going?' he asked, tapping the thermometer to ensure it settled correctly. The air conditioning in the cellar was working hard, but it seemed to be doing its job. The thermometer still read below thirty degrees, and that was in the middle of the maelstrom in the tank. Maréchale nodded and checked another tank, the Vosne, and nodded at that one too. It was as if he was having a private conversation with the wine. He tapped off a little of the Vosne too, swirled it, held it up to the light and sniffed it. He muttered a few words of approval, and then tipped it into the spittoon. The Nuits-Saint-Georges received a similar treatment, and similar approval. He grinned at the policeman, and said words to the effect of so far so good.

'How's the stuff from the east side of the seventy-four doing?' Truchaud asked. He still felt affection for their lesser wine, even though it was by now in the much larger Laforge fermentation tanks with all the other Laforge basic Bourgogne.

Maréchale knew exactly what Truchaud was asking. 'Bringing up the quality of the grapes they are fermenting with,' he replied with a grin. 'Don't tell Marie-Claire that I said that,' he added, and wandered off, presumably to the large hangar-sized cellar where the Laforges made their wine. From both their fermentation rooms, however, the wines burrowed ever deeper under Nuits-Saint-Georges. Once all the variations of fermentation had finished, the young wines would be transferred into the traditional 225 litre barrels called *pièces*, some brand new from the coopers, some less so. Safely in their barrels, they would mature silently in the darkness, until they were bottled at least a year later. What the wine did during that year was still a mystery to most men, but that was nothing compared to what caused the maturing that took place in the bottles. Science had not given any answers to how and why wine aged in the bottle. Some clever dickies had tried to speed the process of bottle aging up so they could make last year's wine taste like it had aged a decade and they might make their money quicker. That didn't work, they just spoilt the wine instead. Good thing that they didn't abuse a Grand Cru in their experiment. Truchaud was far from sure he wanted to know those particular secrets.

The previous year's Clos de Vougeot and Echézeaux were still waiting to be bottled. That was a job for the coming winter, when it would be really too brutally cold for a man to wander out in his vineyards without a fur lining to his coat and hat.

Truchaud looked over his shoulder down into the darkness of the cellar and muttered to the oak barrels in a cartoon Austrian accent, 'I'll be back,' and chuckled to himself. He climbed the old stone steps, which were surely far older than the courtyard and the house on the surface. The wear in the middle of those steps told of many hundreds of different pairs of feet that had trod them before him.

He looked around the yard and rubbed his hands together. Yes, it was now colder outside the cellar than it was down there. Winter was just about upon them, not visibly yet with frost on the vines, but that wouldn't be long now. He went into the house and put the kettle on and made himself a cup of coffee. He picked the mug up and took it upstairs to his room. His little CD player was in his room and not in the sitting room in the house where the family had watched the telly. It was just like it had been when he was a teenager, when the boys had the record player in their room so that they wouldn't annoy their father with 'that racket'.

He ran his fingers through his small rack of CDs; the lion's share of his collection was still in his flat in Paris. He was beginning to wonder not when, but whether he would be going back there. Ah, there it was — his fingers pulled out the Alkan jewel box, as if they would pull anything else out at the moment. Even the Grateful Dead were second choice to that extraordinary *Concerto for Solo Piano* at the moment. He put on his headphones and plugged them into the machine, and those chords of the first theme hit him in the middle of his head just as they had ever since he first heard them a week or so ago. Their majesty and power yet again thrilling him in a way he couldn't remember being thrilled before. He lay down on the bed, just like the superannuated teenager he sometimes felt himself to be, and let out a long breath.

He felt his phone ring. He looked at the screen to identify the caller, and could sense his thrill intensify. Oh yes, that was when he felt that before. He pulled off the headphones and flicked the CD player to pause and said 'Hello' into the phone.

'Commander? It's me, Sergeant Dutoit.'

'Hello Natalie,' he replied, more to a friend than to a sergeant. 'How are you, and what can I do for you?'

'I thought you ought to hear it from me first, that I'm leaving the force.'

Stunned, Truchaud spluttered, 'What?' and then, 'Why?'

'I'm going to have a baby,' she said simply, 'and they're not going to let me out on active duty. Well, there's no way I'm going to go and sit in a typing pool, so I've given in my notice.'

'You're having a baby?' Truchaud was still stunned, and he felt wetness welling up in the corners of his eyes. 'Do I know the father?'

'Yes,' she said but didn't go any further.

'Go on.'

'Well, I have been aware of my clock ticking for a while now. I'm not that far from thirty and, well.' She stopped for a moment, and then rather awkwardly, 'I wanted any child of mine to be powered by some good-quality genes. He or she was going need that to amount to anything in this world, which is going to be a very strange place when they reach adulthood. Well, despite my doing pretty much everything I could to attract your attention last summer, it became fairly obvious that the Truchaud gene pool was inaccessible, so when I went back to Paris, I started to look in other places.'

'George!' exclaimed Truchaud. 'George Delacroix! I might have guessed.' 'Gorgeous' George Delacroix was one of the constables on his team, who had had a serious car accident in the spring, but was now a hundred per cent fit and back on duty. He and Natalie had also played the distraction so often together — a beautiful, blonde, and brutally handsome man doing whatever was needed in a public place was always going to distract any felon from the approaching law.

'Gorgeous George!' Natalie spluttered down the phone, 'As if! You know he's as queer as a four franc note, don't you?'

'Huh?' said Truchaud. No, he didn't know that actually, but then why would that matter? It didn't matter about the sexual orientation of a sperm donor, surely?

'No, it isn't George, it's Clément Lucas.'

Truchaud didn't immediately recognise the name. 'Who?'

'Commander Lucas.' Oh, now he knew who she was talking about, the Parisian oil slick had had his hands all over the girl of his dreams. 'He didn't want to do any of that turkey baster stuff though, he would only do it the traditional way. He's rather sweet in so many ways and is really looking forward to doing all sorts of things with his son, like taking him to the Parc des Princes to see a game or even to see a Johnny Hallyday concert if he's still alive. I haven't dared tell Clément yet that she might turn out to be a girl; it doesn't appear to have crossed his mind. We are getting used to each other though, so it might not have been such a strange decision anyway.'

'So he's called Clément, is he?' said Truchaud at a loss as to what to say. 'I never knew. We always just called each other Lucas and Truchaud, we never seemed to need anything else.'

'Yes, he's called Clément,' Natalie replied, and the phone went silent.

'Isn't there some sort of rule about commanders bonking junior officers?' Truchaud said brutally.

'There probably is, but the divisional commander only found out about it when I resigned, and why I resigned, and it appears that intentional parenthood trumps casual sex, so everyone is happy about it. Apparently the rules date back to the time after the war, when there was a drive to repopulate France again.'

'Oh,' said Truchaud. 'Are you living together?'

'Well, we've still got our separate flats, but I'm spending most evenings at his place nowadays, and I'll probably get rid of my place in the coming weeks. It'll save money, which we're going to need for the baby soon. Isn't it fun?'

She sounded so excited down the phone, exactly the opposite of how he felt. He felt he was going to lose the plot soon. He was either going to become very angry or simply burst into tears. 'Well,' he said, 'Good luck to the pair of you, and if ever you need anything, either of you, you know how to get in touch with me.'

'Thank you for everything, *Chef*. I'll be telling the kids lots about you while they're growing up.'

'Kids,' spluttered Truchaud. 'You mean you're having twins?'

'No, but now we've started, I'm sure we're going to have a family. Do stay in touch *Chef*,' she said, and the phone went dead.

Truchaud unswitched the mute from his CD player, filling the room with sound again, and buried his face in the pillow, muttering the words to *The One that Got Away,* which didn't fit the rhythm of the Alkan at all.

## Thanks

This book fought back! There is an adage that says that once you have written a book, you then have to write a second one, and that's where the trouble starts. *The Charlemagne Connection* couldn't have been more different. It was the best behaved of second books, and the published version was 1.2! The problem was that the ease of the creation of *Charlemagne* put me eight months out of sync with the research that I was going to need to write the third in the series, being the next vintage. Having written the first couple of chapters, I then drifted off to sort out another project, coming back to *Romanée* in September 2014, which I spent picking and sorting grapes. The book you have just finished is the results of eighteen months of pain and confusion, at least partly due to the atrocities in Paris such as the Charlie Hebdo affair. For a long time I wanted the plot to go somewhere else and tried various different directions, some of which leave traces in the book. Then the events in Nice in 2016 persuaded me that the original story I had planned needed telling, and here it is.

Thank you to Chris Pollington, my inside man at Berry Brothers and Rudd, the wine merchants in London, by appointment. Aside from letting me know where all the best places to eat in Nuits-Saint-Georges, despite what they looked like from the street, he proof read this manuscript to make sure that all things viticultural are correct, and as far as I can tell, I have followed his suggestions. Any that I have missed are my fault, or Truchaud's, after all he is a policeman and not a winemaker, and are not however Chris's responsibility.

Sarah Williams is the sort of editor a writer wants at his back. She has lived this book with me in all sorts of strange places. One day we must tell you about Lost City West Virginia. Who knows, maybe one day Truchaud will find himself there! Sarah, thank you for turning this book from something that I had come to hate at one point, into a manuscript that once again I care about.

All at Crime Scene Books, the little imprint that feels more like a family than a business, thank you all for supporting me and my label-mates, hopefully we can all pay you back this year.

## Also by R.M. Cartmel

The Inspector Truchaud 'wine and crime' mystery series by
R.M. Cartmel:

*The Richebourg Affair* (2014)
*The Charlemagne Connection* (2015)

*'This is an intelligent and well-researched story by a writer who clearly loves
the wines and people of Burgundy. It is a Grand Cru of a novel that will
delight both crime fans and oenophiles.'*
L C Tyler, award-winning author of the John Grey historical mysteries and
the Ethelred and Elsie series

*'A well-crafted treasure of unforgettable characters.'*
Jeffrey Siger

*'R.M. Cartmel was born to write.'*
Sharon Powell

*'After an explosive start, R.M. Cartmel's latest vintage offering slips down
very easily, with an intriguing finish.'*
Jasper Morris MW

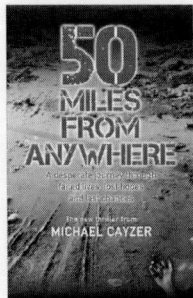

**R.M. Cartmel writing as Michael Cayzer:**

*50 Miles from Anywhere* (2015)

*'Michael Cayzer doesn't shy away from a truth
that is sometimes unpalatable, but he still
manages to show that, even in the most awful
of circumstances, there remains a relatively
good side to people.'*
C. Jeffries

## *Also by Crime Scene Books*

The Amy Lane psychological thriller mystery series by Rosie Claverton:

*Captcha Thief* (2016)
*Terror 404* (2017)

'*Rosie Claverton has produced a highly original heroine with truly authentic strengths and flaws. Definitively recommended.*'
Zoë Sharp, creator of the best-selling Charlie Fox series

'*Rosie Claverton has played the alchemist, and created literary gold.*'
Crime Fiction Lover

The Jocasta Hughes forensic thriller mystery series by Candy Denman:
*Dead Pretty* (2017)

A historical thriller by S.W. Williams:
*Small Deaths* (2017)

True crime by Julian Hayes:
*The Poison Cell* (2017)

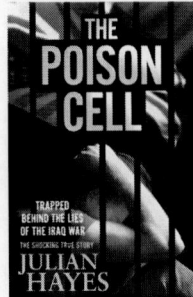